THE DOSSIER OF

SOLAR PONS

#1

THE DOSSIER OF

SOLAR PONS

#1

BASED ON THE CHARACTERS AND SERIES
CREATED BY AUGUST DERLETH

BASIL COPPER

EDITED BY STEPHEN JONES

CONTENTS

EDITOR'S NOTE

Unfortunately, while going through Basil Copper's papers, I was unable to find any of his original manuscripts for the Solar Pons stories. It is possible that these—along with all his correspondence with August Derleth—were amongst the uncatalogued material sent several years ago to the Contemporary Collections repository of the Howard Gotlieb Archival Research Center at Boston University.

We have therefore used the best sources available to us at the present time, including existing texts hand-annotated by the author himself, in the compilation of these volumes. I have also taken the liberty—where required—of returning his work to the English spellings and punctuation that the author originally intended. SJ.

EXPLANATION BY DR. LYNDON PARKER

THE APPEARANCE OF another volume of reminiscences of my old friend Solar Pons calls, perhaps, for
some explanation. It has been on my conscience that a
number of uncollected cases of the one whom the late Sultan
of Turkey was pleased to describe as "The Prince of Detectives",
have been lying gathering dust in my files.

The work of retrieving these, deciphering the rough notes, and
putting them into order for publication has taken a considerable
time, but I trust those many admirers of Solar Pons will not be
disappointed in the results. As a concession to popular request,
I have selected only those reminiscences of a longer nature which
reveal my friend's pre-eminent gifts and which occasionally
highlight the more humorous facets of his character.

The greater length of these cases has enabled me to indulge
the reader in the matter of setting, milieu, and atmosphere. The
result in *The Dossier of Solar Pons* will, I trust, enable those
enthusiasts for the work of the great detective to revel once again
in the thrill of the chase.

It is time now to begin. The game's afoot!

—Lyndon Parker, M.D.

THE DOSSIER OF

THE ADVENTURE OF
THE PERPLEXED PHOTOGRAPHER

✍ 1

IT WAS A wild evening in early April and the rain had been tapping icily at the window panes of our apartments at 7B Praed Street, when what I later came to call the Adventure of the Perplexed Photographer began. My old friend Solar Pons was in one of those restless, nervous moods that descended on him like a blanket when time hung heavily and he had spent most of the day morosely studying and annotating records in his commonplace book with occasional pacing turns about the room.

His examination of the rain-sodden street did nothing to improve his temper and it was with something like relief that I was called out to an urgent case in the afternoon. I was again busy in the evening and, the rain having somewhat abated, returned to 7B in time for an early dinner.

Pons was in a slightly more relaxed mood and allowed himself a thin smile at my sodden and dishevelled appearance.

"Draw your chair up to the fire, my dear Parker. Mrs. Johnson will be in with our meal in a few moments. I fear I have been a far from amiable companion today."

I made a grudging acknowledgement of his graciousness and settled myself in my favourite leather armchair in close proximity to the fireplace, the cheery warmth of which soon relaxed both my limbs and my frosty manner.

The appearance of the beaming, well-scrubbed face of Mrs. Johnson at the threshold, with a heavily laden tray from which ascended wisps of steam and a most agreeable aroma, completely breached my defences and we set to with a will. The table had scarcely been cleared and Pons settled opposite me at the fireplace, with a lit pipe and a glass of whisky and water at his elbow, than Mrs. Johnson once again appeared, this time with a somewhat flustered manner.

"There's a gentleman in the hall below, Mr. Pons. He seems rather agitated and says he must see you at once."

Pons' lean, feral face was transformed immediately. He shot me a triumphant glance from his piercing eye.

"Show him up at once, Mrs. Johnson. I am always available to those select few who alone bring me problems from among the mundane millions of London. Things have been too quiet of late."

I gave a sympathetic nod to Mrs. Johnson who quitted the room; I made to withdraw but subsided in my chair as Pons immediately begged me to remain. I shifted my position so that I could get a clear view of the door as the heavy tread of our visitor followed Mrs. Johnson up the staircase from the hall below.

Mrs. Johnson appeared in the entrance, followed immediately by a tall, heavily bearded man on whose thick-checked ulster raindrops glistened in the light of the room.

"Mr. Bruce Beresford, gentlemen," she announced and went out with the quickness born of long practice, shutting the door behind her.

Our visitor advanced blinking toward us, his arm extended, looking from one to the other.

"Mr. Solar Pons?"

Pons rose from his chair, indicating me with a casual movement of his hand.

"I am he, sir. This is my friend and confidant, Dr. Lyndon Parker."

The bearded man acknowledged my presence with a stiff bow. At Pons' insistence he was already removing his heavy coat, which he laid down on a chair near the fire.

"You have been recommended to me as one of the most able inquiry agents in London."

"Indeed, sir," said Pons drily. "And who may be the others?"

Beresford paused and looked sharply from Pons to myself and then back to the tall figure of my companion.

"The work of Mr. Holmes must always appeal . . ." he began.

"Certainly," interrupted Pons crisply. "And one in your profession would naturally know the major figures in the field. But sit here next to Dr. Parker and I will pour you a whisky."

Our visitor did as my companion said, though he cast a puzzled glance at Pons as the latter busied himself with a bottle of Haig and a siphon. He raised his glass in silent salute.

"You know me, Mr. Pons?"

Solar Pons shook his head, resuming his seat opposite me.

"Apart from the fact that you are a New Zealander, a member of the Signet Club, and a photographer, you are a stranger to me."

Our visitor's astonishment was unfeigned.

"This is remarkable. How could you possibly . . . ?"

"Your accent unmistakably places you as being from New Zealand," said Pons, his eyes dancing. "I have made some little study of the subject of accents. As to the Signet Club, your ring bears the peculiar symbol of that interesting organisation. Your hands are stained with chemicals, a condition peculiar to the photographer who carries out his own developing. When I find that combined with a green patch on your left knee, I conclude that is where you always kneel to take photographs. This afternoon you have been kneeling on grass to do so."

There was a moment of silence as Beresford recovered himself.

"Well, Mr. Pons," said our visitor. "Just so. For a moment I thought you had done something clever."

Pons smiled bitterly and shot me a swift glance.

"Pray continue, Mr. Beresford. I understand you have a problem on which you wish to consult me."

Our visitor stirred in his chair, swilling the amber fluid in his glass.

"You may think me mad, Mr. Pons. Nothing like this has happened to me before. To have one or two plates smashed or stolen, yes, that could happen, but three times is ridiculous. And then this attack on me this evening..."

His beard was bristling with indignation and Pons had a tight smile on his lips as he lifted his hand to halt our visitor's flow of words.

"Come, Mr. Beresford, all in good time. Just drink your whisky calmly and put the events in order."

Our visitor gulped at his glass and flushed.

"Forgive me, Mr. Pons. I am a person ordinarily of a phlegmatic and prosaic nature, but I confess the events of the past twenty-four hours would be enough to upset anyone. Perplexing, most perplexing."

Pons rubbed his thin hands together.

"Do go on, Mr. Beresford. This agency exists to unravel perplexing problems. Eh, Parker?"

"Certainly, Pons," I agreed.

Beresford leaned forward in his chair and cupped his hands round his tumbler to conceal the slight trembling which ran through his robust frame.

"I run a small photographic business off the Strand, Mr. Pons. You may have heard of us. Nothing very fancy. Myself as principal, with two other photographers and my dark-room staff. Though I trust we are not unknown in the larger world."

"Quite so," I said. "I have often seen your work in the sporting press."

Beresford turned a look of approbation on me before proceeding.

"I've been at the game a long time, Mr. Pons, but as the principal I cannot leave it alone. So I often take to the field myself, as it were, picking and choosing the assignments that most interest me. As it happens we have had a rush of work the past few weeks, and the flu epidemic has made things difficult this winter. Both my men were down and one of the dark-room staff."

"I am indeed sorry to hear it," Pons rejoined. "And you yourself have had to take to the field again? Pray continue."

"Well, Mr. Pons," Beresford went on, "only the past twenty-four hours need concern us. As you gathered, I have been taking portraits and action poses of footballers these past two days. Yesterday I was at the Chelsea ground. When I got back to my studio, I found that a whole section of the plates in my leather plate-holder had been smashed. Quite wanton damage, I can assure you. I had left them on the grass near the stadium and noticed nothing amiss at the time. Fortunately, they were unexposed and so no harm was done."

Pons' form had undergone a slight change at our visitor's narrative and now every line of his body expressed intense interest. His keen eyes never left Beresford's face.

"This is quite unique, I take it?"

Beresford nodded.

"It has never happened in my life before. Sheer vandalism, sir. I had one or two calls at private houses yesterday—you may remember the weather was fine in the afternoon—and I took a bus back to my studio. I met an acquaintance on the bus and was busy talking. Judge of my surprise when I checked later to find another section of slides missing from their place in my leather case."

Pons' eyes were positively twinkling now.

"Excellent, Mr. Beresford. This becomes more intriguing by the minute. Do go on."

"Well," said Beresford, giving Pons an indignant look. "That's as may be but it's a serious matter to one in my profession. I had only put the case down on the seat for a few minutes and had stepped across the aisle to talk to my friend."

"So someone sitting nearby could have taken this material?"

Beresford nodded.

"Exactly. Apart from my placing the bag down at Chelsea it hadn't been out of my sight the rest of the day."

The indignation and frustrated rage in Beresford's voice was deepening now.

"This was only the beginning, Mr. Pons! At lunchtime today I came back into my premises to find the front door smashed."

"In what manner?"

"The glass panel had been broken and the catch pushed back. I found my dark-room in disorder and several negatives which were drying had been broken in the manner of the plates at the football ground. I had reason to believe I had disturbed the intruder for the back door into the alley was half-open."

"So that the person who wishes you harm might not have had time to see what he was destroying, Mr. Beresford?" said Pons.

Beresford looked puzzled.

"Eh, Mr. Pons? I don't think I quite understand . . ."

"No matter," rejoined Pons briskly. "You have more to tell me, I take it?"

"I most certainly have," Beresford went on grimly. "Not an hour ago I was coming through a small alley in the Soho area when I was set upon from behind. My hat was jammed over my eyes so that I couldn't see; I was kicked and tripped; and the plates in my hold-all were tipped on to the cobbles and trampled on!"

Beresford's calm had so deserted him that his voice rose to tones of sobbing rage as he described the indignities which had been thrust upon him. There was silence in the room for a moment. Pons sat with his lean, febrile fingers tented before him in an attitude of deep thought.

"My brother-in-law lives nearby," Beresford continued after an interval. "I visited him and cleaned myself up. He advised me to call upon you."

"You have done wisely, Mr. Beresford," said Pons. "This is a most absorbing business which intrigues me greatly."

He glanced at me keenly.

"I would be happy to take up your case, Mr. Beresford. Some private photographs, a football team, and a large number of smashed negatives. What do you make of it, Parker?"

"Vandalism, perhaps?" I suggested. "The whole thing seems pointless."

"Exactly, Parker," Pons chuckled. "Which is exactly why there has to be method behind it."

He lapsed into thought.

"Have you a list of your appointments for the past two days, Mr. Beresford? I think we can ignore events before that since these incidents began only in the last forty-eight hours. You did not, of course, glimpse your assailant this evening?"

Beresford shook his head.

"Unfortunately not, Mr. Pons. By the time I came to my senses all I could hear was the noise of running feet along the alley."

"No matter," said Pons. "I confess I have not been so taken by a problem for a long time."

He got up and went over to his bureau, returning with a note pad and pen.

"If you would be good enough to jot down your engagements together with any other relevant data, Mr. Beresford, I shall be glad to look into the matter. I will step around to your studio in the morning at about ten o'clock."

"I am most grateful, Mr. Pons," muttered our visitor, scribbling furiously, as though the barrel of the pen were the neck of the man who had assaulted him. I could not forbear a quiet smile at his vehemence, though on reflection I had to admit that I should have been twice as indignant had I been in his position.

"Here you are, Mr. Pons."

Beresford moved to Pons' side and passed him the sheet. My companion glanced at it swiftly, his brow corrugated.

"That will do admirably, Mr. Beresford. I see you visited Chelsea again today."

He looked at the almost invisible patch of green on the left leg of our visitor's trousers.

"I take it you had no trouble on this occasion?"

The tall, bearded man drew himself up, reaching for his now dry ulster from the chair.

"I made sure of that, Mr. Pons. I took my bag of plates out into the centre of the pitch with me. Fortunately, the negatives were not among those destroyed this evening."

He inclined his head stiffly.

"Until tomorrow, Mr. Pons. And thank you."

"Until tomorrow, Mr. Beresford."

Beresford buttoned his coat and strode toward the door.

"Good night, doctor."

We listened to his heavy tread descending the stairs. Pons threw himself into his armchair, his eyes dancing with mischief. He gave a dry chuckle and rubbed his hands together.

"A pretty problem indeed. Continue with your analysis, Parker."

"A hoax, perhaps. Or a business rival who is out to ruin Beresford's reputation?"

Pons shook his head.

"You will have to do better than that, Parker. I commend to you the incident of the abstraction of the photographic plates on the omnibus."

I gave a faint snort of irritation.

"Perfectly simple, Pons. The thief could not smash them because it was a public place and he was surrounded by passengers. So he took them to break at his leisure."

Pons' eyes were fixed somewhere up on the ceiling beyond my gaze to where the firelight made a brindled pattern on the white plaster.

"There is that," he admitted. "But as to whether he would smash them is another matter."

And to this maddeningly cryptic remark he would add nothing. I had opened my mouth to draw him out further when there was the sound of a car drawing up outside. Pons crossed noiselessly to the curtains. He came back to stand by the table.

"We are exceedingly popular this evening, Parker. If I am not mistaken the stolid form of Inspector Jamison has just descended from the police car at the kerb outside."

A few moments later we heard the loud, insistent ringing of the bell, the murmur of conversation as Mrs. Johnson opened the door, and then the familiar tread of the Inspector. Pons was already opening the door to admit the Scotland Yard man, who wore a gloomy and worried expression.

"Something serious?" queried Pons hopefully.

Jamison mopped his brow with a handkerchief he took from his overcoat pocket and stared from my companion to me.

"Not only serious, Mr. Pons, but horrific."

"Murder, then?" said Pons.

"Murder in the most sickening circumstances. In a locked room and with a number of singular features."

"Where?"

"Highbury. In broad daylight too. Yesterday afternoon."

An annoyed expression crossed Solar Pons' face and he clicked his tongue.

"Dear me, Jamison. As long ago as that? And no doubt your fellows have been trampling about with their heavy boots."

Jamison coloured and shifted from one foot to another.

"All has been preserved just as Professor Mair was found," he said stiffly. "I would appreciate your co-operation."

"Certainly, my dear fellow. I will just get my coat."

"Coming, Parker?"

I was already on my feet, draining the last of my whisky.

"Certainly, Pons. No doubt the Inspector will enlighten us on the way."

2

We were driving north-east, through rain-sodden streets, before Jamison broke the silence which had descended on the three of us.

"Professor Mair is a wealthy man who retired from the British Museum some years ago," he said at last. "He was an expert on Chinese pottery, I believe. He lives in a large house in Highbury—The Poplars—with a staff of servants, a private secretary, and three relatives. These are his niece, Miss Jean Conyers, and two nephews, Lionel Amsden, a broker in the City; and Clifford Armitage, who looked after the Professor's financial affairs. So far as we can make out the household was a fairly amiable one. Mair had never married and since his parents had made considerable investments on his behalf, he was able to keep up an almost regal establishment at The Poplars. You'll see what I mean when we get there."

Pons made no reply, his intent, hawk-like face silhouetted against the bloom of passing gas lamps, as the police car turned from a main highway into a subsidiary road.

"But just lately the Professor had taken a fancy to move out of London," Inspector Jamison continued. "This caused a minor ripple in the household. The Professor suffered from arthritis and had been advised by his medical man to seek a drier climate."

"In England or abroad?" Pons interjected.

Jamison looked startled.

"That was not made quite clear," he answered stiffly. "But at any rate he intended to put The Poplars up for sale. This was the situation which obtained until yesterday afternoon. Then, at about three o'clock, the people in the house heard the most appalling and inhuman screams coming from Professor Mair's study, which is at the front of the house, on the first floor."

"The servants found the door locked and had to break it down to gain entry. Inside, they discovered a most appalling sight. Drawers and cupboards had been ransacked and it looked as though there had been a tremendous struggle. The Professor lay in front of his desk. A large javelin, one of his collection of weapons, had been taken from the wall and dashed through his body with such force that it penetrated the carpet beneath, pinning him like a butterfly on a card."

"Good Heavens!" I could not help interjecting.

Jamison shook his head.

"You may well say so, doctor. It was one of the most horrible scenes I have ever clapped eyes on and I've seen some things in my time."

"Pray do go on, Jamison," said Pons imperturbably. "I am finding this most absorbing. Were all the family at home?"

The Inspector nodded.

"Niece, nephews, and secretary. They helped to break down the door."

"Ah, yes, the door," interjected Pons slowly. "That does indeed present a problem. You checked the windows, of course?"

Jamison turned an aggrieved face toward us.

"Of course, Mr. Pons. Both the big windows at the front of the study, which face the garden, are three-quarter length. They were securely locked and in any case it is a considerable drop to the garden on to a paved pathway at that point."

Solar Pons sat hunched in thought for a few moments more, oblivious of the lurching of the car or the spitting of the rain on the bodywork.

"But you must have come to some conclusions, Jamison?"

The Inspector stirred uncomfortably on his seat opposite us.

"It is a very complex business. As to motive, both nephews and the niece stand to inherit considerable sums from the Professor's estate as his only relatives. I have had some talk with the family lawyer this afternoon. There is something in excess of a quarter of a million pounds involved."

Pons turned in his corner of the car and his eyes caught mine.

"Motive enough there, Parker, eh?"

I nodded.

"But the locked room . . . And who would be strong enough to wield a harpoon in that manner?"

"A javelin, doctor," Jamison put in. "I had not overlooked that point, Mr. Pons."

He had a little gleam of triumph in his eyes. "I favour young Mr. Amsden. He is over six feet tall and built like a Greek god. Except that only a minute elapsed between the Professor's screaming and the breaking in of the door. As Mr. Amsden was principally concerned in breaking in that very same door, I did not feel I had anything strong enough to go on."

"You were quite right, Jamison," said Solar Pons crisply. "You would have made yourself look extremely foolish had you been misguided enough to have arrested him. There are a number of intriguing aspects here."

Jamison's face brightened.

"You are on to something?"

Pons shook his head irritably.

"I prefer to draw my conclusions from strictly observed data

15

on the spot. I fancy I will need to know a great deal more about The Poplars and its inhabitants before I am able to do so."

And he said nothing further until the wheels of the police car scraped the kerb as it came to a halt in the rainy night before a high brick wall.

◁ 3

Jamison led the way across the pavement to where two large wrought-iron gates were thrown back, framing the entrance to a gravelled drive. By the light of an adjacent gas lamp which threw a mellow glare on to the scene I was able to see why the police car had not driven in to The Poplars. There was a trench dug in the pavement, paving slabs piled high; and across the entry to Professor Mair's mansion heavy boards had been placed. The whole of the frontage leading to the driveway had been excavated and clay and sand filled the gap.

"The Council workmen are doing drainage maintenance here, gentlemen," Jamison explained. "I thought it might be worthwhile keeping this surface clear."

Pons' eyes were sharp and alert in the light of the gas lamp.

"You have done well, Jamison," he said drily. "My precepts appear to have taught you something at last."

The Inspector looked reproachfully at Pons and two tiny spots of red started out on his cheeks, but he said nothing—only waited while Pons went down on hands and knees on the thick boards, examining the trench with his pocket torch.

"A pity you did not call me sooner," he grunted. "Tradesmen and the rain of the past day have done much to obliterate detail which might have told us a good deal. I shall have these boards up as soon as it gets light."

Jamison cleared his throat.

"I think you will find the area beneath the boards may tell you something, Mr. Pons," he said stiffly.

"Let us hope so," my companion replied, looking keenly about him as we walked up the drive to where the large, squat, three-storied mansion of the late Professor Mair stood frowning across a broad lawn to the shrubbery which screened it from the road. The house was a blaze of light and it was evident that our arrival was expected, for a constable ran down the broad front steps toward Jamison, and the massive front door was already being opened by a trimly dressed parlour-maid as we ascended to the portico.

The house had an air of suppressed mourning and one could feel tragedy in the air as Pons and I followed Jamison across a large hall floored in marble. Electric lights in a massive brass lantern illuminated the broad-balconied staircase up which Jamison hurried to the first floor. Pons was darting keen glances about him. A knot of servants stood talking in monotones on the wide landing, but they broke up and went about their duties as our group arrived.

The scene of the tragedy was guarded by a plain-clothes Detective Sergeant who had a muttered colloquy with his superior before ushering us past the shattered rosewood door which had shielded the entrance to the Professor's study. It was a broad, high room lit by green-shaded lamps: two in ceiling fittings, one on the cluttered desk, and another standard lamp which stood near the panelled fireplace.

The fire had long burned out and the place struck dank and chill; the reason for the coldness was obvious from the thing which sprawled incongruously in the centre of the room, amid documents, upturned drawers and other debris. I have long been inured to scenes of post-mortem squalor in my profession, but I have seldom felt the thrill of horror which this room evoked in me.

The body of Professor Mair was spread out in bizarre fashion, his hands crooked in agony about the heavy shaft of the steel-tipped javelin which transfixed his body to the carpet beneath him. Blood had seeped from the wound and made heavy stains on the rug and on the parquet round about.

The Professor was a man of about seventy, with a snow-white beard which was thrown back at an acute angle; the mouth with the broken, decayed teeth was wide open, as though he had been in the act of screaming as he was cut down; and a dark necklace of blood had run from the corner of his mouth on to the collar of his smoking jacket. The blue eyes were wide and staring. It was a horrific and appalling sight and even Pons seemed visibly shaken.

We stood in a hushed semi-circle about the remains for a few seconds and then Pons was himself again; he dropped to his knees with a magnifying glass and busied himself in an examination of the area round the body.

"Nothing of importance there, Mr. Pons," Jamison put in heavily. "We haven't overlooked theft, of course, but these are just papers connected with the Professor's work."

Pons nodded without replying. He was on his feet again now, his keen eyes stabbing about the room. Then he crossed toward the door, taking off his hat and overcoat which he placed on a chair. He came back to me.

"Your department, Parker. Just give me your opinion, would you?"

"Certainly, Pons."

Jamison brought in a bundle of sacking from a pile near the

door and I knelt gingerly upon it to carry out my examination. I avoided the javelin, but Jamison observed, "We have tested for fingerprints, doctor. The murderer wore gloves."

Pons was already near the windows, giving them his usual meticulous examination. He paused on the floor between them, his magnifying glass passing inch by inch across the flooring.

"You are certainly right about one thing, Inspector. No one has been out that way."

Jamison exchanged a satisfied look with the Detective Sergeant, who had come back inside the room and was an interested spectator of the proceedings. Pons next went around the entire room, dismissing the serried ranks of books, which took up three sides, with hardly a glance. He examined the shattered door carefully, noting the key still in the lock. He spent more time on two large cupboards which flanked the door. The Inspector caught the question in his eyes.

"Files, according to Clarence Moffat, the Professor's secretary. But there's been nothing disturbed there, so far as we know."

Pons already had the left-hand door open and was examining the linoleum-covered floor of the interior. He pulled open one or two of the mahogany drawers at the rear of the cupboard and gave the contents a cursory glance. Then he went over to the right-hand cupboard and repeated the process. I noticed he had one of the small envelopes in which he collected specimens ready to hand.

He was at my elbow as I completed my examination, a necessarily brief one in the absence of my case of instruments.

"Rigor mortis has long set in," I said. "Death would have been instantaneous and probably some time yesterday afternoon."

Jamison nodded portentously.

"The same conclusion drawn by the police surgeon," he said. "Of course we shall know more after the post-mortem, but I thought you'd prefer to view the body in situ, Mr. Pons."

Pons nodded.

"Extremely thoughtful, Jamison. Is there nothing further, Parker? Would the javelin have penetrated at one stroke, for example?"

I took hold of the shaft, now that there was no need for caution.

"It's certainly a heavy and fearsome weapon, Pons," I began. "Hello, it's quite loose!"

Even as I spoke, the javelin broke free of the wound and clattered to the floor. Pons had a curious expression on his face. But he said nothing and was already turning to the area above the fireplace where a number of weapons were hung in ornamental display on the wall.

"Obviously this came from the pair here," he mused, his eyes hooded and seemingly half-asleep. He pulled a heavy Malay kris from its scabbard and used it to point at the Inspector.

"Seems rather a strange feature of the décor for a man of peace like Professor Mair, wouldn't you say, Inspector?"

Jamison looked puzzled.

"I don't quite see what you're driving at, Mr. Pons. I believe some of these things originally belonged to the Professor's brother, who was a widely travelled man."

"If you have finished with my services, Pons," I said some-what testily, "I'd be glad to be allowed to rise from my knees."

Solar Pons permitted himself a somewhat bleak smile in that oppressive room of silent death.

"Certainly, my dear fellow. Do forgive me. I was quite absorbed in this little problem before us."

He looked from the corpse to Jamison and then crossed to the fireplace to replace the kris in its scabbard. The envelope had already been returned to his inner pocket. I removed the sacking and dusted my trousers.

"I think we have seen everything of interest for the time being," said Pons crisply, picking up his hat and coat. "And now, if you will allow me, I should like to question the Professor's immediate family."

"They are gathered in the morning room," Jamison volunteered. "There is some refreshment if you would care to partake . . ."

"Thank you but we have already dined," Pons told him. "And now, if you will lead the way, I shall be glad to learn what the late Professor's nearest and dearest have to tell us."

🎵 **4**

As we were descending the main staircase to the hall, a thin, fussy-looking, middle-aged man in a rusty black frock coat and striped trousers came out of one of the ground-floor rooms. He turned a startled face up toward us and I could see the thin strands of black hair shaped carefully across but not concealing the baldness of his head.

"Ah, here is Mr. Moffat, the Professor's secretary," observed Jamison. "Perhaps you would care to have a word with him first. He has been with the Professor for the past ten years."

We had now descended to the ground floor and Jamison effected the introductions.

"Certainly, Mr. Pons," said Clarence Moffat with a nervous smile, when the Inspector had explained our presence there. "Anything I can do to help?"

He led the way into a small room tastefully furnished and with oil paintings of classical subjects in heavy gilt frames lining the walls. Jamison had not exaggerated the scale and value of the late Professor Mair's possessions, I reflected, looking at the pictures. The nearest appeared to be a genuine Watteau. At Pons' insistence the secretary sank into a deep leather chair by the fire opposite Pons. Jamison and I remained standing.

"Where were you exactly when the tragedy occurred, Mr. Moffat?" asked Pons, lowering the lids over his eyes and tenting his bony fingers before him.

"I was reading in this very room, Mr. Pons, awaiting the professor's summons. He usually goes through private papers directly after lunch and then calls me to take dictation for one of his articles."

Pons nodded and sat in thought for a moment though I could see that his eyes were keenly regarding the secretary from beneath his half-lowered lids.

"What then?"

"It was just at five to three, Mr. Pons. I heard these horrible screams. I ran upstairs. Some of the servants and members of the Professor's household joined me. We had to break the door in."

He put his hands up over his eyes.

"It was a dreadful sight, Mr. Pons. I hope never to see such another. But then you have seen for yourself."

Pons nodded. He ignored Jamison's puzzled frown and turned back to Moffat.

"What were your exact duties, Mr. Moffat? I understand from the Inspector here that Mr. Clifford Armitage, one of the Professor's nephews, looks after his financial affairs."

The secretary inclined his head.

"That is so, Mr. Pons. I deal with all the Professor's correspondence and take stenographic dictation and so forth. Mr. Armitage deals purely with the late Professor's financial affairs, which are extensive. When I receive a letter which has financial implications, I pass it to Mr. Armitage and he reciprocates as regards communications concerning my sphere. Our duties slightly overlap but not to any great extent."

"I am sure you will not misunderstand me, Mr. Moffat, but as far as you know, had Professor Mair made any financial provision for you in his will?"

Dull patches of red were standing out on the secretary's pale cheeks now. He shook his head.

"The Professor did not take me into his confidence regarding such matters, Mr. Pons. But no doubt Mr. Armitage could enlighten you."

He moistened his lips and then went on hesitantly.

"He did indicate something on one occasion. He has left me a small annuity, but I have no idea of the actual amount."

Pons made a slight bow. His eyes were sweeping round the room now and he seemed to have lost interest in Moffat.

"You told the Inspector, I believe, that the files in the cupboards upstairs were intact?"

"That is so, Mr. Pons. I have made an exhaustive check and to the best of my belief there is nothing missing."

"Very well. Thank you for your assistance."

Pons uncoiled his lean, spare form from his chair, and Moffat got up with evident relief. We were walking back toward the door when it was opened to admit a tall, slim girl with dark hair whose sombre clothing and haggard features proclaimed her grief at the sinister happening of the previous day. She stopped on the threshold, evidently surprised.

"I am sorry, gentlemen. I hoped to find Mr. Moffat alone."

"It is quite all right, Miss Conyers," said Jamison. "We have just finished. This is Mr. Solar Pons and his colleague, Dr. Lyndon Parker. I suggest we all go through into the morning room."

Miss Conyers nodded, an alert expression in her hazel eyes as she came forward to shake hands, first with Pons and then myself.

"Allow me to express my deep sympathy, Miss Conyers."

The girl made a slight bow, her lips parted as her eyes searched Pons' face.

"Thank you, Mr. Pons."

Her eyes moved on and sought the secretary's.

"I would appreciate your presence in the morning room, Mr. Moffat. Mr. Amsden is being tiresome again."

The secretary excused himself quickly and hurried through the door. Pons stood with his hands behind his back and looked at Miss Conyers intently.

"I gather there is no love lost between the two of you, Miss Conyers?"

The girl shook her head, her mouth a firm, set line.

"My cousin is a boor, Mr. Pons," she said decisively. "He is the one disruptive element in this household. Why my uncle ever let him live here is beyond my imagining."

"On what is this impression based, pray?"

We were walking back through into the hall now, and the girl had stopped at the foot of the great staircase. Jamison hovered on the fringe of the conversation, evidently ill at ease.

"It is nothing palpable, Mr. Pons. It is just that we have never got on since childhood. We took an instinctive dislike to one another. His presence in this house is a constant irritant and he seems to take a delight in thwarting my will in household matters."

"We all have our crosses to bear, Miss Conyers," said Solar Pons drily, looking blandly around at the outward evidence of wealth which lay so ostentatiously about us.

"Now that we have a moment alone," he went on, "it is true to say, is it not, that Professor Mair intended to sell this house?"

The girl had a ghost of a smile on her lips.

"It is indeed, Mr. Pons. His health necessitated a less foggy atmosphere than that of London in winter. He had made some preliminary arrangements to purchase a property on the south coast. And advertisements of this house were to appear in the national newspapers in a week or two. It did not suit Lionel, I can assure you. It would have meant the loss of a comfortable billet since he needs to be near the City for his stock-broking activities."

Pons' eyes were fixed toward the floor and he had an abstracted air now.

"Just so, Miss Conyers," he murmured absently. "And now, Jamison, I think we might join the others."

The morning room at The Poplars was all of sixty feet long, one side facing the garden with its dense shrubbery, the two end walls occupied with glass cabinets containing various *objects d'art*. But I had little time to observe the appointments of the room, my attention being immediately taken up with the altercation taking place between two men in front of the fireplace.

Moffat, I had already met. The man with whom he was engaged in low-toned argument was indeed a giant. Blond and handsome in a brutal sort of way, he had a face in which coarseness and sensuality fought for supremacy. He was well over six feet in height, with a deep chest and neck muscles like those of a bull. He wore a suit of loud tweed, and the heavy flush of anger on his cheek and brow denoted frustration and disappointment.

"I tell you it would be foolish to carry out Uncle's wishes now," he said. "The old man has gone and who knows what intentions his will might have revealed."

A third figure near the fire moved toward the group in a conciliatory manner as we came up. He was a slim, open-faced young man with a shock of brown hair. Dressed tastefully and quietly in a light grey suit, he formed a marked contrast in his slender dapperness to the brutal giant in front of him.

"This is hardly the time and the place, Lionel," he began placatingly.

Then he broke off, a smile on his face, and came down the room toward us.

"Mr. Solar Pons, is it not? I have seen your photograph in various journals. They do not do you justice."

Pons smiled thinly, his glance raking the room to where the sullen figure of Amsden pawed the carpet with the toe of his shoe like a petulant child.

"This is Mr. Clifford Armitage, who saw to Professor Mair's business interests," said Jamison briskly. "Dr. Lyndon Parker."

"Delighted, doctor," said Armitage, relinquishing Pons' hand and hurrying to me. His blue eyes studied my face.

"Dreadful business, but most interesting to see such distinguished people at work."

"You do me too much honour, Mr. Armitage," Pons protested. "But will you not introduce me to Mr. Amsden?"

"Lionel is too worried at present as to how much money he will lose over Uncle's death," put in Miss Conyers waspishly. "If he would restrain himself from horse racing, gambling, and other forms of debt, he would be better advised."

Amsden raised his brutal face and looked at his cousin loweringly.

"Go to blazes, Jean," he said in a sneering voice. "And as for Mr. Smart Aleck Pons, we have no need of such amateurs in the house."

As Armitage raised his hand in protest, Pons smilingly waved his apologies away.

"I have seldom been received with such courtesy," he said ironically. "I understand Mr. Amsden's feelings well."

The giant stared at Pons incredulously.

"The devil you do."

He took a step nearer.

"Oh, well, no hard feelings, Mr. Pons. I've been more than usually tried today and I lost over a hundred on the three-thirty."

"You have my deepest sympathy."

Pons took the giant's outstretched hand. Amsden had a wide smile on his face. I saw that he was exerting enormous pressure on Pons' hand. The smile on my companion's face widened a trifle. His own knuckles were white now, and I saw beads of perspiration on the huge stockbroker's face. He winced with pain and bit his lip. He suddenly let go Pons' hand and fell back, massaging his fingers.

"Damnation on it," he said in mingled tones of disgust and admiration.

"The game is not entirely unknown to me," said Pons, flexing his own fingers and giving me a brief, mocking glance.

"And now, if you will all sit down, there are a few questions I would like to ask."

5

It was past midnight when Pons had finished his questioning, and we were jolting back in a cab to our quarters at 7B Praed Street before he broke the brooding silence which had enveloped him since we left the house. Then he leaned forward in his seat opposite me, his eyes gleaming.

"What do you say, Parker? You know my methods. Apply them."

"Why, Pons," I said. "There is some mystery, certainly, but I should be inclined to put my money on the Inspector's choice."

"Lionel Amsden?"

I nodded.

"He is built like a bull. Assuming the crime was committed by a member of the household or staff—there was certainly no one else in the house at the time according to the statements made—he would be the only person with strength enough to drive that javelin through the unfortunate Professor's body. It is obvious that nothing was stolen and that the desk was ransacked to make the crime look like casual theft."

Pons straightened himself and stretched his bony legs.

"You are definitely improving, Parker."

I must confess I felt a slight warmth spring to my cheek at his unaccustomed praise, but I had no time to bask in the glow for Pons' mobile features had changed expression again.

"The desk was most certainly a somewhat clumsy attempt to divert suspicion and make it look as though the murder was a by-product of burglary. No, no, Parker, there are deeper waters here. But what inclines you to the Amsden theory?"

"He is certainly an unlovable character," I said strongly. "He is at loggerheads with other members of the household, notably

Miss Conyers. And if we are to believe what she and some of the servants say, he has gambling and other debts."

Solar Pons' eyes were dancing and he interrupted me with a short laugh.

"Ah, Parker, there speaks your Puritan streak. I fear that if we arrested people for murder on the strength of their gambling debts, the jails the length and breadth of England would be full to bursting. No, Parker, we must look elsewhere for the cunning perpetrator of this brutal crime."

"But you cannot doubt that Amsden could have done it," I burst out, conscious that my hold on my temper was fraying.

"Explain then, if you will, the method by which the crime was committed," my companion said in that maddeningly assured manner of his.

"Supposing that, pressed by debt, he sought an interview with the Professor. That he asked for an assurance about his inheritance or perhaps a loan to get him out of his difficulties. Amsden lost his temper—no difficult thing with him—and the two men struggled. He seized the javelin and murdered the old man. When his screams aroused the household, he transfixed him with the javelin and rushed out of the room."

"And the locked door?"

Solar Pons had a mocking smile upon his lips now but I plunged on.

"He went a few yards along the corridor and then ran back, making a great deal of noise. He was at the door, and held the knob, while he broke it in."

Pons opened his eyes wide and sat back for a moment.

"That is quite breathtaking, Parker, even for you. But it will not do, I'm afraid. The wreckage of the door certainly indicates that it was locked with the key from the inside at the time it was broken open. There were five people outside the door when it was smashed. No one went near it afterward; in fact the room was full of people. So we can be sure the key was not tampered with. In addition, that portion of the lock on the lintel was torn out of its retaining screws."

Pons closed his eyes and pulled reflectively at the lobe of his ear, as he was wont to do when hot upon the scent.

"No one has yet commented upon one of the most curious aspects of this matter, and it certainly does not seem to have occurred to our good friend the Inspector. I submit that a man transfixed by a javelin dies quickly. He has little time for screaming. I commend that singular fact to your ratiocinative faculties. As a doctor it should have particular significance."

I fear that I stared at Pons open-mouthed, but at that moment the cab turned and deposited us opposite the familiar doorstep of Number 7B Praed Street.

"We must be back at The Poplars in good time tomorrow," Pons went on as we climbed in single file up the stairs to our quarters.

"Don't forget that you promised Mr. Beresford to be at his studio at ten o'clock," I said.

"Ah, yes, Parker, I fear that little matter had temporarily slipped my mind in the stress of the greater crime."

We were in the sitting room and had switched on the light when I was arrested by a curt exclamation from my companion. Pons was standing by the light switch, staring at a sheet of paper he had taken from his pocket, his eyes dancing with excitement.

"I fear my deductive faculties have become somewhat atrophied, my dear fellow."

I recognised the appointments list our photographer visitor of that evening had scribbled down for Pons.

"I fancy that Mr. Beresford's problem must have priority after all, Parker."

He handed me the sheet of paper. At first I could not see what he meant. Then, halfway down Beresford's list of photographic assignments were the five words which had occasioned Pons' excitement: Professor Mair, The Poplars, Highbury.

"But what does it mean, Pons?"

"It means that I am on the way to identifying the man who smashed our visitor's photographic plates. Good night, Parker. I should lose no time in seeking your bed as we must be up betimes in the morning."

6

It was still cold and windy, but the rain had ceased and a pale sun shone the next morning. At nine o'clock when we set out for Beresford's studio, Pons insisted on walking to the Strand. He was singularly uncommunicative but persisted in humming some popular tune in a cracked monotone which added to my sense of mounting irritation. It was still a quarter to ten when we skirted St. Martin's, crossed Duncannon Street, and set off along the south side of the Strand.

Beresford's studio was in a narrow thoroughfare of tall red-brick properties running down to the Embankment, and we mounted narrow stairs to the third floor where, according to the large brass plate, the studio was situated. A glazier was already at work repairing the clear glass panel in the main door of the premises, and our client himself obtruded his bearded face into the gap in the pane in such a droll manner that Pons himself could not forbear a brief smile.

"Come in, come in, Mr. Pons," cried our client, visibly relieved.

He led the way through to a cluttered office where large photographic studies adorned the walls. We passed from this apartment into a narrow corridor leading to Beresford's dark-rooms. It seemed an extensive warren, and Pons' alert eyes were darting keenly about him as we rounded the end of the passage and walked into the room where the photographs were finally dried and finished.

Two men were at work here, but after a brief word with their employer they left us alone. The chamber in which we found ourselves was a large one; two big photographic enlargers stood on a solid wooden bench; there were racks of plates standing out to dry and a tap dripped mournfully in the corner. Unlike the darkrooms there were windows here which let in the daylight, and a door in the far wall led down an iron staircase into a small mews at the rear of the premises.

Pons had seen all this at a glance and now he produced a magnifying lens from an inner pocket and turned to Beresford.

"It is a pity that your assistants have continued working here, Mr. Beresford, but I must just pick up what information I can."

He was over by the door as he spoke, examining the framework and area round the coarse coconut matting in front of it. He had two or three of his small transparent envelopes and transferred something carefully from the surface of the mat to one of the envelopes with a pair of tweezers. Then he was up and down the iron staircase with ferret-like gestures, to Beresford's evident bewilderment. His eyes sought mine and I turned away with inward amusement.

We stood for a few minutes more while Pons bustled out into the main offices to glean what information he could from the shattered front door. When he rejoined us a little later, his lean features were alight with satisfaction. He closed the door behind him and waved our client to a wooden stool. I seated myself on a bench near the open door while Pons remained standing.

"Now, Mr. Beresford, I see from your list, that you had a photographic assignment two days ago at the home of Professor Mair."

"Ah, yes, Mr. Pons. I remember. The Poplars, Highbury. But it was of no importance. Merely illustrations for a brochure. The house was coming up for sale. Now, at Chelsea..."

"Tut, tut, Mr. Beresford," Pons interrupted, the edge of his voice slightly corroded with irritation. "You may forget Chelsea and its footballers. That was an effect, not the cause. Your presence at The Poplars, *au contraire,* was of paramount import-ance."

Beresford's face was a picture; his expression clearly indicated that he thought my companion had taken leave of his senses, but he was too polite to say so.

Solar Pons' tall form was quivering with excitement as he leaned toward our client.

"Now, Mr. Beresford, pay close attention to my questions. A brutal murder was committed at The Poplars two days ago. Your answers may go a long way toward closing the net on a very cunning adversary."

Beresford's jaw dropped.

"A murder, Mr. Pons... I'm not sure I understand."

"You do not read the papers, then?" Pons grunted.

Beresford shook his head.

"I have been extremely busy this last week. And what with the worries of the past forty-eight hours..."

"No matter. Tell me, Mr. Beresford, how did you come to be commissioned to take pictures at The Poplars?"

"Mr. Dartmouth, one of the principals of Swettenham and Fuggle, estate agents of Highbury, for whom I had done a great deal of work, telephoned these premises to seek my help."

"I see. At what time did you arrive at the house?"

"At about two-thirty, Mr. Pons. The rain had ceased and the sun was shining. It seemed a good opportunity."

"Quite so," said Pons.

He gave me a brief glance before resuming.

"Did you take photographs inside the house or out?"

Beresford shifted his bulk on the stool.

"Miss Conyers received me in the hall of the house, Mr. Pons. She gave me specific instructions, and I then set to work to photograph the grounds and the exterior of the house."

"I see. And you were there at three o'clock that afternoon?"

"Certainly, Mr. Pons."

Beresford's bewilderment was plain to see at that moment.

"Patience, Mr. Beresford. We are coming to the kernel of the matter. So I am right, am I not, in assuming that you did not set foot beyond the hall; that you took no interiors of the mansion; and that your work consisted of photographing exterior and grounds?"

"Exactly, Mr. Pons. I finished and left the property at about a quarter past three because it was then beginning to rain."

"You did not see Miss Conyers again?"

Beresford shook his head.

"I had no reason to, Mr. Pons. I had the young lady's instructions, and proofs would have been submitted in the normal way."

Pons nodded and scratched his ear with a familiar gesture.

"What exactly were you doing at precisely three o'clock or a minute or two before, Mr. Beresford?"

Our client sat on the stool, deep in thought for a moment or two.

"I was photographing the main façade of the building, Mr. Pons. I took two or three studies to make sure. I like to be thorough, you see."

"I'm sure you do."

Pons looked disappointed.

"And these photographs were among those destroyed by the vandal who stole your property and attacked you?"

Beresford's face lit up.

"By no means, Mr. Pons. As luck would have it, I had placed these slides in a large pocket in my overcoat."

I was astonished at Pons' reaction. He slapped his thigh with a resounding crack and his face was transformed.

"Excellent, Mr. Beresford! My time has not been wasted this morning. What I want you to do is to prepare your largest and clearest print sizes of these studies. And then I want you to enlarge certain portions of the negative."

He took Beresford back into the dark-room while I remained behind, slightly bemused by the change in Pons' attitude. My friend appeared galvanised into action on his return. He took me by the elbow and rushed me with undignified haste from Beresford's premises.

"Come, Parker, I must consult with Jamison. Then we must return here for the finished prints within the hour. There is no time to lose. Jamison must bring a blank warrant with him next time he visits The Poplars."

And he would venture no further explanation to my hurried questions as we clattered down the staircase.

⌘ 7

After a snatched lunch, early afternoon found us speeding back to Highbury in a taxi. Jamison had already been apprised of our intentions by telephone, and had promised to have the entire household assembled for our arrival. Our client, Mr. Bruce Beresford, sat opposite us, astonishment plain on his honest, bearded face, but pleased, nevertheless, to be the centre of the drama which promised to unfold on our arrival. He carried a portfolio of photographs with him and as soon as we had made ourselves comfortable in the interior of the cab, Pons and Beresford had held a hurried consultation from which I was excluded.

"Excellent, Mr. Beresford, excellent," Pons murmured at length. "The enlargement is disappointing, it is true, but then it would have been miraculous had things turned out the way they have a habit of doing in fiction. Eh, Parker?"

He smiled conspiratorially at me, and I confess I could not resist a waspish reply.

"I can hardly give such an opinion, Pons, when I am deliberately kept outside your confidence."

Pons' smile widened fractionally.

"Say not so, Parker. It is merely that I cannot resist a small artistic gesture which I am saving for the finale. All shall be made clear in due course."

He turned back to Beresford, leaving me to nurse my ruffled feelings.

"You will have the satisfaction of knowing, Mr. Beresford, that your little puzzle and the discomfort to which you were put, has been responsible for the unmasking of as cold-blooded a murderer as I have ever come across."

Beresford's expression was frankly lugubrious now.

"I confess, Mr. Pons, I am as much in the dark as ever."

He started putting the prints back into the heavy cardboard folio with a wistful sigh. Pons leaned forward to him.

"Patience for just a short while longer, Mr. Beresford. I can assure you that your visit to The Poplars, your photographic exploits, and the bizarre events which followed all have a perfectly logical explanation. Ah, here we are at our destination."

A light rain was falling as we paid off the cab. Before we went into the house, Pons pulled back the heavy plank covering of the roadworks outside the main gates of the mansion and carefully examined the indented footprints in the soft clay and sand beneath. He shook his head, replacing the boards with a frown.

"Just as I expected, Parker. There has been a deal of toing and froing. Not enough to obliterate the traces of what I seek, fortunately. No, it will have to be shock tactics, I think, with a dash of bluff in the final analysis."

Beresford and I exchanged a glance behind Pons' back as we went up the drive, but I am afraid our client was unable to obtain much comfort from my expression. We were received in the hallway by Miss Conyers.

"We have followed the Inspector's instructions, Mr. Pons," she said drily. "The others are gathered in my uncle's study at your express request. I presume you would wish to go there directly."

She shivered slightly.

"Though why we should be subjected to such an ordeal when the morning room would be more convenient . . ."

"I have a very good reason, Miss Conyers," Pons interrupted

smoothly. "The body has long been removed and the room tidied, so I do not see why the study should not do as well as any other apartment. And it is vital for my little demonstration."

Miss Conyers shrugged, her displeasure evident on her mobile features. A man-servant hovered in the background but she dismissed him. She herself led the way up the curving stair to where the shattered doorway led to the chamber of death.

A plainclothes detective-constable stood guard at the door but at Pons' sudden gesture refrained from announcing us. Instead, Pons turned to our hostess, glancing keenly round the corridor.

"These bedrooms. To whom do they belong?"

Miss Conyers's face bore traces of puzzlement, her brow furrowed with surprise, as though Pons had asked an outrageous question.

"The first is my own; then my cousin Clifford's, next to mine. Beyond is Moffat, my uncle's secretary; and the last door in the corridor is that of Lionel Amsden."

Pons paused outside the first door.

"Just so. You have no objection to my inspecting these rooms?"

"No, of course not, Mr. Pons."

Miss Conyers moved swiftly toward the door of her own room, but Pons stopped her with a brisk gesture.

"It will not be necessary, Miss Conyers. I hardly think the crime belongs to the hand of a lady. It is just these last three rooms which interest me."

Beresford and I stood somewhat impatiently in the corridor as Pons quickly opened the door of Clifford Armitage's room. He stood sniffing the air keenly.

"A strange perfume, Miss Conyers. It seems to permeate the whole corridor."

"We had some bad coal, Mr. Pons. We keep fires burning in the bedroom grates. I got Travers, one of the footmen, to light some scented candles to take the odour away."

Pons nodded, seemingly satisfied with Miss Conyers' answer and his eyes looked thoughtfully about the corridor.

"This will not take a moment, Parker."

He darted into Armitage's room and I glimpsed him through the half-open door, kneeling on the bedroom floor, going thoroughly over the carpet. He glanced quickly into the half-empty grate in the room. Apparently satisfied, he moved down the corridor and repeated the process with the two remaining rooms, a faint smile on his lips. He spent rather longer in Lionel Amsden's room, and when he returned to us the smile on his face had broadened. He rubbed his lean fingers together in satisfaction.

"Not a word of this to anyone, Miss Conyers," he said sharply. "And now for our little final tableau."

Miss Conyers led the way back into Professor Mair's study. Though the room had been tidied and its gruesome centrepiece removed, the chamber seemed still to exude a brooding atmosphere of horror—an atmosphere it had worn when the Professor's body lay grotesque and distorted on the carpet, which still bore signs of bloodstains and disfigurement.

The massive form of Lionel Amsden stirred in the shadows beyond the desk. There was a sullen, sneering look on his face as he lounged by the fireplace, as though daring Pons to challenge him. But my companion hurried instead directly to Inspector Jamison who sat behind the late Professor's desk, toying with a pencil and notebook and looking as though the tangled web of passions that lurked below the surface at The Poplars was completely beyond him. As indeed it was, I reflected with some satisfaction as I went to stand near the fire opposite Amsden.

All eyes were on Beresford as he bustled in behind me with his large portfolio of photographs. The secretary, Moffat, twisted his thin lips as he sat completely dwarfed by the huge leather armchair in which he reposed. The only person who appeared completely at ease was Clifford Armitage, whose frank, open face wore a welcoming smile as he caught sight of me. Pons had finished his brief consultation with the Inspector now and sat easily on the edge of the desk.

"This is Mr. Bruce Beresford," he said by way of introducing our companion. "He came to me with an interesting problem yesterday—a problem whose solution is central to the death of Professor Mair in this room. Therefore I thought it only right that he should be present this afternoon."

Miss Conyers crossed in front of me and sat down in a chair midway between the big windows which faced the garden. Pale sunshine spilled in now, staining the rich patterning of the carpet a deep carmine and seeming, to my somewhat overheated imagination, to re-echo the sinister theme of blood. Pons turned back to Jamison and bowed ironically.

"With your permission, Inspector."

Jamison nodded stiffly back.

"Please continue, Mr. Pons."

"I presume you have good reason for this melodramatic farce, Mr. Pons?"

Lionel Amsden's sullen face was flushed and his speech slurred. He looked insolently at Pons, who stared imperturbably back at him from his position on top of the desk.

"Reason enough, Mr. Amsden."

"Please be silent, Lionel," snapped Miss Conyers. "You have been drinking."

Amsden gave her a clumsy bow, his eyes flashing fire.

"It is not unknown, cousin dear..."

Inspector Jamison rapped on the surface of the desk with his knuckles, and in the heavy silence which followed Pons said, "Professor Mair's sudden and tragic death confronts us with a number of interesting and interrelated problems. Chiefly, those of motive, method, and culprit."

His eyes wandered round the room, probing each of us in turn.

"My friend, Doctor Parker here, inclines to one theory; yet his solution to the locked-door problem was childish and clumsy—if he will forgive me saying so. And yet, like so many seemingly insoluble puzzles, the answer is simplicity itself. Money, of course, was the motive, and I am certain that in the final analysis we shall find embezzlement at the back of it. Money undoubtedly missing from Professor Mair's estate funds, and when he expressed a desire to sell his house and move elsewhere the murderer, afraid of what such a move would involve—solicitors, the overhaul of accounts, and so forth—became alarmed and sought a drastic solution to his dilemma.

"At an hour in the afternoon when he knew that the Professor was alone in his study, he sought him out, first making sure that other members of the household were peaceably engaged in their normal pursuits in other parts of the house. Seeking the Professor's presence on some banal pretext, he locked the study door behind him to ensure remaining undisturbed. He killed the Professor with one blow from a kris he took from the wall over there. He had little time to clean it and there are still traces of blood on its tip."

"Eh?"

Jamison was on his feet with an alarmed expression; he went heavily to the corner of the study indicated by Pons and took down the weapon, sliding it gently from its scabbard.

"You are right, Mr. Pons," he muttered.

"I am well aware of that, Jamison," said Pons smoothly. "I observed as much within a few minutes of entering the room yesterday."

"But the javelin, Pons?" I protested.

My friend smiled broadly; he was evidently enjoying the effect he had created.

"You are an excellent physician, my dear Parker," he said gently. "But like many untrained people your eye sees only the surface aspect. It was obvious to me that the murderer was endeavouring to implicate Mr. Amsden here. He was a natural candidate owing to his sporting proclivities and his athletic build."

Amsden had turned from the mantelpiece now; the sullen look had gone from his face and his lower jaw had dropped.

"The person who killed the Professor," Pons went on, "was a far smaller man than Mr. Amsden. After he committed the crime, he replaced the kris in its scabbard. Wearing gloves, of course, he then took the javelin and, putting all his weight upon it, forced it as far as he could into the original wound. You will remember the weapon fell out quite easily when you touched it, Parker."

"I remember, Pons," I said somewhat stiffly.

"I do not blame you, my dear fellow. It was a first-rate piece of theatrical dressing and would have deceived most of us.

Though I have no doubt your post-mortem will reveal the true state of affairs readily enough, Jamison."

The grim-faced Inspector had come back to the desk now and was wrapping kris and scabbard in his voluminous handkerchief. He looked gloomily at my companion.

"Well, Mr. Pons?"

"We are looking for a clever, rather slightly built man with a good knowledge of figures," said Pons. "One who took the opportunity, when ransacking the room for effect, to abstract the one account book which might have implicated him. This is mere guesswork for the moment in the absence of anything stronger, but it is all part of the pattern."

He glanced at Moffat who, with ashen face, had struggled up in his armchair and was staring at Pons and the Inspector strangely.

"But the locked door, Mr. Pons?"

Clifford Armitage came toward us, shaking his head.

"I must confess I cannot see how anyone could have got out from this locked room."

Pons shot a quick glance at the secretary, Moffat.

"He never did get out, Mr. Armitage," he said calmly. "He was here all the time."

I looked from Jean Conyers in her seat between the windows to Mr. Bruce Beresford's honest, baffled face. I am sure the blankness in their countenances was fully reflected in my own. Pons went quickly back toward the door.

"The key was turned, the door was locked; let there be no mistake about that. It wanted but a few minutes of three o'clock. The Professor lay dead upon the floor, the room ransacked; the javelin was in place in the ready-made wound. The scene lacked only the master-stroke. The man we are seeking then gave vent to the most bloodcurdling series of screams that he could devise. Something he knew could not fail to bring the household running. He was not mistaken. Within some thirty seconds members of the family and staff, alarmed at the noise, were pounding at the door.

"But before that happened, our man crossed the room rapidly and secreted himself in the left-hand cupboard, one of a pair which flanks the door. There, with great daring, and keeping the cupboard door a fraction ajar so that he could see what went on in the room, he waited with great self-control until the room door was smashed in.

"Then, when he was certain, in the confusion when everyone was clustered in horror round the corpse of Professor Mair, he quietly let himself out of the cupboard, which was, of course, behind the people in the room, and joined the edge of the group as though he had just run in from the corridor."

"Brilliant, Pons!" I could not forbear saying.

"Elementary, my dear Parker," rejoined Pons.

The secretary had found his voice.

"But how could you possibly know this?" he said snappishly.

"For the simple reason that I found traces of his presence in the cupboard, Mr. Moffat."

There was an oppressive silence in the room now. Inspector Jamison's eyes were large and inquiring, but he did not presume to interrupt my friend's exposition.

"I found what I was looking for," Pons went on. "A mixture of sand and clay originating from the road excavations outside the house here. One would expect members of the household to bear traces of this because they were bound to cross the end of the drive entrance going to and fro on their lawful occasions. But there was no reason for anyone to be in that cupboard unless he were the murderer. When we find the same mixture of sand and clay on the floor and mat of Mr. Beresford's dark-room, then it is absolutely conclusive."

Jamison shook his head.

"Just a moment, Mr. Pons. Apart from the fact that I have no idea who Mr. Beresford is, what can his dark-room have to do with it?"

"I am coming to that, Inspector," Pons continued with a thin smile. "In the excavation outside the house I found a distinctive shoe print which had an unusual V pattern. I found part of the same imprint on the floor of the cupboard. I have examined the bedrooms here this afternoon and in a necessarily brief search could find no such shoe. And I have observed that no members of the family were wearing such a shoe. But Miss Conyers told me of a strange odour from the bedroom fires. Smoke from shoe leather makes that odour. It was so strong, in fact, that the servants had to light perfumed candles to take away the smell. I found small traces of shoe leather in one of the fireplaces here this afternoon, which dispelled any lingering doubt I might have had. With my proximity the murderer was forced to take a chance and burned the shoes, piece by piece, over the past two days."

"But why did he wear such distinctive shoes, Pons?" I said.

"He intended to leave a trail for the police. So that they would think the murderer was someone from outside."

Pons' eyes had a faraway look.

"We are dealing with a rare breed of dangerous animal, Parker. One who took infinite pains to concoct the perfect murder. That was why he had to destroy the shoes."

The secretary was on his feet now.

"Very ingenious, Mr. Pons, but you will still need something better than that."

"Indeed, Mr. Moffat," said Pons imperturbably, "and this is where Mr. Beresford comes in."

He turned to our client, who put down his album of photographs on the desk in front of Jamison.

"A series of bizarre events happened to Mr. Beresford only yesterday. He is, as most of you know, a photographer of some distinction, who was commissioned by Professor Mair to photograph this house for the brochures when it was advertised for sale. Mr. Beresford came here at precisely two-thirty p.m. the day before yesterday. He took exterior photographs of the grounds and the façade of The Poplars.

"Miss Conyers received him, and I presume that the other members of the family did not know of his presence. This then is the situation shortly before three o'clock: the door is locked, the crime committed, and the murderer cannot turn back. Just wishing to make sure that everything is quiet, he walks to one of those windows at the front of the study and looks out into the grounds.

"At precisely that instant Mr. Beresford photographs the façade of the house and with it the image of the murderer looking out of the window of Professor Mair's death chamber."

There was a murmur from those gathered in the room, and I noticed the stupefaction on Beresford's and the Inspector's faces. Pons could not suppress a chuckle.

"Astonishing, is it not? And one of the most unusual situations it has been my pleasure to be concerned in. Just imagine this man's dilemma. His plan has been carefully laid. In a few seconds he will scream to bring the household running. He is fully committed to his plan—indeed, the crime is already a *fait accompli*. But he knows Mr. Beresford will be back with the completed photographs. Still his nerve does not fail him. He must recover Mr. Beresford's negatives at all costs."

"Of course, Mr. Pons!"

Light had broken in on Beresford's face. He came forward and pumped Pons' hand.

"Not so fast," said Pons. "Our man carries out the rest of his plan perfectly and then hurries off. He dogs Mr. Beresford's footsteps, steals plates, and smashes others. All to no avail. The real plates, due to a simple error, are in Mr. Beresford's pocket and not in his carrying case at all."

Pons' eyes raked the room. The massive form of Lionel Amsden at the mantel seemed to have shrunk; Miss Conyers' body was drawn up on her chair as though she were afraid to miss a syllable of Pons' discourse. Armitage and Moffat were tense and silent, their eyes never leaving Pons' face. At the desk Inspector Jamison and Beresford wore expressions of eager expectancy.

"You remember, Parker, that I told you the murderer would not necessarily need to smash the plates."

I nodded.

"Since they were stolen on a bus, the thief could not possibly smash them there."

"Naturally," said Pons easily, "but if our man also happened to be a keen amateur photographer, he might well wish to develop the plates himself to see whether he had been caught in the death room at the time of committing his crime. Remember, Mr. Beresford only had to fix the date and time of this photograph and the hangman's rope awaited."

Pons stirred from the desk top and stretched himself.

"I looked for evidence of chemical staining on the fingers," he said softly. "There are such stains on the hands of a man in this room. Apart from Mr. Beresford, that is."

Pons permitted himself a brief smile.

"I wonder what he said when he developed a scene showing the muscular forms of football idols."

He turned to the folio which Beresford was unfolding.

"Thanks to the photographer's enlarging skill we now have an excellent likeness of the murderer standing at the window of this study a few moments after committing his abominable crime."

Pons turned and advanced toward Moffat and Armitage, holding up the large expanse of pasteboard. There was a strangled cry and the group broke up. The blue eyes of Clifford Armitage were distorted and there were flecks of foam at his mouth. He made feeble attempts to ward off the photographic enlargement Pons was thrusting toward him.

Then he turned with a galvanic movement and rushed across the room. Miss Conyers screamed and there was a moment of confusion.

Inspector Jamison moved quickly to intercept him, but Armitage was quicker still. He swept up a bronze statuette from the desk and felled the Inspector with one blow. Before the officer had slumped to the floor, Pons was blocking the path to the door, but Armitage had already turned. His hands over his face, he ran for the window; there was a splintering of glass and woodwork and then nothing but the pale sunlight driving in and the wind lashing the curtains.

Pons' face was white as he came toward me.

"Regrettable, Parker, but it could not have been foreseen. Your department, I think. While you are below I will see to the Inspector."

I ran down the stairs three at a time, but I knew it was already too late. And so it proved. Clifford Armitage, that most cunning and strong-nerved of murderers, whose wits had only cracked at the last, lay at a weird and unnatural angle. He had fallen onto the cement path, and it took me only a moment to confirm that his neck was broken and life already extinct.

Pausing only to give instructions to the detective-constable to cover the remains with a tarpaulin, I hurried back upstairs, considerably relieved to find Inspector Jamison slowly regaining consciousness, a large bump on his forehead already discernible and his temper nowise improved by his experience. When I had made him comfortable on the divan and one of the servants was applying a cold compress to his forehead, Pons drew me to the other end of the study.

"A bad business, Parker, but I fear we had little chance of getting him into court."

"But the photographs, Pons . . . " I began.

Pons shook his head gravely.

"My little charade, as I called it, was a charade in truth. It was bluff, I am afraid, but bluff which nevertheless brought down the curtain on an enterprising and ruthless killer."

He showed me Beresford's enlargements as he spoke. They indeed showed part of the façade and windows of The Poplars, but the muffled figure looking out from behind the white lace curtains was quite indistinguishable.

"Ironic, is it not?" said Pons when I had told him of Armitage's fate.

He glanced over my shoulder at the white face of Jean Conyers.

"I am sorry indeed to have put you to such an ordeal, Miss Conyers."

The girl shook her head.

"I am deeply in your debt, Mr. Pons."

Pons looked from her to Lionel Amsden who had come up

sheepishly behind her and was hesitantly extending his hand to my companion.

"You might remember, Miss Conyers, that surface impressions are not always reliable. Eh, Parker?"

He smiled at her expression and then turned back to Beresford and the secretary at the desk.

"Well, Mr. Beresford, you have brought me a rich and rare experience."

"I am greatly in your debt also, Mr. Pons."

"Well, well, we shall see, Mr. Beresford. In the meantime, no doubt, you and Dr. Parker could join me in a steak and a bottle of wine at Simpson's this evening?"

"Delighted, Mr. Pons."

Solar Pons turned back to me, his eyes twinkling at my expression. "If there are any other small points on which you are not quite clear, my dear fellow, no doubt they can await our return to Praed Street."

"I do not think so, Pons," I murmured. "For once I have little to say."

Solar Pons clapped me on the shoulder and led the way out of the room.

"The long arm of coincidence in the shape of Mr. Bruce Beresford has enabled me to bring to book a most cunning and ingenious murderer," he said.

The Sealed Spire Mystery

✑ 1

I T WAS A bitterly cold day in the memorable winter of
1921 when my friend, the eminent consulting detective
Solar Pons, was involved in one of the most strange and
bizarre adventures I have ever had occasion to chronicle. For
some days it had threatened snow, and though the expected fall
did not materialise, every morning found hoarfrost glittering
on the pavements and railings of the houses round about.

But our apartments at 7B Praed Street were warm and comfortable and Mrs. Johnson, our amiable landlady, kept the fires
heaped with coals so that I soon came to resent having to attend
to the importunate demands of my patients. I had only just
come in to lunch on the morning in question and Pons, who
had been engaged in some abstruse chemical experiments, was
in an unusually amiable mood.

I make the comment because he had recently been through
a period in which his exceptional powers had lain dormant and
it was my experience that such times hung heavily on his hands
and brought a wearisomeness of spirit when such an active brain
lay fallow. He put down the pipette with which he had been

precipitating some yellow solution into the steaming beaker before him and laid aside his apron.

"Ah, Parker. I am glad to see you, my dear fellow. If you will just give me a minute or two to wash my hands, I will be with you shortly. I trust the confinement was not too difficult a one?"

"Moderately so, Pons," I replied. "Though there were one or two anxious moments."

Pons gave me an enigmatic smile as he passed from the room. I read *The Times* for a few minutes and then, seeing that it wanted but a short interval to one o'clock, rang the bell which indicated to Mrs. Johnson that we were ready to partake of lunch. The meal was already on the table and our good landlady had already descended to her own quarters before Pons reappeared. He sat down opposite me, rubbing his lean hands briskly together.

"How on earth did you know I had been to a confinement, Pons?" I said irritably.

My companion's eyes were dancing with suppressed mirth.

"Ah, my simple observation has finally sunk home, Parker," he replied in that superior manner he affected. "There was no great difficulty in the matter."

He turned to survey the windows overlooking the street as a particularly sharp gust of wind rattled the casement.

"A few days ago you had occasion to let drop that you felt Mrs. Bracegirdle's confinement might be a difficult one. Here on the table earlier this morning I find a brief note from Mrs. Johnson conveying the information: *Mrs. Bracegirdle. Urgent.* Therefore, I infer that the happy event is due. When you come in looking irritated, your hair hanging over your eyes and your waistcoat buttoned crudely, at least two buttonholes out of alignment, it is no great matter to deduce that you had to off-coat and buckle to and that the confinement had been a trying experience."

I looked guiltily at the waistcoat in question, tried to bring an affable smile to my ruffled features, and rebuttoned the offending garment.

"You are absolutely correct, Pons," I said, "and I will not give you an opening by commenting on the simplicity of the method by which you arrived at your conclusion. But it was a deucedly difficult birth, though mother and children are doing well."

Pons raised his eyebrows.

"I am glad to hear it, Parker. Twins, I assume."

"A boy and a girl," I said. "I am relieved to have that little matter disposed of, as it has rather been hanging over me for the past few weeks."

"And Mrs. Bracegirdle too, I should imagine," Pons observed blandly.

And with that he set to and for the next few minutes we endeavoured to do full justice to the excellent dish of roast beef and Yorkshire pudding Mrs. Johnson had provided. We had disposed of the dessert and were on the coffee and cheese before my companion broke silence again.

He then made some observations on a particularly gruesome trunk murder, which was occupying an inordinate amount of space in the more sensational papers, to which I gave some perfunctory answers. In truth I had not followed the case very closely, but judging by Pons' shrewd observations on the conduct of the police in the matter, he had come very close to the heart of it.

I was on my second cup of coffee and disposing of my final

portion of cheese when Pons, who had risen from the table with his habitual nervous manner and had crossed to the windows commanding the street, gave a muffled ejaculation.

"What do you make of him, Parker?"

I replaced my cup in the saucer with some asperity and rose from the table, not without some difficulty, and made my way to his side.

"I only wish you would let me finish a meal in peace, Pons," I said.

Pons' eyes were dancing with mischievous humour.

"The exercise is an aid to digestion Parker," he observed gravely. "Whereas the old gentleman who is dancing about so agitatedly on the pavement opposite will not be there for much longer and you will have missed a valuable opportunity forever."

"Opportunity for what?" I said, my ruffled spirits written only too plainly on my face.

"Why, for the deployment of those ratiocinative gifts which you have developed so rapidly of late, Parker. What do you make of him?"

I pushed past Pons somewhat unceremoniously and looked beyond the curtains to where an old gentleman in black was in fact behaving in the curious manner alluded to by my companion. Despite the cold wind which blew along Praed Street, making pieces of paper dance in the frosty gutters, he would first stand still, then move on a few yards as though undecided, but then return to the same spot as if in an agony of mind.

His rusty black suit had obviously seen better days and he clutched an antiquated umbrella in one hand and a small black briefcase in the other. With the wind whistling about the skirts of his coat he was oblivious of the curious glances of the passersby in that busy thoroughfare.

"A man of some seventy years," I said.

"Elementary," Pons commented.

"Retired, probably. Poor, perhaps. Most likely a businessman, judging by his case. Hatless, which may mean he is absent-minded. The Lost Property Office is not far from here. Perhaps he has found the umbrella and wishes to return it."

"And finding the office closed, vents his rage by waving it in the street," added Pons, dissolving into laughter. He caught sight of my rueful face and checked himself.

"I am sorry, my dear fellow, but the delightful absurdity of your diagnosis was too much for my sense of humour."

"Very well, Pons," I said, choking back my feelings. "Perhaps it was not one of my better efforts in the deductive field. But he is certainly past seventy years of age."

"That much is evident," said my companion. "Not a businessman. And certainly not retired. Unless my eyesight deceives me, he is wearing clerical garments."

I looked again, and grudgingly agreed.

"It may be so, Pons. But how do you know he is not retired?"

"The clergy do not normally retire all the while they are clear-minded and able-bodied," said Pons. "The specimen before us, who betrays such indecision in Praed Street, is strong, in good health and evidently in full possession of his faculties. He could not venture abroad hatless on such a bitterly cold day unless this were so."

"You may be right, Pons," I ventured.

My companion gave a tight smile and went on.

"He is certainly not seeking the Lost Property Office, Parker. It is my contention that he is debating whether to come here to consult me or not. The conclusion therefore is that something has occurred which has made him forsake his usual habits, even to quitting his house without his hat in such inclement weather. Wherever it was, it was some distance away."

"How can you say that, Pons?"

I fear my short temper must have showed in my voice, for Pons gave me a regretful look; but the even tenor of his discourse did not change.

"Strange as it may seem, Parker, it has either been raining or the ecclesiastical gentleman has been swimming, for I can clearly see droplets of moisture shining on his umbrella from here. Therefore, he has come from outside London, where local conditions may be a little warmer, for it has certainly not rained in the capital this morning according to the wireless."

"You may be right," I conceded.

"The gentleman concerned, possibly a Rural Dean, is due to attend the conference which begins at Church House, Westminster, tomorrow," Pons went on. "The case contains his overnight things and a paper he is to present on his own particular subject at the conference. The problem with which he is concerned is something to do with either of these matters. He has come up a day early to lay some facts before me, inasmuch as the Conference does not begin until tomorrow afternoon."

I could contain myself no longer.

"Come, Pons! This is the wildest conjecture."

Pons laid a lean finger alongside his nose. He looked at me curiously.

"We shall see, Parker, we shall see. His uncertainty has been thrown to the winds. He is crossing the road and in a few minutes, I fancy, he will be here."

Pons was indeed right, for even as I moved to tidy our lunch table there came a ring at the front doorbell. Pons seated himself in his favourite armchair near the fire with a mocking smile on his face and awaited the measured tread of Mrs. Johnson on the stairs.

🖎 2

"Dr. Glyn Campbell, gentlemen," she announced with a conspiratorial air.Close on her heels appeared the elderly gentleman we had already spent so much time in observing from the window. Closer to, he was, as Pons had said, of robust and sturdy appearance, though half-frozen and very much out of sorts. His broad, red features were roughened with the cold and his faded blue eyes wept behind his gold pince-nez. His old-fashioned clothing had a slight greenish tinge, as though it was not only old but mouldy, and the scanty white hairs on his head were dishevelled and much whipped about by the wind.

He put down the ancient umbrella carefully, leaning it against a leg of the dining table, and looked hesitantly from Pons to myself as Mrs. Johnson quit the room. He clutched the bag to himself and placed it on his lap as my companion motioned him to a chair. I noticed that the umbrella was indeed, as Pons had said, flecked with moisture.

"Mr. Pons?"

Pons responded with a slight bow.

"Allow me to present my friend and colleague, Dr. Lyndon Parker. Dr. Campbell is the Rector of Shap, in Surrey."

The faded blue eyes focused sharply.

"Ah, you know me, Mr. Pons."

57

"As soon as our landlady had announced you," said Pons. "Your writings are not unknown to me."

"Poor things, poor things, Mr. Pons," said our visitor deprecatingly, but the expression on his face nevertheless indicated his pleasure. He put out his reddened hands toward our fire and rubbed them to restore the circulation.

"May I offer you refreshment, Dr. Campbell? Some coffee, perhaps? There is plenty in the pot. And I fancy you will find some brandy on the sideboard, Parker."

"It is too good of you, Mr. Pons," protested the Rector as I moved to the sideboard to get the bottle and a fresh cup and saucer. When our visitor was comfortable with the coffee cup in his hand, I saw that Pons had been studying him carefully.

"You are in some trouble, Dr. Campbell, evidently, or you would not be here. You have come early for the Conference, I take it?"

"Why, yes, Mr. Pons. I am to read a paper at the opening session at Church House, tomorrow."

Pons could not forbear shooting me a mocking glance as he eased his long form in his leather chair.

"The rain must have been unpleasant this morning and entirely unexpected in your part of Surrey, given the weather we have been having of late. Yet you came away so precipitately I daresay you mislaid your hat?"

Dr. Campbell put down the cup in his saucer with a faint clinking in the silence of the sitting room and stared at my companion with wide eyes.

"That is exactly so, Mr. Pons. I could not ignore the rain on my way to the station so I seized the umbrella, quite forgetting my hat in my agitation."

Pons nodded and tented his lean fingers in front of him in the attitude with which I had long become familiar.

"You are also Rural Dean, as your gaiters would indicate. I had occasion to consult *Crockford's* during a case recently and I came across your entry in so doing."

"Yes, Mr. Pons."

The old gentleman relaxed in his chair and favoured both of us with benevolent glances.

"Exactly so, Mr. Pons. And it is partly in connection with my duties as Rural Dean that I find myself in my present predicament."

"Let us just hear your little problem, Dr. Campbell. I have no doubt that we shall be able to do something to resolve your difficulties and three heads are better than one."

"You do me honour, Pons," I protested not without a touch of irony, and I was inwardly amused to see that the inflection of my voice was not lost on the good doctor, whose mild eyes positively beamed with pleasure.

"Well, Mr. Pons," he began without further preamble. "I am, as you say, Rector of Shap and Rural Dean of Stapleford. Though how you guessed I had come for the Conference and had travelled a day early to consult you is quite beyond me."

Pons smiled thinly, avoiding my eye.

"An inspired guess, merely, Dr. Campbell. I could see by your garb that you were a senior churchman. It did not therefore seem out of the way that you had come to London for the Conference. There has been a deal about it in the newspapers lately. You carried a bag which indicated that you intended to stay in London overnight. Assuming that you intended to call upon me, it therefore followed that you had come a day early, since the Conference does not open until tomorrow. I hazarded a further guess, and knowing you to be perhaps a Bishop or at least a Rural Dean, from your dress, I inferred that you would be presenting a paper to your colleagues, as you have just confirmed."

Dr. Campbell drained his coffee, which had been liberally laced with brandy, and gave a sigh of satisfaction.

"I see my faith in you has not been misplaced, Mr. Pons. I had some hesitation, I do not mind admitting, but only because I feared that a consultant of your eminence might laugh at me."

Pons shook his head.

"Grave happenings often turn upon comic events, Dr. Campbell. I shall not do that, never fear."

Thus reassured our visitor clasped his hands about his knees and immediately plunged into his story.

"I hardly know where to begin, Mr. Pons, though I will do my poor best. But the strange events which have been taking place these past months have me completely bewildered and worried. Even my secretary, young Isaac Dabson, is as much in the dark as I. And when I found today that the paper I am to deliver at the Conference tomorrow was not in my case, but some trashy children's comic instead, I thought I should burst with rage and indignation, which is most undignified for one of my cloth."

Our visitor looked so concerned and yet at the same time so comic that I was hard put to it to retain a straight face and Pons' eyes held a twinkle, though his grave expression did not alter. He did not, as I thought he might, immediately recall the Rector to the main tenor of his story but instead asked him what to me sounded like an irrelevant question.

"You have a secretary, Dr. Campbell?"

The venerable churchman nodded gravely.

"You wonder at such a humble country parson as myself running to such a luxury, Mr. Pons?"

As my companion moved to protest, Dr. Campbell waved his apology away.

"It is no secret, Mr. Pons. I have private means. My parents left me well provided for, and my writings on specialised subjects bring me in a second sizeable income so that I do not have to rely my stipend. I am a lifelong bachelor, as no doubt you are already aware. I need a secretary, Mr. Pons, for otherwise the demands of authorship would take up an inordinate amount of my time, to the neglect of my parish duties."

"I am certain that is so," said Pons. "Mr. Dabson has been with you a long while?"

Dr. Campbell inclined his head.

"Almost a year now. He is excellent at his work though I fear he must doubt my sanity sometimes with the events of the past months. I also have a housekeeper who cooks for us, and that completes the ménage at the Rectory."

"Just so, Dr. Campbell. Pray continue."

"Well, Mr. Pons," our visitor went on earnestly, "the events of which I am complaining started about six months ago in the most commonplace way imaginable. I found, on awaking one morning, that my slippers had disappeared from the bedroom. This discommoded me somewhat and it was not until after breakfast that I discovered them. Dabson had gone into the study to transcribe some of my notes of the day before and found them beneath the cover of his typewriting machine."

"You were present on that occasion?"

"Yes, indeed, Mr. Pons. I remember we made a joke about it, but young Dabson cast me a curious look. He had just bought the machine—I believe in being up to date in our methods, Mr.

Pons—and he caught the buckle of one slipper in the ribbon carrier and was afraid he had damaged it."

"It follows, of course, Dr. Campbell, that you did not yourself consciously place the slippers there?"

Our visitor shook his head vehemently.

"Certainly not, Mr. Pons. And since Mrs. Jenkin and Dabson denied all knowledge of the matter, I was forced to pass it over in a somewhat joking manner. Truth to tell I thought little of it, curious as the circumstance was, and a few days later it had become quite lost to my mind in the absorption of everyday tasks."

"I take it anyone could have removed the slippers from your bedroom?"

"That would not be too difficult, Mr. Pons. And there are a number of parishioners in and out of the house all day in the normal course of events. But for what purpose?"

Solar Pons smiled thinly.

"That is presumably why you have consulted me, my dear sir. I am already intrigued and doubtless you have more to tell me."

Dr. Campbell nodded, his normally benevolent eyes carrying a grim expression.

"As I said, things began in that mild and innocuous manner. But a few days later other articles were missing until it seemed that hardly a week passed without some stupid and pointless abstraction of items I needed for the prosecution of my work. It has got to the stage of absolute persecution, Mr. Pons!"

Dr. Campbell glared belligerently for a moment or two and then relaxed, encouraged perhaps by Pons' alert and concerned expression.

"Pray be more specific, Dr. Campbell."

"Well, sir, not two days following the slipper episode, my notes for a speech before the Royal Society disappeared. I found them eventually in the hands of a statue in the garden. That was but the prelude to a series of farcical and meaningless episodes in which I began to assume the aspect of a laughing stock in the village."

Dr. Campbell sighed and his face bore such a harassed expression that the laughable aspects of his story were quite expunged from my mind.

"My hat disappeared, sir. It reappeared at the top of the church flagpole, in full view of all the village. I opened my briefcase in the pulpit to deliver my sermon and produced instead two kippers in greaseproof paper. They stank, sir, if not exactly to high heaven, at least to the church roof."

Pons stretched himself in his chair and permitted himself a thin smile.

"Dear me, Dr. Campbell, this is distressing indeed. Please continue."

Dr. Campbell wagged his head.

"Well, Mr. Pons, the unfortunate and ridiculous incidents which ensued would make a catalogue that would take me all day to relate were I to recall them all. Needless to say no one owned up to the authorship of these strange happenings, and it began to get about the district that the Rector was a little odd and absentminded. That did not bother me at first but the affair has reached such absurd proportions that it has even got to the ears of my Bishop. I fear that if the press were to get hold of it, my scholarly work would suffer."

Pons put the tips of his fingers together and leaned forward.

"Just so. I take it more serious things have happened in addition to these rather light-hearted episodes."

Dr. Campbell shot Pons a reproachful glance.

"Light-hearted is perhaps hardly the term I would have used, Mr. Pons," he said disapprovingly. "But I can see how it would look to an outsider."

"But you have not suffered anything other than annoyance and slight inconvenience," Pons persisted.

"That is true, Mr. Pons," returned our visitor. "Perfectly true. But it is a harassment, sir, a perfect harassment. And one which has reached such proportion as to impinge seriously upon both my professional life and my integrity."

My companion's eyes flashed.

"I did not say the affair was trivial, doctor; merely that the incidents you have described appeared so."

Dr. Campbell appeared mollified.

"Well, that is certainly so, Mr. Pons, as far as it goes. But there were two more incidents of late which had somewhat more sinister connotations. And then my speech today. That is a serious inconvenience and means I must return to my parish."

"Could you not telephone your secretary?" I asked.

Dr. Campbell shook his head.

"He is away in the north for a few days, visiting his sister. And my housekeeper would not be able to do anything about it. Besides, the text of my address might well be hanging from the bell tower by this time."

He said this with a sibilant drawing-in of his breath and a tilt of his determined jaw that boded distinctly un-Christian thoughts, and a brief silence fell before he resumed.

"The latest incidents?" Pons prompted.

"I ask your pardon, Mr. Pons. These are deep waters for me and my mind has not its usual lucidity. The petty irritations I have spoken of have continued at the rate of about one or two a week for the past six months. Only this past fortnight the pattern has changed."

He sighed heavily.

"I mentioned earlier my duties as Rural Dean. One of them consists of delivering an annual address at the Church of St. Mary's at Stapleford. This is in connection with a Conference of Diocesan Candidates—I am sure I need not bother you with the details, gentlemen. There is bound to be a dreadful scandal over this."

He looked sombrely at Pons.

"Among the congregation was an old friend, the Rector of Channock in Yorkshire. He is inordinately fond of cats. Sheba, his favourite Persian, invariably travels with him. I had brought my bag with me. I have it here."

Here our visitor's eyes flickered to his lap. "Truth to tell, it felt inordinately heavy. I put my hand in it to find the notes for my speech when I was surprised to encounter fur. Not to put too much strain on your patience, Mr. Pons, imagine my horror when I drew forth not my notes, but the corpse of Pattenden's favourite cat. Strangled, sir, with a length of wire. The Conference broke up in uproar; I was almost assaulted by Pattenden; sadist and murderer were among the terms flung at me; and I made, in addition to Pattenden, a number of enemies for life!"

Dr. Campbell lapsed into silence again. I glanced at Pons and saw that his expression had changed. The alertness was still in his eyes, but there was something else there; compassion and understanding.

"A frightful experience, Dr. Campbell," he said gently. "I believe I recall a paragraph or two in the newspapers."

The Rector nodded.

"I was fortunate that nothing more was made of it. I left

the Conference immediately, of course, and returned home, dreadfully upset. Naturally, I wrote to Pattenden immediately to protest my innocence, but have heard nothing since. I do not blame him. I should have acted similarly in his position."

Campbell drew his thickset shoulders up.

"I will draw briefly to a close, Mr. Pons. The latest disaster was averted, I am glad to say. A few days ago I found an intimate item of ladies' apparel in the pocket of my jacket in which my handkerchief usually reposes."

A shudder passed through our visitor's frame.

"You can imagine the effect of this, gentlemen, had I produced it at the Ladies' Guild meeting I was due to attend that afternoon. I had already received a summons from my Bishop for this coming week.

"Two days ago I received an extraordinary letter, which I have brought with me. This morning I found my galoshes filled with cold tea. On arrival in town I discover the loss of my address for tomorrow's Assembly."

He paused, temporarily out of breath.

"You have indeed cause to be put out, Rector," said Pons soothingly. "Naturally, I shall take the case. We will return with you on the next train if Parker is agreeable. And we will examine this letter and hear of any further adventures en route."

✍ 3

Pons frowned at the light rain which was starring the windows of the railway carriage. "Before I examine the letter you have given me, Dr. Campbell, you mentioned earlier that one thing happened this morning which prompted you to rush out, quite forgetting your hat."

Dr. Campbell, ensconced on the seat opposite us, clicked his teeth in a highly audible manner. The three of us were quite alone in the compartment, so that we were able to continue the extraordinary dialogue which had begun in Praed Street.

"You will yourself begin to think that my senses are affected, Mr. Pons. It was not just the cold tea and the galoshes this morning. No, you are right. I had opened the hall cupboard to get out my umbrella when I found this notice pinned to the inside of the door."

He reached in his bag and came up with a large folded sheet of cartridge paper. As he held it up toward us I could see that it had written on it in large block capitals, with what appeared to be black crayon: CAMPBELL—YOU MUST OPEN THE SEALED SPIRE!!!

"What do you make of it, Mr. Pons?"

My friend sat in silence for a moment, his chin resting on his slim fingers as he stared at our client sombrely.

"Intriguing, in the extreme. What is the sealed spire?"

Dr. Campbell looked irritated. He passed the paper to Pons who spread it out on the seat next to him and studied it intently. Then he compared it with the sheet of blue notepaper Dr. Campbell had already given him. He absorbed its contents without comment and passed it to me.

"Your parish would seem to harbour more than one eccentric, Rector," he said drily.

Dr. Campbell chuckled throatily, his mild blue eyes dancing with mischief behind the gold frames of his spectacles.

"Capital, Mr. Pons. I see that I did correctly in consulting you. There is some ridiculous legend connected with the spire. My church is of the Norman period, as you probably know. The spire above the bell chamber has been sealed for a long time.

There is, in fact, a large chamber above the bell frame but it was never used for anything more than storage. It was so difficult to get to that a previous incumbent had it boarded up. There is still access today, but the locked trapdoor has not been opened for years."

He paused and looked mournfully at the sodden landscape beyond the windows.

"When I first came to Shap twenty years ago, I went up there. There was nothing other than some old, broken furniture, bare boards and dust, Mr. Pons. I had the trapdoor relocked and so far as I know no one has been there since. But a ridiculous legend has grown up about what the local people call the sealed spire. An old lady in the village, Mrs. Grace Harbinger, is always writing me letters on the subject. Her mind is a little affected, I think. The thing is a confounded nuisance, and a national newspaper got hold of the story some years ago.

"It has become rather like Joanna Southcott's Box, Mr. Pons. Open the sealed spire and all the problems of the world will vanish."

He chuckled again.

I had sat with the piece of blue notepaper in my hand, without reading the message on it, while this dialogue between Pons and the Rector ensued.

"Why do you not simply open the spire and scotch the rumours?" I asked, conscious of Pons' approving glance.

Our client bristled.

"For the very good reason, Dr. Parker, that I will not lend myself to superstition and nonsense. The sealed spire chamber, as they call it, is nothing less than a quite ordinary box-room, filled with old furniture. I will have no truck with such idiocy. And I will not open that room either to please Mrs.

Harbinger or the local press. And if you had read my articles on science and religion, doctor, you would not ask me such a question."

"I am sure that Parker meant no harm, Dr. Campbell," Pons said mildly. "The question would appear to be a logical one on the face of it."

Dr. Campbell looked hurt and he clicked his teeth again.

"I am sorry, gentlemen," he said contritely. "I should not have spoken so, but I have been sorely tried of late."

A brief silence ensued after this apology, and I occupied the awkward pause by perusing the note Pons had handed me. It was indeed a remarkable document. It was dated three days previously and headed, The House upon the Green. It was brief and to the point:

Dear Rector,

As I have constantly pointed out, the sealed spire must be opened if the world is to survive. Your implacable attitude to my repeated requests over the years compels me to bring this case before your Bishop at the earliest opportunity. The whole village joins with me in calling upon you to obey the dictates of conscience. The Sealed Spire must and will be opened! Its revelations will be of inestimable benefit to mankind. You deny our rightful requests at your peril.

Yours,

Grace Harbinger.

I read this extraordinary missive again.

"What do you make of it, Parker?" asked Pons with a grim smile.

"She is obviously deranged," I said indignantly.

"Is she not? But there is more here, Parker, than meets the outward eye. She speaks of other letters, Rector."

Our client nodded uncomfortably.

"Oh, yes, Mr. Pons, as the good lady hints, this has been going on for years. I have drawers full of such letters at home. Dabson is quite resigned to them. Mrs. Harbinger lives not a hundred yards away, on the green facing the Rectory, yet once and sometimes three times a week she essays the long walk to the village stores to post a letter which she could cross the green to deliver by hand."

Pons sat quietly, his fingers toying with the lobe of his left ear.

"Even so, Dr. Campbell, eccentric or not, she would appear to be a formidable opponent. Her enmity would only add fuel to the present furore about you. It is an interesting point."

And he would say nothing further until the train had decanted us onto the platform at the small station of Shap. Our client's Rectory was only a few hundred yards distant, set next to the ancient Norman church, in a delightful rural setting which time seemed to have passed by.

We walked through a path that skirted the churchyard to the hamlet of old timbered houses that seemed even quieter now that they were bound in the icy grip of winter. As Pons had surmised and Dr. Campbell had confirmed, it had rained earlier in the day and moisture glinted on roofs and hedgerows, the dampness adding an extra chill to the air so that I was glad when we had arrived at our destination.

We preceded our client through an ancient lych-gate that faced the green, and he pointed out a low, timbered house on the far side from which smoke ascended in slow spirals against the lowering sky.

"That is Mrs. Harbinger's residence, gentlemen."

"I think I shall pay the lady a visit later in the day," said Pons, glancing at the bulk of the church behind us. "I have a fancy to hear firsthand her thoughts on The Sealed Spire."

"By all means," said the Rector somewhat uncertainly. "But it is a pleasure I fear I must forego. I have had enough of the lady's thoughts on the subject to last me a lifetime."

Pons and I exchanged an ironic glance, and then we had turned to follow Dr. Campbell up a narrow paved path that arched between twin lawns to the façade of a gracious Georgian house adjoining the church on its far side.

We were met in the hallway by a pleasant, middle-aged woman with a worried face.

"Ah, Mrs. Jenkin," said our host. "This is a good friend of mine, Mr. . . . ."

"Rutherford, at your service," interrupted Pons smoothly, ignoring the Rector's startled look. "This is my partner, Mr. Parker. We are antique dealers, come to appraise some of Dr. Campbell's rarer pieces."

The Rector had recovered himself by now and his eyes were glinting behind his gold-rimmed glasses.

"Of course. I should have warned you of this visit, Mrs. Jenkin, but it had quite slipped my mind."

The housekeeper gave her employer a sharp look and then smiled at us.

"Will the gentlemen be staying to tea? I take it you'll want it at the usual time."

"Yes, Mrs. Jenkin, in about an hour. I have had to return unexpectedly but shall be returning to town on the early evening train."

"Very well, Rector."

71

Mrs. Jenkin disappeared about her duties as we followed Dr. Campbell down the hall and into his study, a big room lined with leather-bound books, in which a cheerful fire was burning.

"I thought it best not to advertise my presence here, Rector," said Pons, looking around the room keenly. "If we are to help you, that is."

"You know best, Mr. Pons," said Dr. Campbell diffidently. "Though I am sure you would be more comfortable here."

"Parker and I will be more free if we stay at the inn for one or two nights," said Pons.

He looked at the travelling bag which I had put down in a corner of the study.

"We have brought things for a short stay, and I do not anticipate this business will take more than a couple of days."

"I am very glad to hear you say so, Mr. Pons," said the Rector, crossing to sit in an easy chair by the fire. "Please regard the Rectory as your own. Dabson is away and Mrs. Jenkin is most accommodating and easygoing. If you need meals or anything during the day, you have only to ask her."

"That is very good of you," said Pons, inclining his head. "If you will excuse me."

He went round the study with quick, catlike movements, stabbing glances at the shelves, now and then taking down a book. He was particularly interested in the Rector's big mahogany desk, which was set in a corner near the window overlooking the green. He walked around a smaller desk between the window and the fire, on which a typewriter stood hooded.

"This is where Mr. Dabson works?"

"Yes, Mr. Pons. I fear he is a somewhat chilly mortal and

prefers to be nearer the fire. I find the spot near the window suits me better."

"Quite so."

Pons was over near the Rector's desk again, scrutinising the photographs and prints which hung on the wall. I had removed my coat by this time and went to sit opposite the Rector near the fire, observing Pons' movements and keeping my own counsel.

"What do you make of this, Parker?"

I went quickly over to join him. Pons had indicated a photograph of a group of young men who sat in formal stiffness on chairs in long rows, against the ivy-covered background of some venerable pile. There were names printed on the photographic mount, identifying those in the group. The picture was so old that it was quite yellowed by time, but it was nevertheless remarkably clear. To my astonishment Pons got out his magnifying glass and was studying the faces carefully.

"With your permission, Rector."

So saying he removed the picture from the wall. As he did so he gave a muffled exclamation. I went to his side, stooping to pick up the thick sheaf of typescript stapled together which had slipped from behind the picture. Pons took it from me, studying it, his brows set in firm, corrugated lines.

"Your missing address if I am not much mistaken, Dr. Campbell."

The Rector crossed to us with swift strides. He took the material, his hands trembling with suppressed anger. He bit his lip and looked at Pons diffidently. My companion laid his hand upon his arm.

"Have no fear, Rector. Your wits are not in question so far as I am concerned. These are deep waters, Parker."

Dr. Campbell smiled hesitantly and then turned to the fireside, slipping the notes in his briefcase, which he proceeded to lock. I went back toward the fire with Pons as he placed the picture upward on the secretary's desk, near the fire.

"Now, Parker, give me your opinion."

I searched the rows of faces hesitantly. Pons' hand obscured the printed legend at the base of the frame.

"Why that is surely the Rector," I said, indicating a young man of about thirty who sat in the front row of the group, eyes slightly closed against the sunlight. Dr. Campbell had joined us.

"Quite right, Dr. Parker," the Rector said wryly. "Theological college. A long time ago now, I am afraid."

He turned the frame over, looking for the label on the back.

"Dear me," he said softly. "I see it was taken in 1880. How time flies!"

Pons gave me a quizzical look in which wry humour was mingled.

"Quite so, Dr. Campbell. I have a fancy for such historic photographs. With your permission I will borrow it for a while. I have the names underneath and intend to do a little research in *Crockford's* later."

The Rector looked puzzled; indeed, his blank-faced incomprehension must have matched my own, though he said nothing but went to a small collection of books on his desk and came back with the requisite volume. He looked nostalgically at the picture again.

"Many of them are gone now, I'm afraid, Mr. Pons. At least two in the South African War. And another three in the Great War, you know. Dollond, Carstairs, and Digby. Though they were even then in their fifties, they volunteered to serve as chaplains. A terrible waste, gentlemen."

I joined in Pons' muttered agreement with the Rector's sentiments and went back to the fire, considerably puzzled by Pons' interest in the photograph. He spent the next hour roaming restlessly about Dr. Campbell's study and then, at his own request, ascended to the first-floor bedrooms alone. By the time he rejoined us for tea, which we took in a cheerful side-parlour with flowered wallpaper, he was in an inordinately expansive mood, rubbing his thin, sensitive hands together and humming tunelessly under his breath.

"We progress, Parker, we progress," he said. "And when we have seen Dr. Campbell off on his train, I have one or two little experiments to make."

"I must confess, Pons," I commenced with some irritation, when my companion stopped me by laying a warning finger alongside his nose. He waited until Mrs. Jenkin had brought fresh toast and withdrawn before he broke the silence again.

"I must impress upon you, Parker, that I am Rutherford during our short stay in Shap. It is of the utmost importance that you remember this if we are to do any good. If the person responsible for the mischief against the Rector knows that we are here, he will go to ground and we shall lose a golden opportunity."

"I am sorry, Pons," I said contritely, aware of my *faux pas* too late and that Dr. Campbell's beaming eyes were turned upon me.

Pons' lips were set in a hard line as he regarded me severely.

"It must be Rutherford when we visit Mrs. Harbinger, Parker. I do beg of you to be on your guard, my dear fellow. And now, Dr. Campbell, allow me to pass you another slice of this delicious toast before I subject you to any more questions."

After tea Pons spent half an hour immersed in *Crockford's,* making notes from time to time and checking with Dr. Campbell on those former colleagues who were deceased or overseas. His lips were set in a firm line and his brow frowning so that I knew better than to interrupt him. I passed the time smoking by the fire, and our present circumstances were so cheerful compared with the coldness of the weather outside that it was a considerable effort to turn out again when we accompanied Dr. Campbell to the station to catch the six-thirty p.m. train. The bloom of the gas lamps gilded the sparse white locks of our client gold as he stood at the carriage window to bid us good-bye.

"Make yourselves at home, gentlemen," he said. "I shall be away three days and shall, I trust, have good news of you on my return."

"Two days should see this business through, Rector," said Pons with a thin smile.

We waited until the anxious face of our client was no more than a blur in the darkness, and Pons then led the way briskly up the platform and back toward the village. The rain had held off but the wind was cold and bleak in the extreme. I carried our travelling bag but I was puzzled to see that Pons still had a large holdall he had brought from the Rectory.

I had assumed it was part of our client's luggage but Pons had retained it on the platform. He did not volunteer any information and it did not seem as though it contained anything of great importance. A walk of a few hundred yards only brought us to the Blue Boar, an imposing establishment with a white Georgian portico. There we secured two comfortable rooms in the names of Rutherford and Parker.

I had no sooner unpacked our scanty belongings before Pons was tapping on my door.

"Now, Parker," he said, his eyes dancing. "Best foot forward. First to Mrs. Harbinger's, then back to the Rectory. And remember I am Rutherford all the while I am within the environs of Shap."

"I will try to remember, Pons," I said stiffly.

A few minutes later we were ringing the doorbell of The House upon the Green. Mrs. Harbinger was at home and a trim parlourmaid showed us into an oak-panelled drawing room and went to announce us to her mistress.

Mrs. Harbinger turned out to be an imposing-looking woman of about seventy with snow-white hair and heavily rouged cheeks. The effect was bizarre against the whiteness of her complexion. She wore a strange-looking gown, mauve in colour, belted in at the waist like that of a mediaeval chatelaine. Around her neck was suspended a gold chain bearing a curiously shaped gold locket.

"Well, gentlemen," she snapped. "State your business. I am an extremely busy woman."

Pons wasted no time in coming to the point.

"My name is Rutherford. This is my partner, Mr. Parker. We are Rutherford and Parker, one of the most respected firms of antique dealers and appraisers in the West End of London."

Mrs. Harbinger sucked in her breath and her eyes had become shrewd. She looked around at the valuable antiques that adorned her drawing room as though she were afraid we would abstract them.

"What is that to me?"

Pons smiled winningly.

"Not a great deal, evidently, madam. But we are staying with the Rector of Shap across the green yonder. He is an old friend and we are making an inventory of some of his pieces. I was interested in gaining access to The Sealed Spire since I had heard something of the legends about it. Dr. Campbell does not seem too keen on the subject, but I understood you were something of an authority on the matter."

An amazing change had come over Mrs. Harbinger; she took a step forward and raised one clawlike hand in the air.

"Sit down, gentlemen, sit down. Anyone who can assist that obdurate man in opening The Spire and, by so doing, benefiting England has my full support."

Pons lowered himself into the rocking chair indicated by our hostess.

"Some sherry, gentlemen?"

Pons graciously assented and while Mrs. Harbinger was busy with a decanter and glasses, deliberately lowered one of his eyelids at me in a most provocative manner. When we were sipping delicately at the sherry and making appropriately appreciative comments on its mellow flavour, Mrs. Harbinger had been studying us intently.

"What do you hope to find in The Spire, gentlemen? Antiques? I fear you will be disappointed."

"Oh, so you know what it contains?"

Our strange hostess nodded.

"Documents, gentlemen. Not *objects d'art*. But documents of such richness and distinction that the whole world will recognise the importance of The Sealed Spire."

The long form of Pons stirred uneasily in the rocker.

"I do not quite follow you, madam."

Mrs. Harbinger gave my companion a weary look, followed by an audible clicking of the tongue.

"The Great Scroll of Thoth, the Golden Book of Horus, the Twelve Pentameters of Ishtar are only a few of the priceless treasures concealed within the chamber of The Sealed Spire, Mr. Rutherford."

"Indeed!" said Pons, raising his eyebrows.

Mrs. Harbinger clicked her tongue again.

"I can see you are an unbeliever, sir."

"Not at all," interjected Pons hastily. "It is just that it is rather difficult to see how such gems of wisdom could have become concealed in such a manner."

The impatient look had not left Mrs. Harbinger's face.

"It is too long a story to go into now. You must just take it from me that my researches have yielded up incontrovertible proof. If you can assist me to gain access to The Spire, I will be incalculably in your debt."

Pons held up a hand deprecatingly.

"I cannot promise anything, Mrs. Harbinger. But I can assure you that my partner, Mr. Parker, and I will use our best offices to those ends."

A gleam of malicious triumph had appeared in the mauve-gowned woman's eyes.

"Very well, Mr. Rutherford. You will not find me ungrateful. When can you let me know?"

"Within the next few days, Mrs. Harbinger."

Our hostess stood up, a calculating look on her face. It was plain the interview was at an end. I hastily drained my sherry and a few moments later, after more protestations on Pons' part in his assumed role of Rutherford, we found ourselves outside again and striding back across the green to the Rectory. Pons chuckled as soon as we were out of earshot.

"What do you make of her, Parker?"

"Mad," I said vehemently. "Like this whole business."

Pons' brows were knitted.

"Ah, then you can see no pattern emerging?"

I shook my head.

"None of it makes sense to me, Pons, if you want my candid opinion."

"Nevertheless, there is a strand of sanity here, amid the apparently inconsequential trappings of this affair," he said mysteriously.

He chuckled again.

"Even allowing for the current interest in Egyptology, I fear Mrs. Harbinger will be disappointed by the contents of The Sealed Spire if our client's remarks are to be believed. Cobwebs and old furniture, was it not, according to Dr. Campbell?"

We had gained the Rectory porch by this time and Mrs. Jenkin admitted us with a smile. She ensconced us in the Rector's study and, with the warming announcement that supper would be served at half-past nine, withdrew to leave us to our own devices.

Once again Pons sat at the Rector's desk, busy with his notations and the photograph of Dr. Campbell's theological class of long ago. I had resumed my seat at the fireside, and we sat so in heavy silence for some time. Finally I could keep quiet no longer.

"What do you find so absorbing in that picture, Pons?" I said irritably.

Solar Pons stirred at the desk. He held up the photograph.

"It contains the clue to the whole problem, Parker."

"You must be joking, Pons!"

My companion shook his head.

"Just come here a moment."

I crossed to his side, looking at the yellowed faces of those young men of the South African War and the Great War in silence.

"Well, Pons?"

"Allowing for the fallen, those deceased and those removed to other countries, there are seven who might be suitable for my purposes. But only one within striking distance."

He tapped the glass covering the photograph.

"The Rev. George Neville Stoner, Rector of Chislington, some twenty miles from here."

I stared at the picture of the hook-nosed, lantern-jawed young man with piercing eyes in silence.

"None of this makes sense to me, Pons."

"Nevertheless, Parker, I commend the Rev. Stoner to your attention," said my friend enigmatically.

∽ 5

We were standing so when the front door slammed. Immediately, Pons motioned me to silence. We were once again sitting on either side of the fireplace, the picture back in its place on the wall, when the study door opened and the startled form of a young man stood framed in the opening.

"I beg your pardon, gentlemen, I had no idea..."

"Come in, Mr. Dabson," said Pons, rising. "I am afraid Dr. Campbell did not see fit to tell you of our visit. You have returned unexpectedly, I see."

The secretary flushed.

"Isaac Dabson, at your service, gentlemen. Any friends of Dr. Campbell's . . . "

Pons rose from the fireside and I followed suit as he introduced us to Dabson in our assumed identities.

"You must forgive us for usurping your quarters," said Pons, waving the secretary to a chair. "We can easily withdraw if you so desire."

"I would not hear of it," Dabson protested. "I found the north rather dull and came back a few days early."

"You had rather a dusty journey, I see," said Pons pleasantly, stepping forward to brush some cobwebs from the collar of the secretary's jacket. Once again the black-haired man flushed.

"I have just been across to the church to consult some documents in the vestry," he said hurriedly.

"Quite so," said Pons. "We hope to have that pleasure tomorrow. We are antique dealers and appraisers from London, you see. The Rev. Campbell is a personal friend of long standing and asked us to put a value on some of his older pieces."

The secretary relaxed in his chair.

"Indeed, Mr. Rutherford. Well, I am sure that if you are friends of Dr. Campbell's, everything is in order. When do you expect him back?"

"He intends to break off from the Conference and return tomorrow night," said Pons smoothly. "It is this business of The Sealed Spire. Mrs. Harbinger's persistence has rather worn him down, I fear. He told me this evening that he will open The Sealed Spire once and for all to scotch these rumours she is spreading about the village."

The secretary's pale face bore a strange, almost furtive expression. For a brief space this hook-nosed young man with the wild eyes reminded me of something, though I could not quite place it in the stress of the moment. I gazed at Pons open-mouthed, I fear. But the secretary had recovered himself by now.

"Ah, well, perhaps it might be for the best," he said affably. "Dr. Campbell has, I know, antagonised some of the local people over his attitude toward The Spire. And I must confess, gentlemen, that he has been acting most peculiarly of late."

Pons nodded.

"We are staying at The Blue Boar, Mr. Dabson. The Rector will be telephoning me there tomorrow. I will get Mr. Parker to let you know whether Dr. Campbell is returning or not."

Dabson gave Pons a slight bow; there was an ironic expression in his eyes.

"That is indeed good of you, gentlemen. And now, if you will forgive me, I will seek my quarters. It has been a long and tiring journey."

Pons smiled pleasantly.

"By all means, Mr. Dabson. Good night."

He stood immobile until the door had closed softly behind the retreating form of the secretary. Then he crossed to the fire and dropped back into his chair.

"A cool customer, our Mr. Dabson," he observed. "Now, what do you make of all this, Parker? You have all the threads in your hands."

"Well, Mr. Rutherford, it seems fairly obvious that the Rector is being persecuted," I said. "And it seems equally obvious that the vindictiveness of Mrs. Harbinger is behind it."

Pons stared at me thoughtfully, his fingers tented before him.

"You improve, Parker. A distinct improvement."

"I thought you would see the logic of my argument, Pons."

Solar Pons shook his head impatiently.

"I meant that you had managed to remember my *nom de*

plume," he said severely. "As for the rest of your thesis, you are sadly off the track. Do you not see the significance of the photograph? And the fairly obvious motive behind these apparently insane happenings?"

I shook my head.

"Mark my words, Pons. This Mrs. Harbinger is obviously unhinged."

"A fair assessment, Parker. But she is being used by the cunning instrument behind all this. There is the touch of a master-hand somewhere here. Someone who is actuating the puppets from afar."

"At any rate, there is little more we can do tonight," I said. "Supper will be ready shortly. Have you seen *The Times*?"

I passed Pons that authoritative journal, and he had no sooner settled with it in his chair than he levered himself upright with a muffled ejaculation, his eyes sparkling.

"There, Parker, there is your motive writ plain."

I stared at the Home News page in bewilderment, running my eye across the single-column headings. They seemed incredibly dull: RESULTS OF BOLTON BY-ELECTION; WAR PENSIONS REVIEW; NEW BISHOP OF DURHAM. Then I found what had so obviously excited Pons. ARREST OF BIRMINGHAM MAN. CHARGED WITH TRUNK MURDERS. I read the article with blank incomprehension. Then I put the paper aside.

I do not see how this can possibly assist us, Pons."

Do you not, Parker? Well, my dear fellow, leave it for the moment. We must not overtax your brain too much this evening."

And with this faintly insulting remark he puffed away at his pipe until Mrs. Jenkin tapped at the door to say that supper was ready and waiting.

Pons was out and about a good deal the following day, and I spent most of the time in the lounge of The Blue Boar, for the weather was again inclement and an icy rain was spitting spitefully at the windows of the hostelry. We had an early dinner at six o'clock and just after seven, Pons tapped at the door of my room.

"If you would just step over, Parker, I would like to rehearse you for our little charade this evening."

I followed him back to his own room with rising curiosity.

"Now if you would just pay attention, Parker," said Pons when he had locked the door behind us, "this is the *modus operandi*. At precisely eight o'clock I would like you to present yourself to Mr. Isaac Dabson at the Rectory and give him the following message. Tell him that the Rector has telephoned through and is on his way home. He will go directly to the church and open The Sealed Spire. I think we have already established that this is his intention."

"Will Dabson not think this a curious arrangement, Pons?" I protested.

My companion shook his head.

"I think not, Parker. We have both discussed this matter with the Rector. Mrs. Harbinger has been on about The Spire for years. Dabson has been with the Rector for a year and is *au fait* with the situation. I fancy that your message will have the desired effect."

"What effect, Pons?" I asked.

Solar Pons smiled enigmatically.

"All in good time, I fancy, Parker. Much depends on this scene setting, so I rely on you, my dear fellow. You must also introduce into the conversation as naturally as possible that Dr. Campbell desires Mrs. Harbinger to be told of his intentions."

I nodded.

"I see, Pons. You intend Mrs. Harbinger to be present. But I fail to see how the opening of The Spire will assist us in our purposes."

"All will be made clear, Parker," Pons interrupted curtly. "Now, I have just a few more preparations to make."

He put his finger alongside his lips as though to enjoin caution and took up the bag he had brought from the Rectory and placed it down near the wardrobe in the corner. Then he opened one of the doors and went behind it so that he could use the mirror. I sat in a chair by the bed and smoked, passing the time as best I could.

I could see only Pons' legs, but I judged there was a good deal of activity going on before the mirror and from time to time a lean hand came out from behind the wardrobe door and rummaged in the bag.

As used as I was to Pons' strange variety of disguises, I could not resist a start of surprise when a dry cough interrupted me. Looking up, I beheld Dr. Campbell in front of me. The stoop; the redness of the face; the white, wispy hair; the gold-rimmed spectacles; even the somewhat quirky walk; all were uncannily duplicated. I stood up and stepped toward him.

"Pons!" I cried. "You have excelled yourself."

My companion smiled and straightened his body. Now that I was up close I could see that it was indeed he, but the impersonation was remarkable. I saw now what he had brought in the bag from the rectory. An ancient umbrella and some of the fusty, antique clothes of our eccentric client completed the picture of an elderly cleric.

I see you approve of my little charade, Parker."

"I think I have made that clear, Pons," I said, "but I am not quite certain in my mind as to its exact purpose."

"Ah, Parker, small villages like Shap have many eyes and ears," replied my friend, his pupils sparkling behind the spectacles. "At an appropriate time this evening I shall make my way down the back stairs of this hotel, carrying this empty case. When you have delivered your message to Dabson, you must cut through the churchyard and meet me in the church porch. I have already obtained the necessary keys from the Rector, though he does not know my intention of entering the sealed chamber."

"What do you expect to find, Pons?"

"Certainly not the Great Scroll of Thoth!" rejoined my friend, his eyes glinting with humour. "But I fancy this evening will see some surprises. We will first break open the trapdoor to gain entry. This will give us time to inspect the room. Then, when Dabson has been given sufficient leeway to collect Mrs. Harbinger, I intend to quietly disappear from the church. You will remain in The Spire and I will then make a far more public entrance into the churchyard. I fancy that will precipitate the necessary reaction."

"Ah, you are acting as a decoy, Pons?"

"Something of the sort, Parker. But surely you must have guessed what little game is being played by now."

I shook my head.

"I am completely in the dark, Pons."

Solar Pons stared at me in silence for a moment.

"Yet you have all the components of this little puzzle in your hands. No matter. Things will resolve themselves before the evening is out, I fancy."

✍ 7

The rain had stopped but there was a slight mist rising from the damp earth as I walked past the churchyard and paused at the drive leading to the Rectory. Gas lamps bloomed at the edge of the green and a comforting glow came from the houses around. The village of Shap, which had seen so many strange and scandalous events exploding about the head of its Rector, was apparently innocuous and quiet.

But I wondered just what thoughts and schemes were maturing beneath the bland façades of the trim houses and particularly behind the cosy red curtains of Mrs. Harbinger's dwelling.

Mrs. Jenkin opened the door at my ring, a smile of welcome on her face.

"Mr. Dabson is in the study, Mr. Parker. Do you wish me to announce you?"

I shook my head.

"I can find my way, thank you."

Young Mr. Isaac Dabson was sitting at the Rector's desk when I entered the room at his command to come in. He rose with a frank smile of welcome on his face and shook hands affably.

"I am sorry if I appeared a little irritable last night, Mr. Parker, but I had a long and tiring journey."

"I quite understand," I said. "I regret having to disturb you. I have a message from my colleague. Dr. Campbell telephoned him at the hotel a short while ago. He asked me to tell you that the Rector is returning to the village tonight, when he will go to the church to open The Sealed Spire."

The secretary's eyes were alive with interest.

"Had he any instructions for me, Mr. Parker?"

I shook my head.

"Only that he desired you to let Mrs. Harbinger know of his intentions."

Dabson nodded, his face heavy with thought.

"Do you know when he expects to arrive in Shap?"

"Some time after nine o'clock," I said casually. "There will be plenty of time to let Mrs. Harbinger know."

The secretary drew himself up.

"Certainly, Mr. Parker. Thank you for your courtesy over the message. And now, if you will forgive me, I have much to do this evening."

We shook hands again and I bowed and withdrew. Mrs. Jenkin was coming across the hall to let me out as I closed the door. I hesitated and then decided not to tell her anything; if Dabson wished to take her into his confidence, he could. But Pons, though he had not mentioned the housekeeper specifically, would not wish to involve her, I felt sure.

So I merely wished her good evening and a few minutes later, having crept cautiously round the rear of the churchyard, where I joined the path leading from the direction of the railway station, I found myself in the gloom of the church porch. I had only a few minutes to wait before I heard the faint gritting of a shoe on the wet flagstones and Pons was at my side. I could see by the faint light of a street lamp which penetrated the churchyard at this point that he still wore the clothes and make-up of Dr. Campbell. He put his hand on my arm and drew me deeper into the porch toward the massive oak door.

"Excellent, Parker. I take it the first part of our little scheme has been put in motion?"

"All went well, Pons," I whispered. "Dabson seemed inordinately interested."

Pons chuckled drily. He was already inserting a key into the lock and gently exerting pressure. A few moments later we were within the musty interior of the church. Pons left the door unlocked and, waiting for our eyes to adjust to the gloom, led the way down the aisle, away from the altar, to the rear of the church.

"We have no time to lose, Parker," he said crisply. "Whatever is in The Spire must be dealt with before I make my public entrance."

He waved away my hurried questions and, using a small pocket torch whose beam he kept low to the ground, drew back the curtains leading to the vestry.

"I have been studying the plans of the church and, if I am not mistaken, Parker, the tower entrance should be somewhere here."

As he spoke the faint beam of the torch centred on a low, Gothic archway barred by a varnished oak door. This had the key in the lock, and swiftly we ascended a narrow, winding wooden staircase and were soon on the platform directly beneath the peal of bells. Pons ignored them and went on up a rough wooden stair that came out on to a small landing. I was close at his heels and waited while he took out his magnifying glass and examined some faint marks in the dust on the floor.

He chuckled to himself and centred the beam of his torch on to a wooden trap door in the ceiling. I then saw that the padlock which secured the hasp of the trap had a key in its lock.

"Just as I thought," said Pons calmly.

He tested it carefully.

The lock is well-oiled too. I fancy The Sealed Spire is not so little-trodden or such sacred ground as Mrs. Harbinger fancies."

He threw open the trap, fumbling inside on the floor. He

found a heavy metal switch and yellow light flooded on to the narrow stair.

"Every modern convenience, Parker," said Pons, ascending into the chamber above.

"Be careful, Pons," I said, pressing up the ladder behind him.

As I groped my way into the small, boarded room beneath the church spire, Pons' tall figure was standing immobile in the centre of the chamber. Even in his persona as Dr. Campbell, I had never seen my old friend look so sombre and so grim.

I followed his gaze round the walls and could not suppress an exclamation of horror.

The Sealed Spire was indeed bare of such treasures as Mrs. Harbinger had indicated. Dust there was, on the floor and on the sheeted masses of old furniture which stood here and there against the walls. But it was not these simple domestic details which engrossed my attention. Round the walls, pinned and pasted to the panelling, there were lettering, sheets of paper, photographs and drawings. They all had two things in common: each item concerned the Rector of Shap; and each without exception was obscene and pornographic.

"Great Heavens, Pons!" I exclaimed. "The man must be mad."

Pons shook his head, his face like iron.

"Scandalous, Parker. I quite agree."

I went over to look at a photograph which certainly featured Dr. Campbell and two naked women.

"What are we to do, Pons?"

"What else, Parker? We must burn this sick rubbish, except for a few items which I shall select to keep as evidence. I fancy we shall be receiving visitors within the hour so we have not too much time."

91

There was an urgency in his voice which I had seldom heard. He was already at work tearing down the material from the walls and from off the furniture. I went to assist him, hardly believing the evidence of my eyes.

"But did you suspect Dr. Campbell when he came to us, Pons?"

Solar Pons clicked his tongue with annoyance and shook his head.

"My dear Parker, you surely do not think Dr. Campbell is responsible for this blasphemous display of perverted taste? Learn to use your faculties. This is entirely in keeping with what we have already learned. The *pièce de resistance*, as it were, of a very clever person's hatred."

I stood bewildered.

"But these photographs, Pons?"

"The merest fakes, Parker. Even you must surely see that studio portraits of Dr. Campbell have been superimposed onto these pornographic studies."

"I am glad to hear it, but if Dr. Campbell is not responsible, what is behind all this?"

"There is no time now, Parker. Tear down the rest of those sheets."

Quickly, Pons selected certain material and thrust it into the travelling bag he still carried. Then he dragged out a metal tray from the side of the room on which reposed an old oil stove. Within a few minutes we had burned the offending documents and other photographs piecemeal and, apart from the smoke hanging in the air, the chamber again appeared normal.

Pons rose to his feet and pushed the tray back into the side of the room again. He glanced at his watch.

"We have some twenty minutes, Parker. When I have descended to the church, I want you to switch off the light and remain here in the dark for a few minutes. I am going now, to walk to the station."

"To the station, Pons?"

Solar Pons nodded.

"At precisely nine o'clock I shall make a public appearance as Dr. Campbell. I shall cross the churchyard with a torch, making as much noise as I can. I shall then ascend to this chamber, when you will switch on the light. We will then await events and, if I am not very much mistaken, we shall swiftly receive some visitors."

I had hardly grasped this and, quite bewildered, completed tidying the room, before Pons had clattered off down the staircase. I waited until I heard him gain the floor of the church and then switched off the light, settling down in the darkness to await his return.

🖎 **8**

The tower shuddered and shook as the carillon in the bell chamber below boomed out the hour of nine. Almost as the last quivering stroke died away into silence, there came the thunderous crash of the main church door below and then the footsteps of Pons in the persona of Dr. Campbell, hurrying down the aisle. Three minutes later I had switched on the light, and Solar Pons was smiling at me over the edge of the trapdoor.

"Quickly, Parker. We have little time to lose."

No sooner had he gained the floor of The Sealed Spire chamber than he was stripping himself of his disguise. I was kept busy putting his discarded clothing into the travelling bag. It was precisely three minutes more before once again the familiar figure of Solar Pons stood before me. He put his hand to his lips to enjoin silence.

But I had already caught the noise; many footsteps across the flagged paving of the churchyard; the murmur of voices; and the rumble as the front door of the church went back again. Pons stood rubbing his thin fingers, a little smile of triumph on his face.

"A few moments more, Parker," he whispered, "and we shall see what we shall see."

The confused babble of voices grew stronger and there was a trembling vibration on the wooden staircase. At Pons' gesture I stood well back while my friend concealed himself behind a dusty chest of drawers which stood at one side of the room. In a few seconds the black-haired figure of Isaac Dabson appeared in the opening. He was pushed into the room by the sheer pressure of people behind him. I caught a glimpse of the triumphant and bizarre figure of Mrs. Harbinger; there were two men with cameras and behind them, insistently pushing their way into The Sealed Spire, still more strangers, presumably people from the village.

By now Isaac Dabson had caught sight of me and his jaw dropped. He looked wildly around the dusty walls, his eyes open in surprise.

"Where is the Rector?" he cried. "What does this mean?"

"It means that your little game is up!" said Solar Pons sternly, stepping out from the shadow and confronting the group. "The Rector is in London at the Conference. My name is Solar Pons. It is perhaps not unknown to you."

Dabson's face was a mixture of chagrin and fear. He drew

apart from the people who were still pushing their way up from the staircase.

"Solar Pons!"

Dabson's face was a white mask, but Mrs. Harbinger had elbowed her way to the front and stood glaring at Pons. She sniffed the air and then looked suspiciously at the heap of ashes on the metal tray in the corner.

"The Great Scroll of Thoth! You have not burned the treasures of the ages?"

"No, madam," said Pons imperturbably. "I have merely disposed of some malicious rubbish set to ensnare an innocent man. Ah, gentlemen, I see we have some cameras present. I do not know what Mr. Dabson has told you but I fear you may be disappointed."

A thickset man wearing a black homburg and carrying a heavy plate camera could not restrain his indignation.

"Hooper of the Shap and Stapleford *Chronicle*," he said, casting a sullen glance at the secretary.

"Where is this sensation you promised us, Mr. Dabson?"

"I fear there is no sensation in The Sealed Spire," said Pons mildly. "Other than that likely to be engendered when Mr. Dabson and I have had a little discussion in private."

"I have nothing to say to you," said Dabson, pulling himself together.

Pons shrugged.

"Dear me, Mr. Dabson, I trust I can get you to reconsider. Otherwise I shall have to set matters in motion with the official police, and you will find them less easy to deal with, I can assure you."

Dabson licked his lips and cast a frightened look back over his shoulder to where the disgruntled journalists and photographers were elbowing their way back down the staircase again.

"I do not understand what you mean, Mr. Pons."

Solar Pons eyed the secretary thoughtfully.

"I think you do, Mr. Dabson. Especially as you are related to the Rev. George Neville Stoner, the Rector of Chislington, if I am not mistaken. There is a strong family resemblance in the features."

Dabson had stumbled back, ashen-faced. He tried to speak but was unable to do so. Pons turned to me with a bleak smile.

"Come, Parker, I think the Rectory study will be the best place for our talk. As for you, Mrs. Harbinger, I trust that tonight's little adventure will prompt you not to put too much trust in such half-witted legends as those of The Sealed Spire."

Mrs. Harbinger glared at us and then marched imperiously down the staircase. Dabson followed, a broken figure.

Pons chuckled.

"A weak tool, Parker, in the grip of a stronger intellect. If you will bring the bag and switch off the light as we leave, I will guide us down with the torch."

9

We were driving northwards from Shap. Pons sat in his corner, his hands thrust deep into his ulster pockets, his brow knotted while clouds of sulphurous fumes from the bowl of his pipe ascended to the roof of the taxi. To my repeated questions he had merely murmured, "All in good time, Parker, all in good time," and lapsed into silence.

We had been travelling for some half an hour when the vehicle passed through the streets of a sleeping village and in through tall iron gates to deposit us at the steps of a white Victorian building.

Pons got down and ordered the driver to wait. I followed him up the steps to where a single lantern burned above the porch. A worried-looking housekeeper answered Pons' peremptory ring.

"Solar Pons to see the Rev. George Stoner," he announced.

The elderly woman looked at us doubtfully. She wore a thick, quilted dressing gown and had evidently been on the point of retiring.

"It is almost eleven o'clock, gentlemen. The Rector is in bed and cannot be disturbed."

Pons took a piece of pasteboard from his pocket and scribbled something on it. He handed it to the housekeeper.

"Kindly give him this. I fancy he will see us."

The woman glanced at Pons' card in surprise, asked us to wait in the hall, and slammed the door behind us. She put on the light in a study to the right, which was furnished with almost sumptuous taste. We waited while the woman's footsteps ascended the stairs.

"Ah, Parker," said Solar Pons coolly, running his eye over the Rector's crowded shelves. "The Ethics of Erasmus; the Gnostic Mass; Marcus Aurelius; Walter Pater. A catholic and devious mind, as I surmised."

I could not resist an exclamation.

"What exactly are we doing here, Pons?"

"Just a little more patience. I fancy that is our man now."

There was indeed a nervous tattoo on the staircase, and the study door burst open to admit a tall, lean, ascetic-looking man with a shock of white hair, a hook nose, and a lantern jaw. He wore a mouse-coloured dressing gown and he stood breathing heavily, looking first at me and then at my companion.

"Which of you gentlemen is Mr. Solar Pons?"

Pons bowed stiffly.

"I answer to that cognomen, Rector."

The Rev. Stoner stepped forward, his face haughty and disdainful.

"Then perhaps, sir, you would be good enough to explain the impertinence written on this card?"

"Certainly," said Pons coolly. "It means, surely, that your persecution of your old colleague, Dr. Campbell, Rector of Stapleford and sometime fellow student, must cease."

There was a long moment of silence while the Rector stared at Pons with burning eyes.

"I take it you realise what you are saying?" he replied with deadly calm. "You would need proof for such a wild assertion."

"We have proof, Rector," said Pons quietly, taking a sheet of paper from his pocket. "Your wretched nephew, Isaac Dabson, has given me a full confession. A weak tool for such malicious work. If you do not do as I say, this document will be placed in the hands of the police."

The Rev. Stoner gave a strangled cry and stared at Pons with eyes which seemed to have become sunken and cavernous.

"Withdraw from the Bishopric of Durham, Mr. Stoner!" said Pons in ringing tones.

He replaced the paper in his pocket.

"If you do not, then I will not hesitate to expose you as a malicious rogue! Come, Parker."

He strode from the room, leaving the shrunken figure of the Rector alone in the study. I hurried at his heels and in a few moments more we were in the taxi driving back toward Shap and our comfortable rooms at the inn. Pons burst into laughter and hunted in his pocket for his pipe.

"Well, Parker, what do you make of such a pretty rascal?"

"I must confess, Pons, that I have not made a good deal of the whole muddled business," I said. "And I am afraid that it does not do too much credit to the cloth."

Pons stabbed the air with the stem of his pipe.

"Ah, Parker, there is a good deal of enmity and professional jealousy in the closed world of scholarship. I knew from the moment Dr. Campbell approached us that there was more to this affair than merely stupid practical jokes. Why should anyone want to play such idiotic and cruel tricks on a country Rector? But he is a brilliant scholar and author, Parker. And in the world of scholarship there are often unsuspected depths beneath the placid surface ripples. Even before I came to Shap, I was convinced that I was looking for something in Dr. Campbell's past which was impinging upon the present."

"You astonish me, Pons."

"It would not be the first time, Parker," said Solar Pons, mischievous lights dancing in his eyes. "When I found that these manifestations had begun only six months ago and that Dabson had become the Rector's secretary a year ago, I found my suspicions crystallising. He would need some months to prepare the ground for these cruel and elaborate hoaxes, of course."

"But the motive, Pons!"

"That was crystal-clear also, and it took only a short while at the Rectory for it to become obvious to me."

"Mrs. Harbinger . . ."

An expression of annoyance crossed Pons' face.

"You disappoint me, Parker, you really do. Mrs. Harbinger was a red herring of only the crudest kind but admirable for Dabson's purposes. His entire purpose in Shap was to discredit Dr. Campbell, and this he proceeded to do by every means at his disposal. The Rector sees no harm in anyone, but it was obvious from the scope and method of the annoyances perpetrated on our client that the agent behind them had to be someone close to him. Dabson was the only person who fitted that bill, and Mrs. Harbinger's vendetta against the Rector and her reiterated parrot cries for the opening of The Sealed Spire put a ready tool to his hand."

Pons broke off for a moment and paused to relight his pipe, which had gone out unnoticed during his conversation with me.

"You may remember I was inordinately interested in the photograph of the Rector and the members of his theological class. I had a shrewd suspicion from the outset that scholarship and professional rivalry were at the basis of the feud and I found a rapid means of ascertaining and establishing certain basic facts about Dr. Campbell, his fellow students and friends. We eliminated, as you recall, many people in the group through the action of war, age, and death. Of the handful remaining only one was suitable for my purposes."

"The Rev. Stoner," I interjected.

"Precisely. He had an unmistakable face—lean, with a hook nose and lantern jaw. When I saw those same traits prominently displayed in the physiognomy of Dabson, the admirable secretary, the coincidence was too great to be chance. I concluded, therefore, that Dabson was a relative of Stoner, who lived only twenty miles away. I established from *Crockford's* that he was a brilliant speaker, theologian, and author. There is nothing like a fellow student to harbour jealousy, rancour, and envy. When the two men follow the same profession, church or no, they are rivals for life, Parker. And Stoner was close at hand to direct the vendetta."

"You leave me sadly disillusioned, Pons."

Solar Pons shook his head, making sure with a sidelong glance that his pipe was drawing properly.

"You make the same basic mistake as the layman, Parker. Politics and religion are two of the greatest causes of strife and dissension on this planet. Eliminate them both and one would go a long way toward lasting peace."

"Come, Pons," I protested. "You go too far."

"Perhaps," my companion admitted. "But in the case of the Rev. Stoner, his hatred for the good Dr. Campbell had assumed paranoid proportions. And in the person of his nephew he found a weak but willing tool. Young Dabson was heavily in debt to bookmakers. In return for financial assistance from his uncle, he agreed to the plan to discredit his employer. I have this from his own lips."

He tapped the pocket of his ulster, in which reposed Dabson's signed confession.

"So that as soon as I clapped eyes on Dabson I was suspicious. In the first instance, he had told the Rector he would be absent in the north. But here he was back again, unannounced. No doubt, to my mind, to prepare fresh mischief. When I saw traces of cobwebs on his coat, I deduced he had been at work in the church, a fact he himself immediately confirmed. He had, of course, been there to prepare the sick material displayed in The Sealed Spire. And it was his whole purpose, using Mrs. Harbinger's malice also to bring the Rector to the point of going there."

"I must confess I am still not clear about this business, Pons."

"It was the *pièce de résistance*, Parker, and would undoubtedly have succeeded had not Dr. Campbell asked for my assistance. It would have been the final scandal which would have broken Dr. Campbell and allowed his rival ascendancy. Why do you think Dabson went out of his way to call in the press and half the village in addition to Mrs. Harbinger? No, Parker, Dr. Campbell would have been a ruined man as many another discredited cleric before him."

"But the motive, Pons!"

The patient look was back on my companion's face.

"It was before you all the time, Parker. It has been in the newspapers the last few weeks, and I particularly drew your attention to *The Times*, where the matter was firmly under your gaze in heavy black type. But you insisted on reading out some asinine conclusions about a trunk murder."

I fear I stared at Pons for a long moment as though thunderstruck. A faintly mocking look had settled on Pons' lean features.

"The Bishopric of Durham, Parker. That was the key to the whole thing. The article, if you had taken the trouble to read it, referred to the selection of the new Bishop, one of the key posts in the Church of England. There were only two candidates, both men of high repute; both authors and brilliant scholars."

"Dr. Campbell and the Rev. Stoner, Pons!"

"Exactly, Parker. And a man of doubtful sanity like Dr. Campbell, who was involved in sexual and other scandals over a period of months in his own village, would hardly be preferred over someone of the Rev. Stoner's character."

I sat back in the cab.

"What a damnable villain, Pons. And I have been extremely obtuse."

"On the contrary, Parker, you have been invaluable, as always. And with your assistance we have persuaded Rev. Stoner to withdraw, and Dr. Campbell's preferment is assured."

"What will you tell him, Pons?"

"Merely that young Dabson was called away due to the illness of a relative. He will not return. And I have no doubt that within a day or two we will see that the Rev. Stoner's candidature has been withdrawn."

◈ 10

And so it proved. Pons and I were at breakfast a month later when he slit open a large buff envelope which had come in the morning's post. A cheque fluttered to the carpet, and I picked it up and handed it to him. He smoothed it and raised his eyebrows.

"From Dr. Campbell. He has been extraordinarily generous, Parker."

"I take it he is to be the new Bishop of Durham, Pons?"

"Ah, you have seen this morning's *Times*."

I nodded, studying Pons' face as he rummaged about within the envelope.

"I fancy Dr. Campbell's advancement will be rapid from now on, Parker. He is seventy, which is a mere stripling as senior churchmen go. I would expect to see him translated to York within five years. Do you realise that by the time he is seventy-eight, our client might well be the new Archbishop of Canterbury?"

"You are joking, Pons!"

Solar Pons put down his teacup and looked at me severely.

"I was never more serious, Parker. But in the meantime a more pleasant duty. Here is an invitation for us both to attend the investiture of the new Bishop of Durham at the end of March. I trust you will be free, my dear fellow."

Pons paused and then chuckled.

"I fancy Dr. Campbell will be none too sorry to arrive at Durham. I fear he will have found great difficulty in persuading Mrs. Harbinger that I have not burned the Great Scroll of Thoth."

The Adventure of
the Six Gold Doubloons

🐚 1

"THE LAWS OF chance operate in quite arbitrary ways, Parker, and despite all man's puny efforts and painstaking care, the best-laid schemes often come to naught."

My friend, Solar Pons, was sitting on the park bench looking at me with a mocking expression. It was a beautiful day in early summer, and Hyde Park was crowded with people strolling or sitting on the grass while London's traffic came as a muffled roar from beyond the tall iron railings. I stared at my companion in astonishment.

"Really, Pons! Your deductive feats become ever more astonishing. That was just what I was thinking."

Pons chuckled.

"There was little magical about it, Parker, I can assure you. For the last fifteen minutes you have been completely absorbed by the activities of those ants on the tree stump just behind this bench. During all that time a band of them has been engaged in the Herculean effort of transporting a large wood splinter to the top of the stump. It must weigh hundreds of times their own weight and yet they have persisted. I noted by your expression that your enthusiasm was entirely with the ants. Yet, just as they were on the point of success, the thing slipped and has tumbled to the bottom again. All is to do once more, and by your crestfallen expression I read, aright it seems, your rueful thoughts on not only the ant but on man's condition."

I joined in Pons' smile.

"Well, well, Pons, my thoughts were somewhat on those lines. Yet I never cease to wonder at your intuitive reasoning."

Solar Pons shifted his lean form on the bench and idly rested his gaze on the people passing on the asphalt path in front of us.

"Unfortunately, Parker, there is so little happening within the orbit of the private consulting detective these days that one is forced into such modest displays in order to prevent the ratiocinative faculties from rusting. Look at this old gentleman approaching, for instance. What do you make of him?"

I turned my gaze on the object of Pons' attention. He was behaving in a peculiar manner, I saw instantly. He wore a suit of rusty black and a scarlet muffler round his neck, despite the heat. His arms shook uncontrollably and tears streamed down his face. Ever and again he stopped on the path and raised his eyes to Heaven, while a stream of half-intelligible comments came from his lips. He was hatless and his long white hair streamed about his shoulders. Altogether he was a bizarre and pitiful sight.

"A man of about seventy-five."

"Elementary, Parker."

"Suffers from *paralysis agitans*. Evidently of long-standing."

"Ah, there I must bow to your medical knowledge, Parker,

though I had already come to much the same conclusion from my own observations."

I glanced at Pons in mild irritation and then turned my attention back to the object of our studies.

"A poor man."

"I think not, Parker. Is that all you have been able to discover?"

"I feel there is little that has escaped me, Pons."

"Come, Parker, you can surely do better than that. An elderly man, fairly well-to-do; a Mason; a drunkard, the habit aggravating his medical condition; afflicted with religious mania also; despite his defects, a car driver. A City man, I would say."

"Oh, come, Pons, you are really playing with me on this occasion! There is no way we can verify these assertions."

There was a little bitterness in my tone, and my friend looked at me in surprise.

"There is all the verification one needs before us, Parker, though you are like most laymen in that facts pass before you without being registered by your brain."

"Very well, then, Pons. I will take up your challenge. Well-to-do?"

"His clothes are of excellent cut. When I see two expensive cigars encased in new wrappings peeping from the breast pocket of his jacket, I conclude that he is reasonably well off. He has a copy of the *Financial Times* showing, where he has carelessly thrust that excellent journal into his coat pocket. That is a highly specialised newspaper which none but City men read."

"I give you that, Pons," I said reluctantly. "A Mason?"

"Pooh, that is simple. The seals are plainly visible on his watch chain. As to his drunkenness you would surely agree, as a medical man, that the redness of his features, particularly the nose, and the broken veins of the face indicate the man who is addicted to spirits. He has stopped not two yards from us, and I venture to observe that you now have olfactory evidence of his condition."

Pons had dropped his voice to a murmur as the object of our attention paused in front of us, and I had indeed caught the heavy reek of whisky which emanated from him. I had to agree with Pons as the old man moved on.

"Your demonstration is an apt one, Pons, but how on earth do you deduce that he is a car driver?"

"Nothing simpler, Parker. He has the keys of a vehicle in his right hand, which he keeps jangling as he walks. It is an alarming fact for a man in his condition, but true. I could see the insignia on the key ring as he stopped before us. He drives a Morris. As to his religious mania, he was quoting from the Book of Ezekiel."

I threw up my hands in despair, and my dejected look brought forth a dry chuckle from Pons.

"Cheer up, my dear fellow. I should be all at sea if called upon to diagnose appendicitis. But here, if I am not mistaken, is an old friend. Superintendent Stanley Heathfield of Scotland Yard and surely not out for an afternoon stroll?"

It was indeed the tall, energetic figure of the Superintendent which strode through the park gates. He looked round him eagerly and then quickened his steps toward us as he caught sight of Pons on the bench.

He tipped his bowler hat in salutation to Pons and included me in his courteous bow. His brown eyes were serious above the clipped, iron-grey moustache.

"I must apologise for this intrusion into your rustic idyll, Mr.

Pons. One of my inspectors, Jamison, telephoned your landlady at Praed Street, and we learned you might be found in the Park."

Pons raised his eyebrows.

"A lucky throw, Superintendent, or did you have assistance?"

Superintendent Heathfield sank down next to Pons on the bench, removing his hat as he did so. With his light-weight, well-cut grey flannel suit he looked much more like the City man than our eccentric passerby of a few minutes earlier.

"We have had men combing the Park, Mr. Pons."

"Ah, it is serious, then?"

The Superintendent nodded.

"Murder, Mr. Pons. In shocking circumstances and with suspects which force us to tread circumspectly."

Pons rose instantly from the bench, every line of his form indicating dynamic alertness.

"I am at your service, Superintendent. You have no objection to Dr. Parker accompanying us?"

The Superintendent shook his head.

"By all means. Delighted to have you, doctor."

The three of us walked across the North Carriage Road toward the Victoria Gate. In the Bayswater Road a police car waited, a uniformed sergeant at the wheel. Behind it stood another vehicle, and Heathfield paused for a word with the driver.

"You may inform the others that they may return to their normal duties. We have found Mr. Pons."

I followed Pons and the Superintendent into the interior of the vehicle, and the driver edged out into the traffic in the direction of Notting Hill Gate. Heathfield came to the point at once.

"You have heard of Elihu Cook Stanmore, I take it?"

Pons smiled grimly.

"One of the greatest blackguards in London. Blackmailer, swindler, thief and forger, among his many remarkable talents. Murder, too, most likely, though I have never been able to prove anything."

Superintendent Heathfield looked at Pons thoughtfully, his eyes bright in the gloom of the police car.

"You have hit it aright, Mr. Pons. We at the Yard have sought the same ends for a long time."

Pons nodded.

"I understand that with advancing years he goes in for less strenuous pursuits nowadays. Blackmail, principally, specialising in society ladies with much to hide."

Heathfield chuckled.

"Correct again, Mr. Pons. Which is one of the reasons we have to go carefully. Stanmore had Royal clients."

Pons turned his head sharply toward our companion.

"I see you use the past tense, Superintendent. Am I to take it that Stanmore is the subject of our inquiry?"

Superintendent Heathfield leaned forward in his seat and made sure the glass screen separating us from the driver was tightly closed.

"Stanmore was found murdered in his study this morning, a dagger driven deep between his shoulder blades. On the desk in front of him were six gold doubloons and a card hand-engraved with the words 'Revenge is sweet'."

Pons stared at the tall police officer for a few moments without speaking. Then he put his hand up and stroked the lobe of his left ear as was his habit when thinking.

"Well, I cannot say I am sorry, Superintendent. A more slimy villain never walked the earth. Frankly, I shall be glad to erase his name from my records. There is no crime more despicable, Parker—no activity more damnable than that of the blackmailer who destroys the innocent indiscriminately with the guilty when they become entangled in his net."

I cleared my throat somewhat nervously.

"Even so, Pons, murder has been involved here."

Pons shot me a humorous glance from his deep-set eyes.

"You do correctly to recall me to my sense of duty, Parker."

He turned back to our companion.

"I take it there is no lack of suspects?"

Superintendent Heathfield pursed his lips.

"That is just the trouble, Mr. Pons. Stanmore's body was discovered only a few hours ago, when his manservant arrived at his flat, so that we have not had time to go through the murdered man's effects properly. But I have seen something of the ledgers and files . . ."

He threw up his hands with an expressive gesture.

"A multiplicity of suspects and a thousand motives," put in Pons succinctly. "What do you say, Parker?"

"Those were exactly my thoughts, Pons," I murmured. Pons tented his fingers before him and sunk his chin as he gazed at the Superintendent.

"I think it would be better if you gave us a brief résumé of the facts, Superintendent, which will prevent me from cluttering my mind with too many preconceived ideas before our arrival. We are going where?"

"Westbourne Grove, Mr. Pons. Stanmore maintained an apartment there, in addition to a hotel suite in the West End and two country houses."

"Crime does apparently pay," I said.

Pons shot me a mocking look.

"Does it not, Parker? I hope nothing has been touched, Superintendent."

Heathfield drew himself up on the seat opposite, humorous lines corrugating his brow.

"I am too old a hand for that, Mr. Pons, and I have studied your methods. The body is in situ; nothing in the study has been moved, pending your arrival."

"That is indeed good to hear, Superintendent," said Pons with a faint smile. "And a model for Jamison to follow."

The police car had turned into Westbourne Grove now, and the driver was idling along the kerb, apparently waiting for Heathfield's instructions. The latter rapped on the glass partition.

"Stop here."

He waited until the engine had been switched off.

"I will be brief, Mr. Pons. Stanmore's body was found this morning by his manservant Dawkins at about eleven o'clock— that is, only some four hours ago."

"That seems rather late, Superintendent."

"Dawkins has duties at Stanmore's hotel suite, apparently," replied Heathfield. "He lives at the hotel. When he had finished there, he came on to his employer's flat, letting himself in with his own key. He found Stanmore lying dead as I have described, and immediately called his local police station.

"The inspector in charge realised the gravity of the affair when the Duke of Leinster's name was discovered in Stanmore's records. Scotland Yard informed the Foreign Office and your brother Bancroft immediately suggested . . . "

"That I should be called," Pons concluded with a smile. "Well, well, Brother Bancroft is wise to be concerned. Is the Duke not currently engaged in peace talks at Geneva?"

The Superintendent nodded gravely.

"Quite frankly, Mr. Pons, even if your brother had not interceded, I should have called you in any case."

"This becomes more flattering by the minute, Parker. Please continue, Superintendent."

"Well, Mr. Pons, in the short time available we have given the flat a thorough combing, as you can imagine. Stanmore was in his study, sitting at the desk, the dagger driven deeply into his back."

"You have traced the weapon?"

Heathfield shook his head.

"So far as we can make out it does not belong in the flat. It is a big, heavy, Eastern thing with a brass handle."

"And the gold doubloons?"

"Stanmore has a penchant for such things. He is something of a collector. These Spanish coins are of the type among his collection. I do not think they are of any great significance."

"Do you not, Superintendent? And the message?"

Superintendent Heathfield smiled wryly.

"There we have a large field, Mr. Pons."

"The flat had not been broken into?"

Heathfield shook his head.

There are no signs of forcible entry, there was no great disturbance in the rooms, and, so far as we can see, nothing has been stolen. Stanmore's blackmailing records were in a locked safe in the study. We only found the key by forcing a locked drawer in his desk. Apparently his murderer had no time to seek out incriminating letters or suchlike."

"Unless he had an appointment with Stanmore, collected the material, and then took his revenge," said Pons.

Heathfield shook his head.

"Unlikely, Mr. Pons. We have established from the manservant that no one knew of the Westbourne Grove address, which Stanmore rented in an assumed name. This was the reason he often left the door unlocked so that his man and the cleaning woman could come and go freely."

Pons frowned, his mobile features serious.

"Yet the servant used his key to gain entry. From what you say, someone could simply have walked in through an unlocked door, committed the crime and walked out again, dropping the latch behind him."

Heathfield nodded.

"It would appear so, Mr. Pons."

"Then that would rule the secrecy theory out of court," said Pons crisply. "Someone must have known of Stanmore's secret address or he would still be alive. It is incredibly difficult to keep such matters from the wider world. Well, well, it does give us some promising material on which to work. How could Stanmore have been surprised in such a manner?"

"You will see in a few moments, Mr. Pons. His desk in the study is in the middle of the room, opposite the fireplace, and he sits with his back to the door."

"So that the murderer could have opened the door and have walked quietly across to get within striking distance," said Pons. "The manservant is trustworthy?"

"We have more or less eliminated him from our inquiries, Mr. Pons. Dawkins had been with Stanmore for fifteen years and was devoted to him."

"A curious devotion," I interjected.

"Was it not, Parker?" said Pons, turning to me. "So much for theorising. Now, if you will just be good enough to descend, we shall see what Elihu Cook Stanmore, six gold doubloons, and a piece of pasteboard have to tell us."

2

The apartment of the murdered man was a luxuriously appointed suite of rooms situated on the third floor; Heathfield took us discreetly up the back stairs so that few people could have been aware of our arrival. A conservatively dressed plain-clothes detective was sitting on a divan in the corridor, smoking, looking indolent and relaxed, but in reality missing nothing. He was already at the door unlocking it before we reached it.

A tall grey-haired man with gold spectacles was standing by a table in the entrance hall, fumbling in a small leather bag as we entered. He looked sharply at the Superintendent.

"He has been dead since about eight o'clock this morning," he said. "Instantaneous, of course. I can't tell a great deal until we get him to the mortuary."

Superintendent Heathfield nodded.

"This is Dr. Garratt. Allow me to introduce Mr. Solar Pons and his friend and colleague, Dr. Lyndon Parker."

The doctor came toward us, a faint flush on his features, and shook hands.

"A distinct pleasure, gentlemen. I have been an enthusiastic follower of your career, my dear sir."

"You are too kind," said Pons deprecatingly. "I fear there is little here to engage such small talents as I possess."

The doctor pursed his lips.

"That may be, Mr. Pons. And I should imagine few would mourn Mr. Stanmore's passing. In my duties as a police surgeon I have seen many things, but I cannot say I shed any tears during my examination this morning."

Superintendent Heathfield smiled grimly.

"Dr. Garratt is familiar with Stanmore's history," he explained. "He has strong views on such matters."

"With which I heartily concur," I could not help asserting.

Solar Pons looked amused.

"Well said, Parker. But we are wasting time. If you would lead the way, Superintendent, we will set to work."

The death chamber into which Heathfield now led us was a long, tastefully furnished study, with heavy velvet curtains at the windows; the windows themselves opened onto an inner courtyard and the blank wall of an adjoining building. The secluded setting was no doubt one of the reasons Stanmore had selected it for his activities, I reflected, looking around me.

None of us had much time for the rows of books which flanked the walls, the open safe in the fireplace wall, or the glass cases which occupied the far end of the apartment. All eyes were on the thing slumped at the rosewood desk about ten feet from the fireplace. Elihu Cook Stanmore had been a man of about sixty-five years old, with a shock of white hair which stood out around his head like thistledown.

He lay awry at the desk, huddled in a big leather armchair, his eyes wide and staring, his face blue and congested. The handle of a large brassbound dagger protruded from his back and was partly concealed by the chair. His hands were clawed in agony and his long fingernails had torn gashes in the blotter before him. I could see that the back of his velvet smoking jacket was literally drenched with blood.

Dr. Garratt had followed us in and stood looking on silently. A tall man with red hair was busy at work at a table some yards from the desk. He nodded at the Superintendent and, in response to the latter's querying look, volunteered, "Plenty of prints, sir, but they're too blurred by the look of things. I shall know more when I get back to the laboratory."

Heathfield nodded.

"I shall want to hear as soon as possible," he said.

Pons had already set to work. He paced restlessly about the study, his eyes probing the desk, the open safe, the documents the Scotland Yard men had been sifting on the side table. Now he stepped back into the middle of the room again.

He glanced at the six gold coins which were lying near one of Stanmore's outstretched hands. A large piece of white pasteboard was on the desk, held down by two of the coins. As the Superintendent had noted, it bore merely the words:

REVENGE IS SWEET

"What do you make of the message, Parker?"

"Done with a thick-nibbed pen, in old English lettering," I said.

"Excellent. Continue."

"The sort of card that can be bought at any stationer's shop, Pons."

Pons' eyes were sparkling.

"You are improving out of all recognition, Parker. I could not have learned much more myself. But I think you will find that the card came from a florist. It is a long shot, Superintendent, but it might be worthwhile checking any florist's establishments in the neighbourhood."

"Very well, Mr. Pons."

Pons stood back, his sharp eyes surveying the corpse and its surroundings intently.

"Your department, Parker. Just give us your opinion to add to Dr. Garratt's."

I bent over the body, taking care to avoid contact with the blood-stained area of the jacket. As I did so, I must have knocked against the swivel chair, for it swung around and Stanmore's corpse slumped farther forward across the desk. I could not repress a small gasp of surprise.

"You are on to something, Parker?"

"This is extraordinary, Pons," I said. "Just take a look, doctor. Stanmore has been stabbed not once but more than a dozen times."

There was a deep silence as I pointed out the multiplicity of cuts in the back of the smoking jacket, indicating wounds from which such a deep seepage of blood had occurred.

"It is evident that someone had more than an ordinary dislike for our friend," said Heathfield sardonically.

"This would have been discovered at the mortuary," put in Dr. Garratt sharply. "I was merely asked to make a superficial examination. I understood that the body was to remain in situ because of Foreign Office instructions."

"Certainly, Dr. Garratt," said Superintendent Heathfield soothingly. "We all understand that."

I shot Garratt a sympathetic glance.

"Purest accident," I said. "I would not have noticed but for bumping into the chair."

Garratt bowed slightly and then went out silently, closing the door after him. I turned to the Superintendent.

"I trust I haven't inadvertently..."

Heathfield chuckled.

"The doctor is a little touchy, Dr. Parker. Think nothing of it."

We stood watching while Pons went rapidly over the contents of the desk. He looked at the broken drawer and then crossed to the safe. He leafed idly through the bundles of letters and other documents on the side table. He raised his eyebrows as he caught the ducal crest at the top of some blue stationery.

"What do you intend to do with these, Superintendent?"

"Normally we destroy all such material after a discreet interval, Mr. Pons. But it does look as though we shall have to question some of these people in the course of our inquiries."

"Naturally."

Pons looked inquiringly round him.

"I should like to see Dawkins."

"Certainly, Mr. Pons. He is in the kitchen. Would you prefer to have him called?"

"No, do not disturb him. I will go through."

But before seeking the valet, Pons turned back. He went over to the glass cases at the end of the room and gazed silently at the long rows of coins which were mounted in velvet.

"The famous collection," he murmured. "What do you make of it, Parker?"

I crossed over to my friend's side and glanced down at the cases. Then I went over to the others and scanned their contents, trying to observe detail as Pons would have done.

"The coins on the desk do not seem to have come from here, Pons."

"Exactly, Parker."

"Perhaps they have been recently purchased and he has not had time to add them to his collection?"

"Perhaps," said Pons. "Though I fancy we shall find a more esoteric explanation when we come to it."

He turned on his heel and went over to the table where the bundles of documents from Stanmore's safe had been stacked.

"I should like to take some of this material away with me."

Superintendent Heathfield raised his eyebrows but merely said, "By all means, Mr. Pons. The Foreign Office, through your brother, has given you *carte blanche* in the matter. We have the material listed, of course."

"Of course."

Pons turned to me.

"Perhaps you would be good enough to make a selection, Parker. The complete series of letters of each subject selected, beginning with the Duke of Leinster."

I busied myself at this task while Pons went back to study the gruesome object at the desk. Heathfield found me a large buff envelope and I put the letters in this. I rejoined Pons, who stood frowning at the corpse of Stanmore.

"I seem to detect a distinct cyanose condition, Parker."

"That is not unnatural in a man of Stanmore's years, Pons," I explained. "One would expect some degree of heart disease in a man of his build and sedentary life."

"Would one not, Parker," said Pons enigmatically, his eyes sparkling. "Well, that is something we shall have to leave to Dr. Garratt and his post-mortem examination. In the meantime there is much to do and Dawkins awaits us in the kitchen."

🖎 3

The valet proved to be a small, subdued-looking man, with dark hair going silver at the temples. He was lean, with a prominent Adam's apple, aged about fifty, and wearing discreet, not to say sombre, clothes. As we entered the large, airy kitchen, he was standing at a board, ironing the trousers of a morning suit. There were traces of shock still on his features and the redness of his eyes indicated that he had been weeping.

He looked up incuriously as we came in and Heathfield wasted no time on preliminaries.

"This is Mr. Solar Pons, Dawkins. He represents the Foreign Office in the matter of the death of your employer, and I want you to listen carefully and answer all his questions."

"Certainly, sir."

Dawkins put down the iron on a table at his elbow and turned wearily toward us.

"You'll forgive me, gentlemen. I know these clothes will be of no more use to Mr. Stanmore in this world, but one must do something and under the circumstances it seemed best to get back into my routine."

"An admirable sentiment, Dawkins," observed Solar Pons, looking at the valet shrewdly. "I understand you have been in the late Mr. Stanmore's employ for some fifteen years."

"That is so, Mr. Pons. Indeed, it will be sixteen years in September."

Dawkins bit his lip.

"Or would have been," he corrected himself.

Pons nodded and walked casually about the kitchen, his eyes darting around the room.

"You seem to keep things extraordinarily neat and tidy, Dawkins."

The valet's thin, pale cheeks flushed.

"I do my best, sir."

"What do you know of Mr. Stanmore's business?" asked Pons with deceptive mildness, pulling at the lobe of his ear.

The valet looked surprised.

"Why, nothing, sir. Mr. Stanmore had business ventures all

over the world. Something to do with property, I believe. I know my place, sir. I never asked and Mr. Stanmore never volunteered information."

"An admirable arrangement between master and man," said Pons. "Did any of Mr. Stanmore's clients ever visit him at home? Here, for instance?"

The valet shook his head.

"Not here, sir. This was what Mr. Stanmore called his hideaway. He had business callers at his hotel suite. And at one of his country houses occasionally. He came here to relax, he always said. He worked on the collation of his collection of coins and read a good deal."

"I see."

Pons was looking at Dawkins attentively.

"Tell me about this coin collection, Dawkins."

The valet shook his head.

"I know very little about it, sir. I'm no numismatist. But I know it was very valuable and Mr. Stanmore set great store by it."

And yet he left the apartment unlocked on many occasions, I believe."

The valet flushed again.

"Well, sir, that was understandable. Mr. Stanmore was always on the premises at those times. I had mislaid my key on more than one occasion and Mr. Stanmore disliked being disturbed, particularly by the woman who cleans three mornings a week."

"She has been checked and cleared of suspicion," Heathfield murmured at this point.

Pons nodded and went on with his questioning of Dawkins.

"So Mr. Stanmore was in the habit of leaving the front door unlocked on those mornings you or the cleaning woman were due. That seems clear enough. Yet the apartment was locked this morning?"

"Yes, sir. I was a little surprised, particularly as Mr. Stanmore knew I was due this morning. But fortunately I had my key with me and let myself in."

The valet faltered and lowered his eyes.

"And found Mr. Stanmore at his desk," said Pons gently. "You did not touch anything?"

Dawkins shook his head.

"I telephoned the police immediately, sir, and put myself completely at their disposal."

"An admirable procedure," Pons continued. "What do you make of those coins on the desk? Doubloons, are they not?"

"I believe they are, Mr. Pons. That was one of Mr. Stanmore's little foibles. Whenever he had concluded a particularly important property deal, he would present a doubloon to his client as a mark of appreciation."

Pons exchanged a keen glance with Superintendent Heathfield.

"Indeed. A quaint little custom, as you so rightly say. These coins did not come from Mr. Stanmore's main collection, then?"

The valet shook his head.

"No, sir. They were what Mr. Stanmore called imperfect specimens, duplicates and so forth. I know little of coin collecting, sir, but my employer laid great stress on the coins in his collection being in mint condition."

"Thank you, Dawkins. That will be all for the present. Hold yourself in readiness in case you should be wanted further."

Dawkins bowed courteously and then bent over the ironing board again as we quitted the room with the Superintendent.

"Well, well, Parker," said Pons briskly. "I think we have seen everything of importance for the moment. I will be in touch, Superintendent. In the meantime I will peruse these letters and let you know my conclusions."

4

A few minutes later we were in a taxi driving across London, Pons at my side, his chin sunk on his breast, the opened envelope of documents on his knee before him.

"We are not going back to Praed Street, then, Pons?"

My companion roused himself from his reverie.

"7B? No, Parker. We must see Lady Mary Hawthorne without delay, before this affair goes any further."

"Lady Mary Hawthorne, Pons?" I said in some bewilderment.

"A well-known society lady who is deeply implicated in this matter," said Pons, tapping the bundle of documents on his lap. "I fear she may do something desperate if we do not put her mind at rest."

"I realise I have not had time to read the documents, Pons . . ."

"Tut, tut, Parker," Pons interrupted irritably, his lean, feral face restlessly turning from side to side. "A glance was enough. It has been in all the papers. Lady Mary is engaged to be married to the Duke of Leinster. It was no doubt that fact that precipitated matters and put a term to Stanmore's life."

He was silent for the remainder of the journey, and it was not until we were hurrying up the steps of a stately mansion near Carlton Terrace that he favoured me with any further observations.

"Discretion, Parker, discretion. After the introduction let me do the talking."

"Certainly, Pons," I protested. "I hope I am not noted for my lack of tact."

Solar Pons permitted himself the fleeting ghost of a smile.

"It is not that, my dear fellow. It is just that sometimes your enthusiasm for my methods gets the better of you."

"Better enthusiasm, Pons," I muttered, "than indifference or scepticism."

Pons looked at me wryly without speaking and then pressed the massive brass stud at the side of the door, which animated the electric bell. It had no sooner echoed in the interior than a grave-faced footman appeared on the steps.

"Take this to your mistress," said Pons curtly, handing him his card. "Tell her it is a matter of great urgency and will not brook delay."

The manservant raised his eyebrows, his genteel façade visibly breached.

"Please come in, gentlemen," he said in a flustered manner. "I will inform Lady Mary that you are here."

He led the way across a hall whose marble floor was in a black-and-white chessboard pattern and left us in a long morning room with pale lemon walls. Cut flowers were massed in bowls and vases everywhere, and the impression was one of unostentatious wealth and elegant good taste. Pons had crossed to the fireplace wall and was examining a pastel study of a strikingly beautiful woman with jet-black hair.

"If that is Lady Mary, the Duke of Leinster is a fortunate man," I ventured over Pons' shoulder.

He gave me an enigmatic smile.

"Is he not, Parker? Yet the course of true love seldom runs smooth, as the well-worn adage says, and I fear that Mr. Stanmore's activities may have put some obstacles in the couple's path."

His observations were dramatically borne out a few moments later when the door to the morning room was imperiously thrown open and the agitated form of Lady Mary herself appeared before us. The portrait did not do her justice, but her beauty was marred at present by the paleness of her cheeks and the wildness of her eye. She came to the point immediately, unerringly arresting my companion's attention.

"Mr. Pons? Your presence here can only mean one thing!"

"Will you not calm yourself, dear lady? I am sure you will be more comfortable by the fireplace. I see you have already heard the news about Mr. Stanmore?"

"It is useless to conceal it in the presence of such a remarkable mind," said the dark-haired woman bitterly.

She sank into the chair indicated by Pons and regarded us with burning eyes.

"Forgive me, Lady Mary," said Pons abruptly. "I am forgetting the social niceties in the stress of the occasion. This is my friend and invaluable colleague, Dr. Lyndon Parker."

Lady Mary acknowledged the introduction with an abstracted inclination of her head and again turned her attention to Pons. For all her poise and the fact that she was in her own house she reminded me of nothing so much as a small animal menaced by a snake. Something of the same sort had evidently occurred to Pons, for he relaxed his manner somewhat and said gently, "You have no reason to fear me, Lady Mary."

There was a strange expression in Lady Mary Hawthorne's eyes as she stared at Pons.

"We shall see, Mr. Pons, we shall see. Your presence here bodes no good."

Pons drew himself up and put out his hand in a commanding gesture.

"Ah, there you do me injustice, Lady Mary. I am here to do good and to right wrong. If it is any scrap of satisfaction to you, I agree that Elihu Cook Stanmore was the biggest blackguard and the most unmitigated scoundrel who ever walked in shoe leather."

Lady Mary had grown deathly pale and she lay back in her chair, her rapid breathing betraying her agitation.

"I see that all is known, Mr. Pons. My letters . . ."

"Are in safe hands, Lady Mary."

Pons drew forth a bundle of blue envelopes tied with pink tape. Lady Mary half-rose from the chair, her right hand plucking at her throat. She made a gesture as if she would snatch them from my companion.

"You have read them?"

Her voice was so low as to be almost inaudible.

Pons shook his head.

"A few paragraphs only of the top letter, which the police had already opened. That and the signature." Lady Mary's breath went out in a sigh of relief. She rose to her feet.

"Let us understand this, Mr. Pons. I am not ashamed of those letters. They were written to a man with whom I was very much in love and who was killed while serving as a pilot with the Royal Flying Corps in the late war."

Solar Pons inclined his head.

"I am indeed sorry."

A little smile was playing round Lady Mary's lips.

"They are passionate love letters, Mr. Pons; I have no compunction admitting it. Their recipient was a man to whom I had given myself wholly and without reserve, physically and spiritually. We would have been married had he survived the war."

"There is no need to tell me this, Lady Mary."

"I would like you to know, Mr. Pons."

"Why did you pay this man Stanmore, Lady Mary? Surely His Grace is too big a man to bother with what is past. Had Stanmore placed this material in his hands, he would simply have handed the letters to you or burned them unread, surely?"

Lady Mary shook her head.

"You misunderstand me, Mr. Pons. I had no fears for Hugo. But his family is one of the proudest and most stiff-backed in the whole of England. His mother in particular. One breath of scandal and the engagement would have been broken off. Believe me, Mr. Pons, that creature Stanmore would have sent these letters direct to my fiancé's mother. And the shattering of the engagement would have broken Hugo's heart. I was not prepared to risk it."

Pons stood deep in thought for a moment. Then he reached out and took Lady Mary's hand. He placed the bundle of letters within it.

"No doubt these memories are fragrant, Lady Mary. You may wish to keep these in a safe place where you treasure such intimate thoughts."

Lady Mary's eyes were wide as she stared at Pons.

"And the price, Mr. Pons?"

Solar Pons shook his head.

"Some things are beyond price, Lady Mary. All I ask is some information which may lead me to the murderer of Stanmore."

Lady Mary was silent for a moment. Her lips curved in a smile of great sweetness and simplicity.

"I greatly appreciate your generosity, Mr. Pons. But even so your price is higher than you may know. As you have undoubtedly obtained a list of Stanmore's victims, may I suggest that you have a word with Hugo himself?"

Pons gave our hostess a shrewd glance.

"I had intended to do so, Lady Mary. And thank you for your gracious suggestion."

He consulted a scrap of paper he took from the buff envelope.

"Lady Mary Hawthorne; the Duke of Leinster; His Grace the Duke of Swaffham; the Honourable Timothy Drexell, M.P.; the Baron Bedale; the Duchess of Ware . . . the list is indeed a noble not to say distinguished one. And when one finds a number of fingerprints on the knife and six golden doubloons, it really gives one pause to think."

Pons' wide smile matched Lady Mary's own.

"I believe you know a great deal more than would appear, Mr. Pons."

"It may be, Lady Mary, it may be," murmured Pons. "But Dr. Parker and I have much to do."

Lady Mary's face was thoughtful as she balanced the bundle of letters in her tiny hand.

"You really are a most remarkable man, Mr. Pons. May I wish you success in your quest. And my deepest thanks."

Pons stooped a moment as he kissed the tips of our hostess's fingers.

"Thank you, Lady Mary. And felicitations on your forthcoming marriage, which I am sure will be happy and long-lived. Good day."

We were crossing the floor and had almost reached the door when Lady Mary called Pons back.

"You will not find the Duke in town, Mr. Pons. He is at his country lodge in Sussex. He will be there for the remainder of this week."

"Thank you, Lady Mary. I will take the liberty of calling upon him tomorrow. No doubt you will have a message conveyed to him."

"I will do that, Mr. Pons. And thank you again."

A few moments later we were outside in the sunshine. Pons laughed as he strode down the steps.

"Magnificent, was she not, Parker?"

"Undoubtedly, Pons," I replied. "But I must confess I have not been able to make much of the conversation."

"Have you not, Parker? Well, perhaps we could run over a few salient points after Mrs. Johnson's excellent supper this evening."

5

Our apartment at 7B Praed Street was blue with smoke. I got up from the table and significantly opened one of the long windows, letting in the cool air of the summer evening.

"Really, Pons!" I protested. "This is becoming intolerable."

"Is it not," he retorted languidly. "Six doubloons, a cyanose condition, several fingerprints, and at least a dozen noble blackmail clients."

"You know very well what I mean, Pons," I replied, looking pointedly at Pons' reeking pipe as I came back to the table. "That infernal thing should be smoked only in the open air."

"On the contrary," said Solar Pons with a smile glinting from behind the stem, "the atmosphere it engenders concentrates the thoughts, sharpens the mind, and has a practical application inasmuch as it asphyxiates the mosquitoes."

"And with them your old and valued friend, Dr. Lyndon Parker," I said with some asperity.

Pons removed the pipe from his mouth and broke into a laugh.

"Forgive me, my dear fellow. I must confess this is rather a burner. It was, as you may remember, a souvenir of one of my most bizarre cases."

"That of Jethro Stringer, the Mad Corinthian of Nether-hampton," I reminded him.

"One of a presentation set as a gift from his grateful son-in-law, Wednesday Lovelace," Pons murmured.

"His intended final victim," I said. "The only one who stood between Stringer and a million-pound fortune."

"Nevertheless, Parker, before you are carried away on a wave of nostalgic reminiscence, allow me to recall you briefly to the present."

"Really, Pons, you began it . . . " I commenced when I was interrupted by the shrilling of the telephone in the passage outside. A moment later Mrs. Johnson appeared.

"Superintendent Heathfield, Mr. Pons."

Pons went out and for the next few minutes I could hear his murmured questions and responses from behind the thick door. Pons' pipe burned on heedlessly on a corner of the table, and I removed it to the safety of a glass vase near the window. I had no sooner resumed my seat than Pons was back, his lean face alight with excitement. He rubbed his thin fingers together and sat down opposite me.

"Ah, Parker, we progress. Dr. Garratt's report was at hand. Heathfield tells me that Stanmore died of heart failure before he was stabbed. I suspected as much."

"This is incredible, Pons!" I cried.

Solar Pons chuckled.

"Is it not, Parker? But not entirely unexpected. Remember, I pointed out the cyanose condition."

"It is sheer madness, Pons," I went on. "Why would anyone want to stab this man when he had already been conveniently removed? And not only stab him once but several times?"

"Twenty-four, to be exact," said Pons imperturbably. "Garratt is able to count accurately, it appears."

"This becomes more baffling by the moment."

Pons shook his head.

"On the contrary, it becomes clearer. There were six doubloons, you will recall. And four thousand pounds had been paid in each case to date."

I fear I was becoming even more exasperated, and Solar Pons looked at me in surprise.

"Always remember, Parker, that what is before one, however outré and extraordinary, must represent the truth. It needs only to be read aright."

"You put great significance on these doubloons, Pons," I cried.

"Exactly," said Pons. "What do you make of them?"

"Stanmore was in the habit of presenting them to his 'clients' as a rather sour way of congratulating them on being bled white, Pons."

Solar Pons nodded.

"Rather colourfully put, Parker, but I get your meaning. Then what was the significance of the six doubloons on the desk?"

"Perhaps he was preparing six more cases of blackmail, Pons."

Solar Pons shook his head.

"You disappoint me, Parker. You have had plenty of opportunity to observe my methods. I commend the doubloons to you. Say rather that this man was being paid back in his own coin. When we find twenty-four stab wounds, the six golden objects, the noble clients and a multiplicity of fingerprints, the affair becomes relatively simple."

"Simple, Pons!"

I threw up my hands in despair.

"And I postulate that the card stating 'Revenge is sweet' clinches the matter. This was a carefully planned affair, Parker. And the man responsible did not want to be disappointed. The card and the coins point to this. And why did the valet not surprise anyone in the apartment? After all, he could have arrived at any time. There was a lookout, Parker; we may take that as certain."

Pons had been fumbling around for a minute or so and now he shot me a sharp glance.

"You have also forgotten the matter of the peace talks. The Duke is heavily involved in those."

I could not resist a sly dig at Pons in retaliation for my present frustration.

"Brother Bancroft should see you now, Pons. Your pipe is over by the window yonder, if you had but the wit to see it."

Pons drew up his eyebrows and fires of humour sparkled in his eyes.

"Touché, Parker, touché. You are developing a definite wit in early middle-age. There is hope for you yet."

And he was soon enveloped in clouds of poisonous blue fumes again.

6

Our destination in Sussex was only an hour's journey by train from Charing Cross, and shortly after midday the following morning we *debouched* from the small wooden station building to find a pony and trap, sent by the Duke himself, awaiting our arrival. We were soon bowling along the dusty country lanes between high banks and blooming hedgerows, with the agreeable scent of freshly cut grass in our nostrils.

"There is a great deal to be said for England at this time of year, Parker," Solar Pons enthused, stretching out his long legs in the trap interior and looking broodingly at the dim blue distances of the far hills as we drove across the undulating countryside.

"I do not think that Elihu Cook Stanmore would agree with you, Pons," I said drily.

"Ah, there you go astray, Parker. That was a matter between him and his Maker. Stanmore is no doubt where he ought to be, and the world is rolling on its way as it should be."

"No doubt you are right, Pons," I conceded.

At that moment the trap swept round a bend in the white highway and the driver pointed with his whip to iron gates beyond which could be seen a long, low handsome house built of the distinctive golden sandstone so prevalent thereabouts.

"Delamere Lodge, gentlemen."

In a short while we had pulled up in front of an impressive flight of steps which led to the massive entrance portico. A tall black-bearded man hurried down to meet us. He was such an imposing figure that I thought for a moment it was the Duke himself. He was dressed in a suit of shaggy tweeds and he looked at us in a most unfriendly manner from beneath beetling black brows. But his manner seemed civil enough.

He merely murmured, "Follow me, gentlemen" and led us through an oak-panelled hall and down a long, green-walled corridor hung with sporting prints and eighteenth-century political cartoons.

"His Grace is in the gun room."

Pons raised his eyebrows but said nothing. At the threshold of the stout oak door which led to our destination the bearded man stopped so suddenly that I almost collided with him. He ignored me and cast his black eyes on my companion, fixing him with a smouldering glance.

"A word in your ear, Mr. Solar Pons. I am very attached to the Duke. If any harm should come to him, you will have me to contend with."

Solar Pons smiled pleasantly. He stood quite at ease, taking the measure of the barrel-chested man who barred the way to the door.

"Your function, I take it, was to stand guard during the murder of the late Elihu Stanmore."

The big man stared wildly at Pons, his complexion beneath the beard turning a dark yellow. Then he gave a snarl and started forward.

"I must warn you that you will find my strength equal to your own," said Pons, coolly stepping back a pace and putting himself on guard.

The big man's mouth dropped, but before there were any further developments, the door was flung furiously open and a tall, aristocratic-looking man in his mid-thirties, wearing a handsome Vandyke beard, stood framed in the lintel.

"What is this, Jefferies?" he cried, his beard bristling with rage. "How dare you presume to treat my guests in this fashion?"

The big man recovered himself. He looked at the Duke not a whit abashed.

"He knows, Your Grace."

"Does he, indeed?" said the Duke of Leinster levelly, looking at Pons with a gleam of irony in his eye. "You had better come in, Mr. Pons. I am honoured to know you, sir. I must apologise for Jefferies. He has a formidable exterior, but he is completely devoted to my service."

"That is quite understandable," said Pons, taking the Duke's outstretched hand. "Allow me to present my friend, Dr. Lyndon Parker."

"I am equally delighted, doctor. Please come in. You'll take some coffee, gentlemen, and stay to lunch? Ask Mrs. Cummings to make the necessary arrangements, Jefferies, if you'll be so good."

The Duke led the way into the gun room, which was a long, high chamber with panelled walls and a vast stone fireplace. The mullioned windows looked out over the spacious grounds, and racks of weapons and trophies of the chase adorned the panelling.

The Duke led the way down the room and waved Pons and myself to two comfortable leather chairs. He seated himself at a bench where he had evidently been polishing weapons, for several cutlasses and a sabre were laid out on the scarred tabletop.

"You'll forgive me for going on with what I was doing, gentlemen."

Pons nodded and walked down the room, examining the racks of weapons.

"You collect Chinese daggers too, I see."

"A foible of an ancestor," replied the Duke carelessly. "It is not a branch of the collection with which I have any great affinity."

"One dagger missing, I notice."

The Duke's eyes flickered toward mine, and I could have sworn a half-smile lingered about his lips.

"It was lost while the collection was being cleaned last year, I believe. I do not know where it has got to."

"Indeed," said Pons. "When last seen it was adorning the shoulder blades of a gentleman called Elihu Cook Stanmore. It had been driven some twenty-four times into his back."

"Remarkable, Mr. Pons," said the Duke of Leinster levelly. "That could not have done a great deal for his health."

"Life was quite extinct," said Pons.

He could not repress a glance of admiration.

"If you do not mind me saying so, Your Grace, you are keeping up an extraordinarily cool exterior in this matter." The Duke put down a cutlass and picked up one of the sabres. He held it pointed toward Pons, a sardonic smile on his face.

"You forget I am a trained diplomat, Mr. Pons. Ah, here is Mrs. Cummings with the coffee and biscuits."

He waited until the elderly woman with the pleasant, motherly features had poured the coffee from a silver-plated pot and quit the room, before he spoke again.

"One lump or two, Mr. Pons? Incidentally, sir, I do not mind admitting that you would have had a very different reception had I not received a telephone call from Lady Mary. I am deeply obliged to you, Mr. Pons, I really am."

There was a faint flush on Pons' cheeks.

"It was a pleasure to be of service to such a gracious lady. Would it be premature to wish you every happiness in your future life together?"

The Duke, who wore a green baize apron over a smart light grey suit, bowed, observing, "That is much appreciated, Mr. Pons. I must say my future depends very much on you."

"I am glad you recognise the fact, Your Grace. Would it also be indiscreet of me to ask how the peace talks at Geneva are going?"

137

The Duke looked at Pons steadily, the coffee cup arrested halfway to his lips.

"Very indiscreet, Mr. Pons. But between these four walls and knowing that your close relationship with your brother is not only one of blood, I am happy to say that Great Britain's position is not prejudiced in any way by the operations of Mr. Stanmore."

I had been a silent spectator of this conversation in mounting bewilderment and now I could not withhold my comment.

"I am afraid this is far above my head, Pons. Would one of you mind coming to the point?"

To my surprise, the Duke of Leinster burst out laughing.

"You have my sympathy, doctor."

He waved the tip of the sabre.

"Shall we give up fencing, Mr. Pons?"

My companion nodded, putting down his cup and reaching for a biscuit.

"I would strongly suspect that what precipitated Stanmore's death was the pressure put on the Duke deliberately to weaken, if not completely vitiate, this country's position in the current negotiations at Geneva."

"Which would have gravely altered the present precarious balance of power in Europe," added the Duke.

"I seem to detect the trembling of the spider's web," said Pons, looking at me grimly. "The delicate hand of our old friend Baron Ennesfred Kroll."

"You don't mean to say so, Pons!" I ejaculated.

"On the contrary, Parker. The implications of this affair go even deeper than I at first envisaged. Will you start, sir, or shall I?"

"You seem to know so much about it, I shall defer to you,

Mr. Pons. Then you shall see whether we were justified. I take it you will make my official position clear to Mr. Bancroft Pons?"

Pons smiled.

"You may be assured of it, Your Grace."

The Duke of Leinster leaned forward to the coffee pot.

"Do allow me to pour you some more of this excellent brew, Dr. Parker."

🖎 7

"What I find surprising, Your Grace, is the fact that you have made it fairly plain that you have a connection with the death of Stanmore," Pons began.

The Duke smiled grimly from his position at the table. He fingered the sabre thoughtfully.

"There is not much point in denying it, Mr. Pons. My family motto is connected with honesty and truthfulness. And I do not run a great deal of risk, surely, when you know by now that that blackguard died before the moment of execution."

Pons stroked the lobe of his left ear with a thin finger and smiled briefly.

"There is that, Your Grace, but the fact remains that murder was planned. And you and your companions are certainly guilty of his death inasmuch as your threats precipitated Stanmore's heart attack."

The Duke looked at Pons gravely.

"Tut, tut, Mr. Pons. This is mere quibbling. I expected your visit, of course. I knew Stanmore would keep records. Unfortunately, we were disturbed by someone before we could make a proper search."

Pons sat back in his chair and tented his fingers before him as he stared at the Duke fixedly.

"You have just reminded me, Your Grace, that I have done you, through your fiancée, some slight favour. I have most of the pieces of this puzzle. I should like to ask you a favour in return. I am not quite clear in my own mind just what hold Stanmore could have had over you."

The Duke put down the sabre with which he had been toying and looked taken aback for the first time since the interview began.

"I will return the favour, Mr. Pons, on the solemn oath of both of you that not a word of what I shall tell you will go beyond the walls of this chamber."

"You have our word, Your Grace."

Leinster nodded. He got up from the bench and took a few nervous pacing turns in front of the empty fireplace which, at this time of the year, contained a mass of flowers. Their red, spiky beauty reminded me of the deeper stains in Stanmore's chamber of death.

"How he came by them, I know not, Mr. Pons, but this unspeakable creature had some love letters written by my late father to a former mistress. He threatened to lay them before my mother. She is a woman of high moral principles who adored my father. The shock would have killed her. I had no choice but to pay him money. I had given him a total of four thousand pounds with the promise, at the time of his death, of more. Latterly he had been putting pressure on me to betray my country."

Pons' face was grim and serious as he listened to this recital.

"You have my word, Your Grace," he repeated. "I am indeed sorry. Stanmore deserved death, if ever a man did."

Pons hesitated as his eyes searched the Duke's face and then he went on.

"Did you know of your fiancée also being blackmailed?"

"Only latterly, Mr. Pons. Mary came to me in great distress. She did not go into detail."

An unspoken question lingered in his eyes.

Pons put him at ease.

"You need not concern yourself, Your Grace. Lady Mary is an honourable woman. The affair concerned nothing but old love letters written years ago to an officer now dead. I am sure Lady Mary will not mind me telling you under the present difficult circumstances. Stanmore also threatened to send these letters to your mother. With your mother's well-known ethical standards, Lady Mary felt she might forbid the marriage. She could not risk that."

The Duke stood in silence for a moment; then his face cleared. He came forward and wrung Pons' hand in silence. I cleared my throat. The noise sounded like a loud intrusion in the silence.

"I am sorry, Pons, but from a layman's point of view, I am not at all sure of this matter."

Pons' eyes were dancing as he turned back to me.

"Let us just reconstruct the crime, Parker. I have already drawn your attention to a number of significant points. It was obvious from the beginning that one of Stanmore's blackmail victims had committed the murder. But the very ferocity of the method aroused my suspicions. One stab wound would have been enough for a man with Stanmore's heart condition. But twenty-four wounds smacked of a ritual. The Chinese dagger was a red herring, merely, and I discounted it immediately.

"The first problem that presented itself, was the secret

141

address. If we discarded the valet, Dawkins, and the woman who did the cleaning, we were left with two alternatives. Someone who found the unlocked door by accident and took the opportunity to dispose of Stanmore; the coincidence was too wild and unlikely. We were then left with the alternative of a carefully planned murder, involving several people. Jefferies?"

The Duke nodded.

"I had him follow Stanmore about London. I like to know my enemy and all his habits. Eventually, about six months ago, he was successful and tracked him to Westbourne Grove. The next stage was to cultivate Dawkins. He frequents a public house, The Jolly Vine, nearby. Over the course of those months the two men became drinking companions. In his cups Dawkins let fall various names of 'business clients' of his employer."

"The people who visited him at his West End hotel," said Pons crisply. "I suspected something of the sort but am glad to have the fact confirmed from your own lips. You not only desired to relieve some of Stanmore's other victims as well as yourself and Lady Mary but you required accomplices to spread the risk. An unusual crime. Death by proxy, one might call it."

Leinster's eyes were sparkling as he followed my companion's reasoning.

"For once a reputation has not been exaggerated, Mr. Pons."

"You discreetly called upon those of your companions in misfortune as were known to you," Pons went on. "They were not only friends or acquaintances but all men in early or middle life, who could be relied upon in a tight corner. I saw many such names in the list I perused."

"You may ask me anything except their names," said the Duke curtly.

"That will not be necessary," Pons continued. "On the morning selected for Stanmore's execution six of you went to his flat. Jefferies remained outside to give the alarm in case the valet arrived early. You would then leave by the back stairs."

The Duke nodded, his eyes never leaving Pons' face.

"Correct, Mr. Pons. We left the building quickly when Jefferies signalled the alarm. A man came up the stairs shortly after eight o'clock. Jefferies was taken unawares and could not be sure that it was not Dawkins. He gave the alarm and we left hurriedly the same way we came, one by one, down the back stairs. In the event it must have been an occupant of one of the other flats—but we were not to know that."

Pons nodded.

"The six of you went into the flat. Stanmore was already at his study desk, his back to the door. You personally led the way, holding the dagger. Stanmore turned round, recognised his clients, choked, and had a heart attack. But you decided to make sure of him. Why?"

Leinster inclined his head thoughtfully.

"Revenge is sweet, Mr. Pons," he said softly. "Stanmore was choking. We could not be sure whether the seizure was fatal or not. We had to make a quick decision. We killed him ritually, as you say."

"By each taking a section of the dagger and guiding it home," Pons went on. "Thus leaving a portion of each man's finger-prints to confuse the police."

"Which certainly had the desired effect, Pons," I reminded him.

"The picture was fairly clear to me at a glance," Pons said. "It was an ingenious notion and would certainly have involved some legal problems."

"But why twenty-four stab wounds?" I asked.

"That was elementary, Parker. The six gold doubloons pointed the way. We knew, after what Dawkins said, that Stanmore gave his 'clients' a so-called bonus in the form of a doubloon when he had drained them dry. This was a case of six clients returning the compliment with interest, as it were. There were six clients. I had noted from the record that each to date had paid Stanmore four thousand pounds."

Light broke.

"Six fours are twenty-four, Pons!" I cried.

"You continue to improve, Parker," said Pons condescendingly. "The florist's card had been deliberately written in a manner that was unlikely ever to be traced by the police. And Stanmore's records contained a multiplicity of suspects, many of whom were so distinguished and powerful that the police would have to tread carefully. But I already had Brother Bancroft's brief and thus concentrated my search in the area of diplomacy, which led me directly to you, Your Grace."

"You have caught me red-handed, Mr. Pons," said our extraordinary host. "What do you intend to do?"

Pons was silent for a moment, his eyes searching the far distance.

"Telephone my brother in due course and tell him that England's secrets are safe in the hands of one of the ablest public servants she has ever had. Although, as a professional, I must frown at murder or attempted murder in all its forms, I feel that on this occasion justice has been done."

"But what are you going to tell Superintendent Heathfield, Pons?" I asked.

Leinster and Pons exchanged a conspiratorial smile. Solar

Pons tented his long, thin fingers before him and looked at me blandly.

"We will think of something, Parker," he said gently. "But I fear this is one case where my ratiocinative faculties have been strained beyond the limit. And I have no doubt that Foreign Office influence will bring a speedy closure of the file."

"You will not find my fiancée and me ungrateful, gentlemen," said the Duke of Leinster, taking my colleague by the hand. "And now, if you will permit me, an excellent lunch awaits us."

ALLEN K '14

THE ADVENTURE OF
THE IPI IDOL

1

"CAREFUL OBSERVATION IS the whole basis of the ratiocinative process," said Solar Pons. "That and the correct deduction of data from the observable facts."

A thick fog was swirling outside the windows of our quarters at 7B Praed Street but within, all was comfort and cheer. I sat with my feet up on the fender, a glass of port at my elbow, while Pons was in his favourite leather armchair opposite, a grey dressing gown draped round his lean, angular form. We had just had supper and, after a busy day spent on my rounds in this bleak January weather, I was more than glad to return to the warmth and pleasant comradeship of the familiar sitting room.

Pons had been unusually quiet after the meal and now he sprawled, his pipe sending curling streamers of blue smoke up to the ceiling, competing with the aroma of the log fire which burned redly on the hearth.

"You have forgotten one thing, Pons," said I. "It all depends upon the person who is doing the deducing. Apart from your brother Bancroft I know of no one save yourself who is so gifted."

147

Solar Pons smiled warmly, his ascetic face a carmine mask in the firelight as he turned toward me.

"You are flatteringly in form this evening, my dear Parker, but I must disclaim so narrow an honour. Many people in all walks of life use the deductive faculties. You yourself have displayed astonishing powers on occasion."

I mumbled some disclaimer and looked at Pons narrowly. In truth he was being rather fulsome this evening so far as my own lamentable lack of talent in this direction was concerned.

"For example," he went on, as though conscious of my inward reasoning, "what do you make of the stick left by our visitor earlier this evening?"

Our motherly landlady, Mrs. Johnson, had apprised us of the visitor. I had been on my rounds and Pons had been for an evening walk; we had fallen in together at the top end of Praed Street and continued so for a while. On our return to 7B Pons had been distinctly disappointed to have missed a possible client.

"A distinguished-looking gentleman, Mr. Pons," Mrs. Johnson murmured. "He waited for upwards of half an hour and then said he had an appointment. He will try and get back later this evening. I told him you took supper at eight o'clock."

"You did quite correctly, Mrs. Johnson," said Pons. "And thank you."

He turned bitterly to me as we mounted the stairs to our quarters.

"You see, Parker, what a mere forty minutes from home to post a few wretched letters may lead to. Here I have been this past month or so becalmed in a desperate sea of aridity so far as criminous happenings in the metropolis are concerned, and I am abroad the one evening a client calls."

Now, as I recalled the circumstances when Pons drew attention to the stick, I could not repress a slight tendency to mischief.

"I should not attach too much importance to this, Pons. Our visitor may have merely wished to read the gas meter."

Pons' eyes twinkled.

"I appreciate your effort to lighten my sombre mood, but I think not, Parker. Pray take up the stick and give me your opinion."

Thus bidden, I crossed to the side table, where our visitor had laid it, and brought it back to my comfortable chair by the fire.

"Some African wood, evidently."

"Good, Parker, good," said Pons, settling himself back and raking about with a metal instrument in the bowl of his pipe.

"A fairly new stick, which nevertheless has had hard wear."

"Elementary, my dear Parker. The fact tells you nothing?"

I turned the stick around. It had a handsome handle of some darker wood and a brass ferrule.

"The ferrule is much worn, indicating that the bearer is lame."

"Highly speculative, Parker," said Solar Pons, stretching himself in his chair and tamping a fresh wad of cut tobacco into his pipe.

"And the plate on the shaft which I can see plainly winking in the firelight from here?"

"I was saving that for the last, Pons," I said. "I was endeavouring to read as much as possible from the actual stick."

"Most laudable, Parker," murmured Pons, half-enveloped in blue smoke again. He put his matchstick down in a brass tray at his elbow and looked speculatively at the correspondence pinned to the mantel with a heavy jack-knife.

"Presented by his friends of the U.P.C. to Col. J.H. d'Arcy, U.D.C. on the occasion of his retirement, March 3rd 1921."

"A handsome piece," I went on. "The Colonel, presumably the owner of the stick, is elderly. Hence his retirement. A civic post evidently."

"A notable reading, Parker," said Pons with a grunt. "Can you tell us more from the inscription?"

"Very little, Pons," I said. "Though the lettering is fairly obvious. It is a local government matter. Naturally, I cannot say precisely but roughly it could be something like 'From his friends of the Upper Penge Council to Colonel d'Arcy of the Urban District Council'."

"Well done, Parker," said Pons with a short laugh. He gave me a look of approval with his deep-set eyes.

"I trust I have not overlooked anything of major importance, Pons," I added with somewhat justifiable pride.

"Just hand me the stick a moment, like a good fellow."

I passed him the object in silence and waited while he examined it by the light of the reading lamp behind his chair.

"Most commendable, Parker," he exclaimed at length. "There are only a few major points you have overlooked."

"And pray what might those be, Pons?"

"So far from being a cripple, Colonel d'Arcy is an active, vigorous man, in his prime, certainly not more than fifty-five years of age."

"Come, come, Pons," I protested.

"In addition he has certainly nothing to do with local government, far less Upper Penge Council, which I suspect does not even exist," went on Pons imperturbably. "He was in the

Colonial Service until last year and served in an administrative capacity in West Africa. They tend to retire early in such climates."

I could not forbear a smile.

"Really, Pons, this is going a little far. But it will be easy enough to disprove when Colonel d'Arcy arrives."

"Or prove, Parker," said Pons quietly. "He keeps a bull mastiff also, if I am not mistaken."

He held up his hand to stop my flow of protestations.

"The stick is of West African hardwood, the handle of another variety of hardwood found in that corner of the world. It is a presentation stick as is clear from the inscription. It therefore follows that Colonel d'Arcy may well have served in the army in those parts and stayed on in the Colonial Service."

"It is possible, Pons," I admitted. "But how do you deduce that he is vigorous?"

"This is not the stick of a lame man," said Pons decisively. "He has had it only a year. It was a presentation stick in which he takes some pride. The brass ferrule is quite worn, which indicates much walking, to my mind. Moreover, the ferrule, as you will see, is worn quite evenly all the way round, which indicates that the Colonel rotates it in his hand as he flourishes it. That is not the action of a person suffering from lameness."

"You may be right, Pons," I said. "But my stab at local government is just as likely to be correct as your Colonial background."

Solar Pons shook his head with a mocking smile.

"Try Urundi, Parker. We may well then arrive at a presentation from the Urundi Planters' Club to the local District Commissioner."

I was silent for a moment.

"You know the man, Pons?"

Solar Pons shook his head and again turned his attention to his pipe.

"And the dog, Pons?"

"There are strong indentations on the shaft of the stick which suggest that a dog is in the habit of carrying it for his master. The impressions are broad and widely set apart, though not easy to see because the wood is hard and the stick is black. Nothing but a big dog would make such marks. I submit a bull mastiff."

"It is a long shot, Pons," I submitted.

"We shall see," said my companion urbanely. "For Mrs. Johnson has just gone to the front door and there, if I am not mistaken, is the footstep of our man on the stairs now."

🖎 2

Mrs. Johnson's cheerful, well-scrubbed face appeared in the doorway.

"The gentleman I was telling you about, Mr. Pons. Colonel d'Arcy."

Pons and I rose as the room appeared to shake. Colonel d'Arcy was indeed an enormous man, more than six-feet tall and proportionately broad. He wore a large checked overcoat against the bitter cold outside and carried a black homburg in his hand. His open, bearded face had a deep tan, and piercing blue eyes looked first at me and then at my companion.

"Mr. Solar Pons? I deeply regret this intrusion, but I simply must consult you."

"Pray come in, Colonel d'Arcy. I regret that I was not at home when first you called. Please take a seat here by the fire. This is my friend, Dr. Lyndon Parker."

"Glad to meet you, Dr. Parker."

The Colonel gave me a bone-crushing grip and paused to take off his coat before sitting down. Pons excused himself and left the room to remove his dressing gown. When he reappeared a few seconds later, he had resumed his jacket and his face had the alert look I had not seen for some weeks. Mrs. Johnson had hovered by the door to see if there was anything we required and now quietly excused herself and left.

I had been rather puzzled by a low panting noise which had persisted for some minutes, and as I moved to offer the Colonel some liquid refreshment, my foot touched something and there was a low growl. Colonel d'Arcy sprang up with a sharp apology.

"Come here, Toto! I hope you do not mind the liberty, Mr. Pons, but I brought my dog with me to town today. He is extraordinarily attached to me, and I did not want to leave him at home, for he pines if I am away for any length of time."

"I am sure he will be no trouble, Colonel," said Pons, looking at me quizzically. "A bull mastiff, I see. Carries your stick, no doubt?"

"Why, yes, Mr. Pons. Which reminds me, I am afraid I inadvertently forgot it when I left your chambers."

"It is quite safe, Colonel. Allow me to pass it to you. You are certainly not infirm, so I assume you do a great deal of walking."

Colonel d'Arcy nodded, taking the glass of pink gin from me with a grunt of satisfaction. He looked approvingly at both of us over the rim as he gave us a silent toast. I poured whisky for myself and Pons and resumed my seat by the fire. The dog Toto crawled toward the fender and looked at his master with unwinking yellow eyes. Pons could not resist a little glance of triumph at me.

The Colonel put down his glass with a satisfied air.

"I do a great deal of walking, it's true. And I treasure this stick."

"A gift, I see," said Pons. "I took the liberty of reading the inscription."

Colonel d'Arcy nodded.

"From West Africa. I was in the Colonial Service there. Retired a year ago."

"At the age of fifty-five, I would venture," said Pons, a malicious glint in his eye.

"Why, yes, Mr. Pons, though I do not see how you could possibly know that."

"Just a guess, Colonel. You were an administrator?"

District Commissioner at Urundi. My friends in the Planters Club gave me the stick."

"Which Toto, as I observed, is in the habit of carrying, I see."

Our visitor looked at Pons once more in amazement and then burst into a short laugh.

"That is true, Mr. Pons, though how on earth you know these things . . . "

"Oh, I was just indulging in a little exercise in deductive analysis from your stick, with Parker here, before you arrived, Colonel. It was not without its amusing aspects. Parker had you down as an elderly invalid who had retired from an urban council."

"Come, Pons," I protested. "That is unfair. I was only making a tentative shot at the facts, at your invitation."

"Life is unfair, Parker," said Solar Pons, leaning back in his chair and favouring me with a reassuring smile. "Have the satisfaction of knowing that you have done no worse in the matter and certainly better than most. But we are forgetting your problem, Colonel, in these little speculations. You do have a problem, or you would not have come to consult me?"

Our visitor nodded. He passed his hand across his thick black beard, and his face had assumed a serious aspect.

"I have indeed, Mr. Pons. It is something quite outside my normal experience."

Solar Pons rubbed his thin fingers together.

"That is what this agency exists for. Please continue."

The Colonel took another sip of his pink gin and rested the glass in his big, capable hands as his sombre eyes probed the glowing depths of the wood fire before him. At that moment I seemed to see him in faraway places in Africa; he must have sat many times like that in the bush, by the warmth of a campfire, with the strange night noises of Africa sounding through the jungle. Then he appeared to recollect himself with a slight start.

"You must forgive me, Mr. Pons, but this business has rattled me a little, I can tell you. As you gathered, I retired last year from the Colonial Service at the age of fifty-five. I had come into some money from a relative who had died and left me a considerable property in England. I was a bachelor, in good health, and I decided that it would be pleasant to return to the U.K. to live in some comfort and to see what life had still to offer. I had missed a good deal of a domestic nature in my years in the wild. Though I am in middle-age, I am a vigorous person and not too ugly, as you see."

Colonel d'Arcy paused and gave Pons a brief smile.

"You had hoped, as do so many returning expatriates, to find a suitable lady who would join her destiny to yours in matrimony," said Solar Pons, returning the smile. "I trust you have been successful."

Our visitor's face glowed.

"Mr. Pons, if you could only meet the young lady in question. Miss Mortimer is the most charming, the most..."

"I am sure that is so," said Pons, interrupting the Colonel's flow. "But I must ask you to keep to the nature of the problem before us."

The Colonel shrugged wryly.

"I do get rather carried away by Miss Mortimer, Mr. Pons," he said. "You do right to recall me to the point, though the lady's position has some bearing on the matter."

He shifted his posture in the chair and looked curiously at Pons' old slipper on the fender, from which an ounce packet of shag projected.

"My uncle, Silas Renfrew, was an eccentric, Mr. Pons. His estate would have passed to his son, my cousin, but he died while I was still in Africa. Instead, my uncle chose to leave the property to me. It is a big old rambling place in Essex, with a considerable acreage of grounds and woodland."

Pons sat with his fingers tented before him, his eyes lidded, every aspect of his body denoting his alertness.

"The legacy was a considerable one also, Colonel d'Arcy?"

Our visitor nodded, bending to affectionately cuff the massive head of the dog stretched in contentment in front of him.

"It was totally unexpected, as I think I mentioned, Mr. Pons. I had saved a good deal on my own account and of course my Colonial pension left me well provided for."

Solar Pons leaned back in his seat and closed his eyes tightly.

"I am afraid I must ask you to be more specific, Colonel. It is the legacy I am concerned with."

The Colonel hesitated a short moment.

"It was in excess of a hundred thousand pounds, Mr. Pons.

In addition I am advised by my uncle's lawyer that the estate itself is worth almost as much again."

Solar Pons opened his eyes and looked at our visitor intently.

"A considerable fortune, Colonel. It was as well to establish that at the outset."

Pons ignored the startled look the Colonel gave him and waited for him to go on.

"Well, sir, I settled in at The Briars, as the estate is called. It is in a lonely spot on the Essex marshes, some miles from Tolleshunt D'Arcy with which my family has a distant connection, I believe. There is a largish village nearby, and some sizeable country houses; otherwise it is fairly wild and lonely country, Mr. Pons. I had been there some months when I met Miss Claire Mortimer, a neighbouring landowner's daughter, who has now consented to become my wife. She is a lady of some thirty-three years and I am a good deal older than she, though she thinks that of no account."

Colonel d'Arcy cleared his throat and drained his glass. I hastened to refill it for him, and our visitor resumed his discourse.

"The Briars is a pretty old house, Mr. Pons, though not as old as some in those parts. It was about this time last year that I settled in with my traps and various trophies. I bought some new furniture and made a few changes, but I kept on the housekeeper and the three or four other members of the existing staff.

"It was from the housekeeper, Mrs. Karswell, that I heard the stories about my uncle, Mr. Pons. He had had some connection with West Africa too, strangely enough, and had an interest in tribal matters. But toward the end of his life he had an abiding fear of something which he felt might be coming for him. As I said, he settled his money on my cousin, Adrian Renfrew."

157

"The young man who died?"

"Under mysterious circumstances, Mr. Pons. Some weeks before, my uncle had occasion to go into his library one evening. He found a small carved idol on his desk, which threw him into a fearful state. It was a crude, primitively constructed thing with tribal markings. The Ipi, I believe, an obscure sect in Africa, who practice devil worship."

"He could not find out where the thing had come from?"

Colonel d'Arcy shook his head.

"No one knew anything about it, Mr. Pons. Or no one would say, which came to the same thing so far as my uncle was concerned. The housekeeper told me all this, you understand. But he evidently took it as some sort of frightful warning and had the grounds locked and the house bolted and barred at night. There were some who said he made money at the slave trade. I don't know how true that is, Mr. Pons. But apparently the warning, if warning it was, was not intended for him, because something struck at his son.

"About a week after the idol came, Adrian was called out into the grounds by a suspicious noise one night. He gave a great cry and said something had bitten him. Indeed, his foot and leg swelled up to an incredible size, and it was obvious he had been stung by something poisonous. Mr. Pons, he died in great agony, within three days, despite all the doctors could do to save him!"

✎ **3**

There was a long silence in the room and I got up and placed another billet of wood upon the fire. Pons sat with the sensitive fingers of one hand stroking the lobe of his left ear in a gesture with which I had long become familiar.

"Do go on, Colonel. This is of absorbing interest. If what you say is correct, some beast of tropical origin was responsible for young Renfrew's death."

"That is so, Mr. Pons. There was a search made, of course, but nothing was ever found. And if it were so, the insect, or snake, would not have long survived in an English winter."

"Do go on."

"Well, Mr. Pons. There is not a great deal more, although what transpired recently did give me one of the biggest frights of my life. A small parcel came for me last week. I have it here."

"Containing an African idol, no doubt," said Pons with a curious smile.

"Exactly, Mr. Pons."

"Pray let me see it."

Our visitor rummaged in the pocket of the overcoat he had left on the chair and produced a small cardboard box wrapped in torn brown paper. The name and address was inked on the paper in rough block letters. Pons took it up.

"Postmarked Colchester, I see. Done with a thick-nibbed pen. The writing tells us nothing. Probably written in a post office. Time of posting ten forty-five a.m.; ordinary string such as one could buy at any ironmonger's. The paper is wrapping paper whose sheets are sold by the million in stationers the length and breadth of the land. The box looks as though it might have once contained an Easter egg. Or it could have come from a toy shop. Let us just have a look at the contents."

He carefully lifted out the ugly object and set it down on a small table at the fireside, where we could all clearly see it. It was indeed a bizarre thing. About five inches in height, the negroid features were difficult to make out, partaking both of male and female characteristics. The statuette was full-length, jet-black, and the cheeks of the creature were gashed and incised. There were yellow and red stripes painted across the face and stomach of the effigy. It was crudely done, as we could all see. Solar Pons put out a forefinger and touched the figurine.

"I am no authority on West African tribal matters, Colonel. What do you make of it?"

"Those are Ipi markings, all right, Mr. Pons. But if that is tribal carving, I will eat my hat."

Pons chuckled and nodded his head in assent.

"I had already come to the same conclusions, Colonel. A crude facsimile of the real thing, possibly copied out of some encyclopaedia."

He moistened his forefinger with saliva and rubbed at the flank of the figure. His finger came away black. He smiled.

"Cheaply constructed, cheaply coloured too. But the thing evidently put the fear of death into Silas Renfrew. Surely you are not suggesting that the arrival of this idol threw you into a state of terror also."

Our visitor burst into a short, barking laugh which made the dog Toto prick up its ears.

"It would take something more tangible to do that, Mr. Pons. No, sir, it was an event which happened last night and which almost cost me my life. About two days ago I found I had mislaid my favourite pair of bedroom slippers. I thought little about it, feeling that perhaps one of the servants had taken them away to polish. Last night, they were back at my bedside."

Our visitor's face had turned deathly pale, and his brilliant blue eyes were fixed upon Pons.

"I was in my pyjamas, Mr. Pons. It was almost midnight and the fire in the room was burning low. My feet were bare, and I was reaching out my hand for my slippers when I saw a shadow crawl, out of the corner of my eye. Mr. Pons, you may believe me or believe me not, but it was the biggest spider I have ever seen; a monstrous, hairy thing that looked to my overheated mind as big as a soup plate."

"Good heavens!" I could not help exclaiming.

Colonel d'Arcy looked at me grimly.

"You may well say so, doctor. The thing was a nightmare. It had evidently been sheltering in my slipper for warmth and was making for the area of the fire. Fortunately I was able to seize the poker and despatched the loathsome creature with a few well-aimed blows. Mr. Pons, it was a tarantula! One bite from that thing and it would have been all up with me."

Pons ran a finger gently along the edge of his jaw and his eyes were serious.

"These are deep waters, Parker. You did well to come to me, Colonel. What did you do with the remains of this creature?"

"I burned it, Mr. Pons. Burned it in loathing and disgust, and then had the servants up, and the whole room turned inside out."

"Nevertheless, it might have assisted us if you had saved the remains," said Solar Pons. "You are certain it was a tarantula?"

Colonel d'Arcy nodded grimly.

"I have seen enough of the brutes in my time."

"Nevertheless, your bizarre and fascinating mystery, Colonel, raises a number of interesting questions. This creature—and possibly something similar that may have bitten young Adrian Renfrew—could not have lived long in an English winter, as you say. Therefore it needed artificial warmth. The supply of such things is necessarily specialised and narrows down the search considerably. No doubt it was packed carefully in your slipper by someone who knew what he was about. Possibly the insect was drugged. The heat in the room gradually died out and the brute awoke and sought warmth. You are indeed lucky, Colonel, that it did not seek it against the sole of your foot."

Our visitor shuddered and beads of perspiration were starting out on his brow.

"This morning, Mr. Pons, I sought the advice of my fiancée. She advised—nay even urged me strongly—to come to you. I thought the matter over all day. Finally, common sense prevailed. I am not a coward, Mr. Pons, but something vile is menacing the inhabitants of The Briars. I do not wish Miss Mortimer involved. I beg of you to return to Essex with me tonight, Mr. Pons. Money is of no object."

Solar Pons held up his hand and rose swiftly to his feet.

"It is not a question of money, Colonel. I had long ago made up my mind to take the case. There is no time to be lost. Have you set a date for your wedding?"

Our visitor looked startled and rose to his feet also.

"In early spring, Mr. Pons. May."

Pons pulled at the lobe of his ear.

"Just over three months. There may be an element of desperation here. No doubt an attempt will be made again. You have not yet told us how your uncle died, Colonel."

"He was a broken man after the death of his only son, Mr. Pons. He was found dead in his study one night. Foul play was not suspected. He had a long history of heart trouble."

Pons nodded, his eyes questioningly on my face.

"It has just turned ten o'clock. There is a train shortly which will take us to our destination within the hour. Are you free to accompany us, Parker?"

"If the Colonel has no objection."

Colonel d'Arcy raised a deprecatory hand.

"I would be greatly honoured, doctor."

"That is settled then," said Solar Pons, returning to his bedroom to throw some things into his overnight bag.

"I will just telephone my locum, Pons," I said, but he had already disappeared. The dog Toto got up with a snuffling noise, evidently glad to be moving again. I helped Colonel d'Arcy on with his coat and then made my call and packed my own bag. Within ten minutes we were en route for Essex.

4

Our client had his own motor-car waiting at the small country station. It was a bitterly cold night with the fog swirling heavily, though a light wind which was moving across the surrounding marshes made it gust and eddy.

"My fiancée is staying at The Briars with her mother at the moment," Colonel d'Arcy explained as he drove carefully along the flat road, the wall of fog swirling uneasily in the yellow light of the headlamps. "She insisted on coming across today straight away."

"An admirable lady," said Pons, sitting back in his corner of the car, his features in heavy shadow. "Though whether it is wise to be with you is another matter."

"You do not think she is in any danger?" said the Colonel in an alarmed tone.

"We cannot rule out the possibility. Anyone close to you may be. We must just keep a close watch on the young lady. Obviously, your preparations for marriage have precipitated matters."

"I do not see, Mr. Pons..." began our client, when a farm cart loomed suddenly out of the fog and we were lurching over the rough with a screeching of brakes. Our client swore and was visibly shaken. He carefully reversed back onto the road and we got out. The big wooden farm cart, the horse standing patiently in the shafts, was three-quarters across the narrow lane.

"We might all have been killed," said Colonel d'Arcy violently. "I will report this to the police by telephone as soon as we arrive home."

"Indeed," said Pons casually, looking carefully about the roadside verge. "You are not the only person who almost came to grief, I see."

He pointed to where zig-zag tyre marks wandered across the frosty grass. He was immediately down on his knees with a pocket torch, examining them while Colonel d'Arcy looked somewhat puzzledly on.

"The driver of this vehicle obviously veered round and stopped."

"Did he not," said Pons.

He had already taken the horse's reins and urged it and the heavy cart up on to the verge, where he tied the animal to some stout iron railings. He looked underneath the vehicle with his torch and came back dusting his hands. "No doubt the driver has gone for help. I see that the back axle is cracked."

"Even so," exploded Colonel d'Arcy, "he should have been more careful and have seen that the animal was tied up securely."

We got back in the car and drove on toward The Briars in sombre silence, the fog waving and eddying in thick, oily swathes. Toto, who had remained crouched at the Colonel's feet, quite phlegmatic even during the near-accident, had not descended to the ground when we examined the wagon but now that we were approaching the Colonel's home, began to exhibit some excitement, whining and growling and wagging his massive tail.

"Before we join your fiancée and her family," said Pons, "I must ask what arrangements you have made regarding your property."

Our client looked surprised.

"Why, Mr. Pons, I have not made a will if that is what you mean. But when I do so, my estate would naturally pass to my wife, the present Miss Mortimer, in due course."

"You have no other surviving relatives?"

Colonel d'Arcy shook his head.

No close ones that I know of. And certainly no one who would stand to benefit by my estate. You surely cannot mean . . ."

"There is no other plausible motive," Pons went on imperturbably. "On the basis of what you have told me, money would appear to be the cause of these dark events which have surrounded your family. Your uncle might have been supposed to die naturally at some future time, due to his heart complaint. There was no urgency about that, though an attempt was made to frighten him with the idol. His son, a young man and his sole heir, died soon afterward under frightful circumstances. The new heir is first threatened and then his life attempted. No, Colonel, there is no coincidence here. A malign, evil brain is working inexorably toward securing your estate. We must be on constant guard."

"Good heavens, Pons," I said, conscious of a faint shudder in my spinal region. "You will be frightening me next."

"I fancy I shall frighten you, Parker, more easily than Colonel d'Arcy," said Pons with a thin smile. "I want him to be on his guard. We are up against a devilish and cunning adversary."

THE DOSSIER OF SOLAR PONS

"In that case I wish I had brought my revolver," I said somewhat tartly.

"Ah, Parker," said Solar Pons in that maddeningly omniscient manner of his, "I took the liberty of packing it for you. I have brought a derringer myself and I fancy that will be adequate armament, both for tarantulas or human adversaries."

And he passed the weapon to me.

"I confess I am confused and bewildered by the whole thing, gentlemen," said Colonel d'Arcy, hunched over the wheel and straining his eyes through the fog. "There are no possible heirs, so how could my estate be the motive?"

"Ah, that is something yet to be discovered," said Solar Pons mysteriously, and he said nothing more until the Colonel's car had crawled through the last few hundred yards of fog and deposited us at our destination.

The Briars proved to be a long, low, stone-built house with wings thrown out at either side, approached through iron entrance gates, the estate road running through a considerable area of woodland and grass before the house itself was reached. The Colonel parked the car on a broad gravel concourse.

Pons and I got down as a welcoming shaft of light came from a door which was flung open at the head of the steps. There were several vehicles parked in front of the lawn which fronted the mansion, and Pons passed a few moments examining them while the Colonel reversed the car. The fog was lifting a little now and as we went up the steps, I could see that the house was handsome, with carved statues set in niches and well-kept stonework.

The door had been opened by a tall, dark-visaged man in a green baize apron and wearing a batwing collar which stood out in sharp contrast to his sombre clothing. He gave Colonel d'Arcy a stiff bow and was already bending forward to pick up our bags.

"This is Vickers, who was my batman in West Africa," said the Colonel. "These are my guests, Mr. Solar Pons and Dr. Lyndon Parker."

The dark-faced man gave us a bow which seemed like an extension of the first.

"Good evening, gentlemen. Your rooms are ready."

He closed the door behind us and turned to our client.

"Mr. Bradshaw has arrived, sir."

"Good. He is my solicitor, Mr. Pons. Would you like to meet him?"

Solar Pons nodded.

"If it is no trouble. We can go to our rooms afterward, Parker."

We followed the Colonel across a gloomy hall with oak panelling, lined with shields and spears of African origin.

"It seems rather late for a call," said Pons.

"Bradshaw probably dined with my fiancée and her mother," the Colonel explained. "They knew I would be back tonight."

As he spoke there was a murmur of voices, and d'Arcy threw back the oak-panelled double doors and ushered us into another large panelled room lit by candles in chandeliers and boasting a massive stone fireplace in which logs burned cheerfully.

A slender, dark-haired girl with wide blue eyes came forward impetuously and kissed our host lightly on the lips.

"We were getting a little worried, darling. Mummy thought something had happened to you in the fog."

The girl turned her frank gaze on to us while a matronly lady with greying hair, obviously her mother, and a thickset man with a silver moustache and hair thickly powdered with white strands came forward from the background.

167

Our client made the introductions and led us toward the long table in the centre of the room.

"You'll want some refreshment, gentlemen?"

"We have already dined," Pons explained.

He looked with mischievous eyes at me.

"But a drink would not come amiss, eh, Parker?"

"To keep the fog out, Pons," I assented.

Our host busied himself with the glasses, and Pons and I found ourselves with the lawyer as the two ladies went across to the fire. Chadburn Bradshaw, our client's solicitor, had very white teeth and a faint tan on his lean face. His voice had a Scottish accent as he wrinkled his brows in concentration.

"Mr. Pons? Not the famous consulting detective?"

"Hardly famous," Pons replied. "But that is my profession."

"You are too modest, Mr. Pons," said the lawyer with obvious interest. "You will find much to tax your wits at The Briars. It has the reputation of being haunted. And on a foggy night such as this . . ."

He laughed as he turned toward d'Arcy, who came up with brimming glasses, which he pressed into our hands. We went over to join the ladies at the fire.

"Best be careful when you leave, Bradshaw. We nearly had a smash on the way over."

Bradshaw raised his eyebrows, lifting his glass in a toast which included Miss Mortimer and her mother.

"You mean the farm wagon?" Bradshaw asked. "Has that not been cleared yet? Fortunately, I saw it in time."

"That is your bullnose Morris outside, then?" said Pons.

"Yes, Mr. Pons. Nice cars, aren't they?"

"Indeed."

Our host had excused himself and was talking to the ladies, but now he came hurrying over, his face bearing a frown.

"An estate matter, Bradshaw? I hope it is nothing serious?"

The lawyer shook his head.

"Just a routine matter, Colonel, which nevertheless requires your signature. I have the papers in your study and it will take only a few moments."

He paused and I became aware that there was a slight draught. I turned toward the door, noticing by Pons' stiffened attitude that he had already taken note of it. There was an odd silence, and then the taciturn servant in the baize apron shuffled in and silently began clearing glasses from the table. It was obvious that he had been listening to the conversation, and I shot an inquiring look toward the solicitor.

"Curious fellow, Vickers," said Bradshaw sotto voce. "I don't trust him. He's always snooping about, and he knows far too much about the Colonel's private affairs."

"Really," said Pons, looking sharply across to where Colonel d'Arcy had paused to give his servant some instructions. Bradshaw shrugged.

"Still, it's no business of mine, Mr. Pons. The Colonel picked up Vickers when he was in the Army in West Africa and hung on to him. There's no accounting for tastes."

"No, indeed," I said.

Bradshaw was moving off with the Colonel when Pons took him by the arm.

"There are one or two matters about this house on which I should like to consult you. Would tomorrow be convenient?"

"Certainly, Mr. Pons. I have an office in Tolleshunt D'Arcy. Anyone will tell you where it is. Shall we say about three o'clock?"

169

"Don't forget you are coming for the weekend," our host interrupted. "I am having a small house party to celebrate our engagement."

"Well, then, it is indeed providential that we are here," said Solar Pons. "Until tomorrow, Mr. Bradshaw."

The ladies had now come toward us.

"You will forgive us, Mr. Pons," said Claire Mortimer. "The hour is late and my mother and I wish to retire. We look forward to making the further acquaintance of you and Dr. Parker tomorrow."

Pons bent and took her hand. It may have been my imagination, but I thought I saw an anguished appeal in the girl's eyes as she raised them to my companion's.

A short while later we all broke up for the night. Our host accompanied Bradshaw out to his car. I was astonished at Pons' behaviour as soon as the two men had closed the front door behind them. He put his hand to his lips and hurried me along the hall, our footsteps muffled on the thick carpeting. We turned an angle in the wall and Pons motioned me to be silent.

It was dark in the alcove and at first I could see only the outline of a figure and something which looked like a table. Light winked on bottles and glasses. Then I saw the manservant, Vickers. He was bending over a glass and carefully measuring out liquid. When he had about an inch in the bottom, he put down his head and sniffed it. He remained like this for a while and then turned to a second bottle. When he had dealt with four in this manner, Pons and I quietly withdrew.

We had already said good night to our host and as we crept up the great staircase, the muffled noise of Bradshaw's car crept away through the fog. We found our chambers without any difficulty, for Vickers had left the doors ajar. When we were out of earshot of the hallway, Pons said, "What do you make of that, Parker?"

"Mysterious and suspicious," I replied, knowing he was referring to the servant's behaviour. "It seems to me, Pons, that we have seldom ventured into a darker and more sinister business than the events taking place under the roof of The Briars."

Solar Pons rubbed his thin hands together, and his eyes were twinkling in the dim light of the hallway.

"I have rarely seen a more promising situation. Pleasant dreams, my dear fellow."

And with that he strode into his room and closed the door.

᳕ 5

The next morning dawned bleakly cold and foggy. Pons was afoot and about long before I made my way to the breakfast table. I saw him through the window in conversation with a man who looked like a gardener, as I greeted my host and his prospective wife and mother-in-law.

It was a lively and pleasant group who chatted like old friends, waited on by efficient servants led by Mrs. Karswell, the housekeeper, a middle-aged, stately woman with reserved manners which concealed great warmth of character. Miss Mortimer and her Mother, who was almost as handsome despite her seniority, put themselves out to be kind, and it was easy to see that Claire Mortimer and our host were deeply attached to one another.

At one point in the conversation she put out her hand impulsively to mine on the tablecloth and said, "Both mother and I are deeply grateful to you and Mr. Pons, doctor, for your help in the trouble which has come upon us."

171

I mumbled some banality and as I studied the girl and the Colonel, aware all the time of Mrs. Mortimer's inquiring eye upon me, I was disturbingly conscious of Claire Mortimer's fascinating character and the sinister implications of the web which, if Pons were correct, surrounded the couple.

I was almost disappointed when Pons joined us, for the conversation immediately turned into brisker channels. His walk had invigorated him, and his lean, hawk-like face was glowing with the cold and the exercise. He rubbed his hands together as he sat down to do justice to the bacon, eggs, and grilled kidneys heaped up generously on his plate.

"Well, Parker," he said genially during the first lull in the conversation. "I trust you have been employing your time usefully while I was out of doors."

"I trust so, Pons," I replied, uncomfortably aware of Miss Mortimer's eyes upon me.

"I have taken the liberty, Colonel d'Arcy," Pons went on, "of begging the loan of one of your cars from your chauffeur round at the stable wing. He seems an amiable fellow and readily agreed, with the proviso that I obtain your authority."

"Certainly, Mr. Pons," said our host with a light laugh. "Metcalfe is a stickler for protocol, I am afraid."

"Another of your West African soldiers?" said Pons keenly.

"No," said d'Arcy, shaking his bearded head. "But he was highly recommended by Vickers and I have been well satisfied with him. Do you wish me to accompany you on your excursion?"

Pons shook his head.

"Parker will drive me, if he will be so kind. I have a mind to sample the pleasures of Tolleshunt D'Arcy, and a tour round the marshes would not come amiss. The mist has lifted a little this morning."

"Even so, Mr. Pons, I should not stay out after dark. It has a habit of thickening up in wintertime, as it did last night."

"Have no fear, Colonel. Parker and I will be back in time for tea at the latest. And no doubt you and Miss Mortimer have much to talk about and a great deal to do in preparing for your forthcoming party."

His gaze rested ironically on his host and his fiancée in turn and the flush in the girl's cheeks was a pleasant thing to see.

"Well, Parker," said Pons in the pause which followed. "If you have quite finished your coffee, we will retire to our rooms to prepare for our little expedition. We would be able to obtain lunch in Tolleshunt D'Arcy, no doubt?"

Our host nodded.

"Certainly, Mr. Pons. There are two good hotels and other establishments."

"Excellent. Until tonight, then."

A few minutes later we were driving away down the winding road through the park in a powerful little covered touring car that the chauffeur had provided. I was unfamiliar with the gears and suffered some tart comments from Pons until I had mastered the vehicle and we gained the main road. Pons was silent during the journey, looking out across the bleak landscape which was wreathed in low-lying mist, now and again touched by a deep red winter sun that hung close to the horizon.

We reached the cluster of houses that was Tolleshunt D'Arcy and after we had parked in the main street, soon found the offices that were our destination for that afternoon. Pons continued silent and absorbed and paced about the streets, now and again making trivial purchases at various shops, engaging in desultory and, to my mind, highly irrelevant conversation with their proprietors.

Later we returned to the car and drove out in a great wide looping circle across the marshlands. The sun had dispersed the mist now and glittered on the hoarfrost that stiffened the grass and turned the coats of the patient cattle in the fields to a pale gold. The scene had a certain bleak beauty, and Pons so far overcame his indifference to what he called the neutrality of landscape that he became quite voluble on the subject.

"We seem to have spent an aimless morning, Pons," I said, as we once again entered Tolleshunt D'Arcy and parked in front of an imposing oak-beamed hotel.

"Patience, Parker, was never one of your greatest virtues," said my companion succinctly.

"But all these conversations and purchases of useless boxes of matches, Pons."

"Method, Parker, method. One learns a great deal about small communities by such seemingly idle chatter."

"Come, Pons, I did not hear anything of any value."

"A correction, Parker. You heard a great deal but you did not deduce anything of any value from what you heard."

I sniffed. We walked through the entrance of The George and seated ourselves at a comfortable table in the agreeably old-fashioned dining room.

"Perhaps you could enlighten me, Pons."

Solar Pons smiled and tented his lean fingers before him as his sharp eyes surveyed the people in the dining room.

"For example, my dear fellow, it emerges that Colonel d'Arcy is an honest and agreeable employer, if these people's opinion is to be respected and I maintain that it is. Miss Mortimer is highly thought of and her family have been here for generations. Mrs. Karswell is a model housekeeper and has the affection of the local community, for which she does much charitable work. Vickers is disliked and receives a character assassination at the hands of these people."

"You astonish me, Pons! I did not gather all this."

Solar Pons shrugged, studying the menu the waiter had produced for us.

"I am not surprised, Parker. After all, it is not your forté. But one reads between the lines. The inflection of a voice, a pause, a lowering of the tones, the merest hesitation in answering a question—these things can tell one a great deal."

"And have you come to any conclusions, Pons?"

Solar Pons smiled.

"Let us say I have some mental reservations and some strong suspicions. Nothing that I would care to talk about at this moment."

And with that I had to be content, for Pons did not speak again until three o'clock had chimed from the church tower and we were walking up the stairs into Mr. Chadburn Bradshaw's comfortable office.

The solicitor's clerk, a burly, middle-aged man with beetling eyebrows, had no sooner ushered us into the book-lined apartment than Bradshaw came bustling over from his desk to greet us. He seated us in two leather armchairs facing his desk and resumed his own seat. Today he wore a salt and pepper suit with a discreet grey tie that bore the symbol of some club or other.

"Would you care for some refreshment, gentlemen? I am afraid I can offer only tea."

This with a wry smile. Pons shook his head.

"Thank you, no, Mr. Bradshaw. We have not long lunched at The George."

"An excellent establishment, Mr. Pons. But this is not purely a social visit?"

Pons came straight to the point.

"You have guessed right, Mr. Bradshaw. Colonel d'Arcy takes you into his confidence, I believe?"

Bradshaw sat back in his seat and drummed with restless fingers upon his desk.

"I have that honour, Mr. Pons. I administered his late uncle's estate. The family were old friends."

"So that you are familiar with the tragic incidents that have taken place at The Briars over the past few years?"

Bradshaw nodded. He hesitated a moment, his eyes focused on the far distance beyond the bookcases.

"You appreciate, Mr. Pons, that I am Colonel d'Arcy's legal adviser. I cannot breach confidences."

"But you could stretch a point or two, Mr. Bradshaw, in the interests of your client. Particularly in a matter involving life or death."

The lawyer nodded. He gave a bleak smile.

"Ah, I see that you are familiar with the incident involving Mr. Adrian Renfrew. Then I am also correct in assuming that your interest in this matter is not merely one of idle curiosity."

Solar Pons crossed one lean leg over the other and bent forward in his chair.

"You would be correct, Mr. Bradshaw. There is no reason why you should not know. We believe the Colonel's life is in danger. That is why I have been retained in the matter."

There was a long silence in the room. Bradshaw gazed from one to the other of us, a serious expression on his face. The red winter sunlight spilling in through the window at his side made a carmine mask of his features.

"Well, of course, Mr. Pons," he said composedly. "That puts a different complexion on things. I am at your disposal so long as it is understood that I cannot do anything which could be construed as a breach of professional ethics."

"Naturally," Solar Pons assured him.

He was sitting bolt upright in the chair now, his figure alert and energetic, his left hand pulling at the lobe of his ear.

"My friend Parker and I have pledged ourselves to protect the Colonel from whatever harm threatens. I too cannot go into much detail for professional reasons. Even consulting detectives—as well as solicitors—have ethical standards."

There were little sparks of humour in Pons' eyes, and the solicitor's own glance was filled with ironic amusement as though he appreciated the point. His whitening hair and the silver moustache were all crimsoned with the dying winter sunlight now.

"What do you wish to know, sir?"

"You administer the Colonel's considerable estate, Mr. Bradshaw. I believe someone is trying to get control of the family's assets. I would like to know if you have any documents in your possession or any knowledge which might lead my inquiries in any specific direction."

The solicitor's face was alight with interest; he drummed his fingers on the desk again.

"You are a very shrewd man, Mr. Pons. There is something, but as to whether I should reveal it to you is another matter."

He hesitated.

"I can assure you that no improper use will be made of the information, Mr. Bradshaw."

"In that case, Mr. Pons..."

Chadburn Bradshaw rose from the desk and crossed to a

green iron safe at the side of the room. He rummaged inside it and presently emerged with a brown cardboard dossier tied with red tape. He brought it back to the desk and undid it.

"What use you make of this information is up to you, Mr. Pons. But it must be made clear that it must not be seen to come from me."

"That is perfectly understood."

"Well, then. There was another beneficiary of Silas Renfrew's estate, you must know. He was a strange and eccentric man, though he had become a good friend to me over the years."

"You interest me greatly, Mr. Bradshaw. Do go on."

"A distant cousin, George Tolliver, is a secret beneficiary of the estate. He and young Adrian Renfrew were great friends as boys, but later Tolliver went to America. He had a bad reputation there, I believe."

"No one knew of the existence of this legacy?"

The solicitor shook his head.

"Silas Renfrew insisted on this. He felt he had behaved badly toward his relative, I think. Only myself and Mr. Renfrew knew of this. And George Tolliver, of course. He would inherit only on the Colonel's death."

"You have not even told the Colonel?"

Bradshaw shook his head.

"Those were Mr. Renfrew's precise instructions."

"What was the amount of the legacy?"

"Precisely fifty thousand pounds, Mr. Pons. I have the document."

He took it from the cardboard file as he spoke and came round the desk to hand it to my companion. Solar Pons bent eagerly over it, his keen, aquiline features intent on the detail. He turned the pages over, studying the signatures.

"Excellent, Mr. Bradshaw. You have been extremely helpful. Tell me, how was Mr. Tolliver informed of his good fortune? Did you see him?"

Bradshaw shook his head.

"He was in America at the time. So far as I knew, Mr. Renfrew informed him by letter, enclosing a copy of the document here."

Pons sat deep in thought for a moment longer.

"Have you any idea where George Tolliver is now, Mr. Bradshaw?"

"Not ten miles from where we are sitting, Mr. Pons. He bought a large house in the area some two years ago. I heard of this through my property interests in the district. Of course, I have not sought him out as it was no business of mine, but the name is the same. And according to reports of his strange ménage I have no doubt it is the Tolliver named in the will."

"What makes you say that?"

"Because of the man's weird tastes, Mr. Pons. He has some sort of private menagerie over there. He keeps tropical snakes and spiders among other things, I understand."

"Why, Pons, this is . . ." I burst out excitedly.

Pons' warning frowns checked my flow and I turned rather shamefacedly to the lawyer. But he evidently affected not to notice my discomfort and sat waiting for Pons' next question.

"I am in your debt, Mr. Bradshaw," said he, rising from the chair. "Now it only remains for you to give me the address of Mr. Tolliver, and I will pay him a call. I think we have time before it gets entirely dark, Parker."

An alarmed look crossed Bradshaw's face.

"You will be careful, Mr. Pons. A confidence, remember."

179

He rose, putting the document back into the cardboard folder.

"Have no fear, Mr. Bradshaw," said Pons, shaking hands. "You have my word."

"Very well, then. Tolliver lives at a place called Whitestone Manor. Some nine or so miles outside Tolleshunt D'Arcy. Just take the main road the way your car is pointing and keep straight on."

"Many thanks, Mr. Bradshaw. It has been a most instructive afternoon. Come, Parker."

✑ 6

A few minutes later we were humming along the straight, flat road through the marsh country on our way to Whitestone Manor. Pons sat at my side deep in thought, his aquiline face clear-minted against the freezing winter background. A low mist was rising again, and for the first few minutes I concentrated on the road, digesting the information we had just received. Finally Pons broke silence.

"Well, Parker, what do you make of it? I know that you are bursting to question me."

"You are perfectly correct, Pons. That man Tolliver and the business of the snakes and spiders. Why, the whole thing fits together as plainly as the nose on my face."

Pons chuckled, taking his pipe from his pocket.

"Does it not, Parker. It certainly seems as if Mr. Tolliver has both motive and opportunity, though how he would insinuate such creatures into Colonel d'Arcy's home must remain conjectural for the moment."

"Such a man could find ways," I said.

"True, Parker, true," Pons nodded, filling the interior of the car with the harsh reek of shag as he lit the tobacco in the bowl of his pipe.

"Old Silas Renfrew was a curious man, certainly, and this bequest throws a fresh light upon matters."

"And remember the manner in which his son died," I continued. "The Colonel said his death bore all the symptoms of a bite from a tropical insect."

"I see that your medical as well as your deductive faculties are working well, Parker," went on Pons, shooting me sharp glances from beneath his brows, as he puffed furiously at his pipe.

"But here, if I am not mistaken, is our destination."

Even as he spoke the white palings of a large house were composing themselves in the light mist which had begun to gather. I drove the car up in front of a heavy oak door, one of three in the façade of the ancient timbered house, and switched off the engine. Silence crowded in, broken only by the melancholy cawing of rooks from some ancient elms which overhung the lawn, now heavily carpeted with leaves. It was a sombre scene, but Pons was cheerful enough as he got out of the car, rubbing his hands together briskly.

"Quite a Gothic milieu, Parker," he said with satisfaction as he led the way up to the front door, which was already being opened by a severe-looking woman with shingled hair.

"Solar Pons and Dr. Lyndon Parker to see Mr. George Tolliver," said my companion crisply.

The woman inclined her head, no sign of surprise on her pale face.

"You will find him in his laboratory. It is the large barn at the other side of the house."

181

And with that she slammed the door. Pons chuckled. He was already walking away in the direction indicated, and I had a job to keep up with him as he followed the paved path. The barn indeed was a massive structure—evidently an Elizabethan tithe-barn—and electric lights burned cheerily behind the windows in its white-painted planking. There was an electric bell push set into the door lintel, and its shrill ring was followed almost immediately by a loud exhortation to go in.

It was agreeably warm in the interior and with the warmth was mingled a sharp, animal smell, acrid and unmistakable—like that in one of the mammal houses in the zoo. The first thing I noticed was cages ranged round the walls at this end of the building; wire and iron structures, in which dark forms could be glimpsed. There were glass tanks containing fish and reptiles; up at the far end, on a large platform, a Bunsen burner burned palely. There were rows of bookshelves and benches. This was all I had time for as the master of this strange domain was already bearing down upon us.

He was a small, rather mild-looking man with steel-framed spectacles and a shock of whitening hair which hung down low over his brow. He wore a sort of smock over his waistcoat and trousers, and a black-and-white striped shirt looked incongruous in juxtaposition with the greenness of the overall. He held out his hand as he came down the steps from the platform and looked at us alertly.

"Welcome, gentlemen. Visitors are rare, but I do not think I have had the pleasure . . . "

"Solar Pons and Dr. Lyndon Parker," Pons explained. "We are staying with Colonel d'Arcy in the neighbourhood, and as we understood you are a relative, decided to take the liberty of calling upon you."

"A distant relative only, gentlemen," said Tolliver, studying us sharply from behind his glasses.

"But will you not come up into my study and remove your coats? If you would like some tea . . . "

"Thank you, no," said Pons affably. "We are due back at The Briars for tea, but since we were so close, we looked in with an invitation."

We were up on the platform now and I studied the books and equipment with mounting interest as Pons and our strange host chatted on.

"Invitation?"

Tolliver looked from Pons to me and then back to my companion again with unconcealed curiosity.

"Well, yes," said Pons with a composure I found difficult to contemplate. "The Colonel feels that he should, perhaps, have been more forthcoming in paying his respects and wishes to make up for it."

Tolliver held up his hand.

"Colonel d'Arcy owes me nothing, Mr. Pons. I am a distant cousin only."

"Nevertheless, he would be delighted if you could accept a little suggestion. He has just become engaged to a delightful young lady and would appreciate the honour if you could come over to spend one or two nights as his guest this weekend. Friday evening was the time suggested."

I could only watch open-mouthed as Tolliver coloured and looked around hesitantly.

"Why, I should deem it an honour, Mr. Pons."

"That is settled, then. Shall we say six o'clock Friday evening?"

"That will do admirably."

Pons nodded as though the subject were closed. He looked round with piercing eyes.

"I see you are a herpetologist, Mr. Tolliver."

Our host flushed.

"An amateur only. Zoology has been my passion since college days."

"You seem to have quite a collection. These bird-eating spiders, for example..."

I was already looking at the creatures in question, and my scalp crawled with loathing at the great furry creature which scuttled across the sanded floor of one of the heated glass cages. In another coil after coil of gold-dusted patterning moved lazily across a tree branch.

"Magnificent, aren't they?" Tolliver continued. "I have some notable rarities. Would you care for a tour?"

Pons smilingly declined.

"I think I have seen enough, Mr. Tolliver."

We were descending the stairs again now.

"I trust you and Dr. Parker will visit me again," said our host when we were once more near the door. He shook hands with Pons and then turned to me. Pons spoke again before I could open the door.

"Do you by any chance know Mr. Bradshaw, the solicitor from Tolleshunt D'Arcy?"

"Yes, indeed. He acts for me in certain matters."

Despite my warning frown at Pons, he continued as though he had not seen it.

"By the way, Mr. Tolliver, you have not lost any specimens lately? Spiders, for example. Or snakes?"

I could not help making a small explosive sound of astonishment, but the effect on Tolliver was electrifying. He cast a worried, almost haggard, look about him.

"I could not possibly see how you could know that, Mr. Pons.

But the truth is that I have. I do not understand how it could have happened. Several specimens have disappeared of late."

He licked his lips nervously.

"I would appreciate it if you did not bruit the fact abroad. My laboratory, as the locals call it, is little liked hereabouts."

"You have my word, Mr. Tolliver."

Tolliver glanced around uneasily.

"The only relief, Mr. Pons, is that the specimens need tropical heat. They would have died quickly outside these walls."

"That is good to hear," said Solar Pons with a dry laugh, gazing at an anaconda which took up most of a large cage opposite. "Until Friday."

"Until Friday, Mr. Pons."

I could hardly wait until we were back in the car.

"Good heavens, Pons, this man has given himself away. And are you mad, inviting him to stay at The Briars?"

"I fancy it will be an interesting weekend, Parker," said Pons, a faraway expression in his eyes as I turned the car and headed back toward Colonel d'Arcy's house.

"It was a liberty, as you say, but as soon as I have explained the situation to our client, I am sure he will co-operate. And now, if you please, Parker, I would prefer to smoke in silence while I get to grips with the problem."

7

"Your health, Mr. Pons!"

Colonel d'Arcy's bearded face was flushed with pleasure and as I looked round the dining table, I saw nothing but contentment on the features of Miss Mortimer, her mother, and about a dozen other guests who were celebrating our client's engagement. The great panelled dining room was a blaze of light from the chandeliers and from the vast stone fireplace heaped with logs, which cast a mellow glow over the tiled hearth and on the replete form of the dog, Toto, which lay with its paws toward the warmth.

Pons and I occupied positions of honour near the end of the table. The only other people present known to us were the lawyer Bradshaw and Pons' invited guest, Tolliver. Colonel d'Arcy himself had welcomed Pons' suggestion, though my friend had given no indication of his inward thoughts on the subject. In truth, there were some half-dozen people already staying for the weekend and The Briars was so vast, the servants so numerous, that Tolliver's presence was hardly noticed.

This Friday evening was the formal engagement dinner, and the Saturday was to be given over to a dance, to which many of the neighbouring gentry and their families had been invited. Pons could be an excellent listener on occasion, even though he might be privately bored, and now he smiled encouragingly as a wealthy farmer on his left went on with a tirade about the scandalously low price of potatoes.

Our host and his fiancée were obviously wrapped up in each other, and Bradshaw was engaged in earnest conversation with Mrs. Mortimer, so I was at liberty to study Tolliver. He affected to be listening to a tall, fair girl who had been placed at his right hand, but all the while his eyes were roving restlessly about the apartment, now at the richness of the table decorations, now at the chandeliers, and occasionally at the sullen figure of Vickers who passed to and from the table on various errands.

"An interesting study, is it not, Parker?"

The low voice of Pons was in my ear, his face alert, his eyes missing nothing that went on in the room.

"Indeed, Pons, though I am not quite sure . . . "

"Of mankind, Parker. Of one's fellow human beings. And there is nothing like a convivial dinner atmosphere, as tonight, for catching them off-guard."

"Ah, Pons, you mean Tolliver. And Vicker's attitude . . . "

Pons' fingers dug into my arm, a warning plainly on his face.

"Hush, Parker, moderate your tones. We do not wish the world to know our business."

He looked round the table coolly, as though enjoying the conversation, while he continued our discourse sotto voce.

"Be on the alert when we retire, Parker. And make sure you have your revolver. If I am not mistaken, something is due to happen this evening."

"So we will not be retiring, Pons?" I said.

He shook his head.

"We must keep on the alert. Fetch your revolver from your bedroom after dinner. We had better keep guard in my room since it is the nearest to the Colonel's."

"Very well, Pons."

As soon as dinner was over I made my excuses to the company and begged a headache to avoid the gathering in the smoking room. I went straight to my own room and disinterred my pistol from my valise. I checked it carefully, but the cartridges were in the chambers and there was no sign that it had been tampered with. I had just put my case away when I heard a faint creaking outside in the corridor.

It was the work of a moment to cross the carpeting and throw the door open. The dark-faced servant Vickers was standing there. He still wore the green baize apron and the dark suit over the batwing collar and sombre tie. Far from being nonplussed he smiled in what I thought a most impertinent manner.

"I just felt you might need something, Dr. Parker."

"There is nothing, thank you," I said stiffly, giving him a disapproving glance.

His smile widened even further. His manner was just this side of insolence.

"How long have you been there?" I asked.

He shrugged.

"Just long enough, Doctor."

And he was gliding away down the corridor before I could remonstrate. I was still fuming when Pons joined me in his room a few minutes later. He flung himself on the bed and chuckled.

"Ah, Parker," said he. "It does not always do to make mysteries where none exist."

"But there's something infernally suspicious about the fellow, Pons," I said bitterly. "He's always hanging about. Surely it is plausible to suppose that he might have had something to do with the young nephew's death and the attempt against the Colonel's life."

Solar Pons looked up at me with that maddeningly omniscient air he sometimes affected.

"Where does that leave our snake and insect man, Tolliver?" he said drily. "You are an excellent doctor, Parker, and your diagnoses are invariably right. But you have not yet learned to apply the same exacting standards to your observation of human nature in action. You will end by having a multiplicity of suspects. You must first draw the correct conclusions from the material before you."

"Mark my words, Pons…" I began heatedly when my companion arrested me with a sudden gesture of his hand. He sprang up from the bed, drawing his own pistol and putting it down on the counterpane within easy reach.

"The guests are retiring for the night, Parker. I fancy we shall soon hear something."

He glanced at his watch as the gruff voice of Colonel d'Arcy sounded in the corridor outside.

"But I predict it will be an hour or more before they settle. I suggest we make ourselves comfortable, and I have taken the precaution of abstracting a whisky bottle and some glasses from the dining room so that we shall not find the period of waiting too tiresome."

So saying he reseated himself in a wing chair near the fireplace as the door of Colonel d'Arcy's room quietly closed and footsteps began to die away down the corridors of the great house.

✒ **8**

More than an hour had passed and the lights had long been extinguished. I eased my position in the chair and waved my hand to dispel the heavy waves of blue smoke from Pons' pipe.

"Patience, Parker," he said softly. "I fancy the time is at hand. If he is to strike it must be done soon because he knows we are on the ground."

We had only a bedside lamp burning in the room and all the time we had been here Pons had been alert, listening for every footfall in the corridor. Half a dozen times he had darted to the room door, opening it a crack, surveying the corridor outside and then returning to his seat. There were two wall sconces still burning in the passage outside, leaving long stretches of shadow, and I understood from Pons that it was Colonel d'Arcy's habit to leave lights on all night whenever he had house guests.

Twice had the surly figure of Vickers been seen by Pons passing along the corridor during that time, but Pons had only smiled at my fulminations and had bidden me to be patient. Now there had been a deep silence for some while though my companion assured me that lights still shone beneath some doors, including that of Colonel d'Arcy.

I had risen from my chair and was taking a turn about the room when Pons jumped swiftly to his feet, holding his finger to his lips. At almost the same instant a terrible scream re-echoed throughout the house. It was a woman's voice, hoarse and resonant with terror and it seemed to come from next door. Pons had already flung open the door, revolver in hand.

"As quickly as you can, Parker. It is life and death!"

I was swiftly at his heels, revolver drawn, as Pons flung himself at the door of Colonel d'Arcy's room. He hurled it open without ceremony. I shall never forget the sight that greeted us. The room was lit only by one solitary bedside lamp which threw a subdued glow across the apartment.

The bed coverlets had been thrown back but our attention was riveted on the end of the bed where the figure of a beautiful girl crouched, a look of absolute terror on her chalk-white face. The body of Miss Claire Mortimer was rigid with shock and horror. She was clad only in a dressing gown and her dark hair was awry and falling across her face.

"There, Parker, there!" said Solar Pons, his iron grip at my wrist.

I wrenched my glance from the frozen figure of the girl up toward the pillow. At first I could see nothing, then, from the tumbled white sheets, flickered the greenish coils of a snake. Its tongue darted from its mouth and a sibilant hissing noise filled the chamber. My throat was dry and my hand unsteady, but Pons' voice brought me to myself.

"A green mamba, Parker. The most deadly snake in all Africa! Your shot, I think."

I raised my revolver, hardly conscious of what I was doing. Yet I was myself again, my nerves calmed by Pons' reassuring presence. He moved closer to the girl, inch by inch, his derringer at the ready.

The crack of my pistol, the acrid sting of powder and the flash were followed by a rain of feathers from the bed, and the bullet cut a vicious gouge in the planking of the floor beyond. Splinters flew in the air as the snake writhed for an instant and then was still.

"Well done, Parker!" said Pons, supporting the fainting girl and dragging her from the bed. I ran to his side and helped him move her to a chair.

"See to that thing, Parker. Make sure it is dead."

Perspiration was running down my cheeks, but my nerves were steady now as I cautiously approached the bed.

"My aim was true, Pons," I said, unable to keep the pride from my voice. Footsteps were sounding in the corridor now, and the room seemed full of people. I was only vaguely aware of Bradshaw, Tolliver, Mrs. Mortimer, and the dark visage of Vickers.

Light flooded the room from a ceiling fixture, and at the same instant I managed to cover the remains of the snake with the bedding. Pons shot me a glance of approval. The bearded face of Colonel d'Arcy appeared. He elbowed his way through without ceremony.

"Good God, Mr. Pons! Claire! What on earth has happened?"

"The lady has had a nightmare," said Pons gently. "All is well now. But I think it would be best if she spent the remainder of the night with her mother. And I should keep this room locked if I were you."

The Colonel instantly grasped the situation.

"It is nothing, ladies and gentlemen. Would you please return to your rooms. I very much regret the disturbance."

The sobbing girl, soothed by her mother, was led from the room, and the remaining guests, with curious glances, shortly followed. Our host hurried away, leaving Pons and me alone in that suddenly sinister room.

"I don't understand, Pons," I said.

Solar Pons ran a finger along his jaw, which was grimly set.

"I am not entirely clear myself, Parker," he said. "But we shall no doubt learn more in a moment."

Indeed, our host returned almost at once and faced us sombrely, locking the door behind him.

"I cannot thank you enough, gentlemen. If anything had happened to Claire... What was it?"

I pulled back the bedding. Colonel d'Arcy surveyed the mamba with sick loathing on his face. He clenched his fists and his features began to suffuse with blood.

"By God, Mr. Pons, we must discover the wicked mind behind this..."

"It is almost over, Colonel," said Pons quietly. "Though I do not know how Miss Mortimer came to be here."

"She complained of a draught in her room," said our host. "Mine was the more comfortable so I gave it to her. The fireplace has more heat, for one thing."

Pons nodded.

"Evidently, he could not have known that," he murmured. "I am afraid Parker and I have made a mess of your floor..."

Colonel d'Arcy stared at us in amazement. He came forward and wrung my hand, then turned to Pons.

"I am not an emotional man, gentlemen, but Miss Mortimer means more to me than anything in the world."

"I understand that, Colonel," said Pons, frowning down at the thing that still lay in bloody tatters on the bed. "But it will not stop here. Our man knows we are on to him. The shot alone would have warned him. He will act quickly. We must act more quickly still."

Colonel d'Arcy looked bewildered.

"I am in your hands, Mr. Pons. What do you want me to do?"

"I think this evil man will strike again before the night is out. This time at you, Colonel. I want you to go to my room or Parker's and spend the night there. No one but the three of us must know of this."

"Anything you say, Mr. Pons. What do you intend to do?"

Pons went to stand by the fireplace, holding out his thin hands to the glowing embers. His lean, feral face had seldom looked more grim.

"First, I would like the disposition of the guests this evening and the exact location of their rooms."

"That is easily done," said the Colonel.

Pons listened attentively as he gave us the information. He nodded with satisfaction.

"Ironic is it not, Parker?"

"I do not understand, Pons."

"No matter. You will in due time."

He turned briskly to the Colonel.

"We must spend the rest of the night in your room, Colonel. I fancy a revolver or a stick will be adequate protection against the menace of the Ipi Idol."

He looked at me, his eyes alight with excitement. "Come, Parker. The game's afoot!"

9

It was three a.m. The night was dark and silent, though a little light came in through a chink in the window curtains. Fog still swirled heavily at the panes. It was cold in the room and my thoughts were leaden. Pons sat opposite me in a wing chair, his face in shadow. The room door was facing me so that I could keep it under observation; Pons' chair faced a locked door which communicated with an adjoining dressing room, which was not being used as a guest bedroom.

It was over two hours since we had come there and I had begun to doubt whether even Pons' rapier-like mind had drawn the right conclusions from the situation. I myself thought it unlikely that the murderous brain threatening the household of The Briars would strike again so soon, but Pons was obviously in possession of a great deal more information which had passed me by.

Three o'clock had chimed from a church clock somewhere far away, and I found myself drifting off into sleep when I was arrested by a hand on my arm and Solar Pons' voice whispering in my ear.

"Hold yourself in readiness, my dear fellow. I think something is about to happen."

There was a faint glow in the room, I saw, as I struggled up in the chair. A light had been switched on in the room communicating with ours. There was a gap beneath the door and the radiance spilled across the carpet so that I could make out Pons' set face and the long, slim cane he held in his right hand. I got up from the chair and would have crossed to the door had not Pons gently pulled me back. He put his fingers to his lips, enjoining absolute silence.

I crouched in the semi-darkness, a pulse throbbing in my throat, conscious of the chill of the revolver I had drawn from my pocket and which now rested in my right hand. A dark shadow passed across the other side of the connecting door. Someone was standing there. Then there came a faint scratching noise. A long silence ensued. I felt Pons' hand on my arm again. A shadow was growing as something passed beneath the door. There was a minute, rustling noise which set my nerves on edge. I was suddenly conscious that Pons had left my side and I felt a moment of panic.

Then the room was a blaze of light, momentarily dazzling me.

"Look, Parker!"

I followed Pons' outstretched hand and felt my throat constrict with nausea. The giant spider scuttled across the carpet toward us. The obscene, bloated thing was covered with hair, and metallic eyes regarded us with alien intelligence.

"A tarantula, Parker! For God's sake, take care. There, you brute!"

Pons advanced, cutting at the carpet with the cane. With a sibilant, hissing noise the thing scuttled back the way it had come. Pons followed it, aiming blows rapidly, but the creature was too quick. It squeezed beneath the door with incredible speed. A shadow moved across the light and then came an agonising scream that I can recall even to this day, despite the gap of years. Even Pons' nerve almost broke.

He hesitated and then unlocked the door and threw it wide. The sight that met us was one of bizarre horror. A man in a dressing gown was sprawled against the wall where he had been sitting, his hands clawed in agony. Beside him was a felt-lined box, with air holes, from which the spider had evidently come. The distorted features, the glazed eyes, the dishevelled hair made the face almost unrecognisable. Then something stirred in the whitening hair and the tarantula sprang to the floor.

"One side, Parker!"

Pons jumped by me and hacked madly at the thing which scuttled between the paralysed man's legs. He cut and slashed and stamped with a savagery I would not have suspected in him, until nothing but a quivering pulp remained. I felt sick but forced myself back to normality.

"What a vile brute, Pons," I said. "Did you know this?"

"I suspected something of it, Parker," said my companion quietly, throwing down the cane.

"Your department, I think."

I approached the curiously rigid body and was astonished to recognise for the first time the solicitor Chadburn Bradshaw.

"Pons! I am astonished. But you knew?"

Solar Pons nodded.

"Almost from the beginning. The facts were fairly clear-cut. But we have no time for that now. Is he still alive?"

I examined the lawyer carefully.

"We shall need to get him to hospital immediately, Pons. We had better arouse the household. He has been bitten on the forehead, certainly, but it looks to me as though he has all the symptoms of a stroke."

Solar Pons stood looking down at the recumbent, vacant-eyed figure.

"Poetic justice, Parker," he said softly. "I do not think we need waste too much sympathy."

10

"Mr. Pons, I am immeasurably in your debt. I can never repay you enough." Colonel d'Arcy's strong, bearded face flashed beaming approval as he looked first at my companion, then at me and finally rested upon Miss Claire Mortimer.

Solar Pons smiled.

"On the contrary, I should thank you, Colonel. I have had one of the most fascinating cases I can recall working on and have tracked down one of the most damnable villains who ever forged a signature."

A cloud passed across our host's face.

"I am afraid Bradshaw's machinations have cost me dear, Mr. Pons. From what the Essex police have been able to tell me in the past week, it looks as though he has made away with a third of the estate."

Miss Claire Mortimer squeezed her fiancé's hand across the table.

"Nothing has been lost," she said softly. "I have property of my own and we can sell off some of the acreage."

Colonel d'Arcy flushed.

"Do not think it is the money alone, Claire," he said heatedly. "When I think of the cold-blooded horror of that devil's schemes and the danger to which I exposed you . . . "

He broke off for a moment, looked at the girl, and smiled.

"As you say, the money can be made good. I am the last person to wish anyone dead, Mr. Pons, but I am glad Chadburn Bradshaw has gone to his maker."

Pons turned to me.

"That was a curious aspect, Parker. Died in the ambulance on his way to hospital, you said?"

I nodded.

"The shock seems to have brought on a stroke, Pons, as much as the bite. It is a most unmedical conclusion to come to, but one might almost have said that fright killed him as much as anything since he might have recovered from the poisonous wound that creature gave him if we could have given him immediate treatment."

"Things are well as they are," said Solar Pons. "I had my suspicions of Bradshaw almost as soon as I arrived here."

"You cannot mean it, Pons."

"I do mean it, Parker. From what Colonel d'Arcy had told me, I knew that money had to be at the bottom of it. It is at the bottom of most crime, and who is better placed to mismanage the funds than the family solicitor. We have already discussed the nonsense of the Ipi Idol and the deaths of Silas Renfrew and his nephew."

Solar Pons shifted in his chair and tamped fresh tobacco into his pipe at Miss Mortimer's smiling invitation to smoke.

"It was ludicrous in the extreme to imagine that a West African secret society would be active in Essex many years after Renfrew's return from those parts. I have no doubt old Renfrew had things of which to be ashamed in his past, and Bradshaw might have hoped that the receipt of the idol would hasten his death because of his advanced heart condition. The police finding a document signed by Renfrew making his solicitor the beneficiary of his estate provides adequate motive."

"But could not Bradshaw have forged that, Pons?" I asked.

Pons shook his head.

"That particular document has been authenticated and provided Bradshaw with the perfect way out. I submit that old Renfrew's condition was such that he did not always know what he was signing. But first Bradshaw had to strike at anyone who came between him and the fortune. He was successful in both the case of Renfrew and the nephew. We cannot know what means he used to kill young Adrian Renfrew except that it was most likely a poisonous tropical insect. He could have obtained such a specimen from a zoological garden or from one of the more esoteric London animal supply shops."

Pons puffed at his pipe, the flames of the burning tobacco making little stipples of light on his strong, ascetic face.

"So much is surmise. Now as to fact. It must have been a considerable shock to him when the old man made you the sole beneficiary, Colonel, after the death of his son. Bradshaw had already made large inroads into the estate money and was desperate for funds. He resolved to strike at you, and he found a ready-made instrument at hand in another distant relative, Tolliver, who quite by chance had come to live some miles off.

"He was also a client of Bradshaw's, which made the whole thing much easier. More to the point, he kept strange pets, among whom were such dangerous specimens as tarantulas and snakes. The police have discovered a heated room at Bradshaw's house, where the specimens he stole from Tolliver were kept at the right temperature until needed. A padded basket kept the insect or reptile warm while being transferred even in this bitter January weather.

"Since Bradshaw was a frequent visitor at both Tolliver's house and your own home, Colonel, he was able to lay his plans with care. Unfortunately for him you escaped his first serious attempt and worse still, were on the alert. He had to move quickly, for your pending marriage to Miss Mortimer would put the fortune even farther beyond his reach."

"But how did you come to suspect him, Pons?" I said.

Solar Pons put his pipe down on the table in front of him and tented his fingers.

"Elementary, my dear Parker. And by the same simple process which made you suspect Vickers of deep-dyed villainy."

I flushed, aware of Colonel d'Arcy's amused glance.

"How was I to know that he was devoted to the Colonel's service and watched over him day and night, Pons? Even to the extent of testing his Colonel's liquor supply for poison."

"You must admit, Parker, that I drew your attention to Vickers' behaviour, but unfortunately you drew the wrong conclusions from it. A man who has been in the service of a person like Colonel d'Arcy for so many years is surely to be trusted. I put more credence in the Colonel's character reading than in village gossip. Vickers' manner was unfortunate, I agree, but his spying was in a good cause. To protect his master."

"Say no more, Pons," I begged. "I still cannot see why you were so suspicious of Bradshaw."

"Even before I had met him," said Pons. "You may recall our near-escape from a dangerous accident on the night of our arrival. I was already on my guard in view of past events— particularly the attempt to kill the Colonel. I knew very well the presence of the heavy vehicle on the road in those dangerous foggy conditions was not coincidence. So I made a close examination of the spot."

"And found where another vehicle had come to grief, Pons." Solar Pons shook his head.

"That was not so, Parker. What I found was the place where the horse and cart had been originally stationed when the axle broke. A car on its way from Tolleshunt D'Arcy had deliberately stopped and drawn onto the verge while its driver went about the business of urging the horse back onto the road. It will, of course, be impossible to prove now, but had Bradshaw lived, I think we should have found that he knew the Colonel's movements on that day; had waited until the next to last train had arrived; had seen that the Colonel was not on it; and had then put his scheme into operation, relying on the fact that there would be no other cars coming from the station that evening. You may have observed that the Colonel's was the only car to be parked there."

"That is all very well, Pons, but what directed you to Bradshaw?"

"The simple matter of the tyre marks on the verge. They were of a country pattern, with heavy V indentations. There was a bullnose Morris parked outside this house that night and the tyres corresponded in every respect."

"Remarkable, Mr. Pons," put in Colonel d'Arcy. He looked enthusiastically at my companion.

"That would not alone have been conclusive but it drew my attention to Bradshaw," Pons continued. "When we visited his offices the following day, he made two fatal mistakes. The first was in disclosing his client's affairs to us. No reputable lawyer would do that, but he skilfully revealed the existence of the non-existent benefaction in favour of Tolliver to provide a motive for murder and misdirect my inquiries. The document he flourished was quite obviously forged, though it was skilfully done. I later compared the signature he had shown me with specimens of Silas Renfrew's own handwriting in this house, and there were a number of subtle differences. Tolliver, of course, was a ready-made suspect, and the presence of dangerous reptiles in his house would have proved conclusive in a normal police investigation.

"But he was frank with me, appeared genuinely worried, and

admitted that specimens were missing from his private zoo. That was enough to clear him in my estimation."

"But why did you put Bradshaw on his guard, Pons?"

Solar Pons chuckled.

"That was quite deliberate, Parker. I wanted him to see that we were on the track, that we realised Colonel d'Arcy's life was threatened. He was a consummate actor but I realised that he was alarmed and felt his whole scheme in peril. A man in that condition becomes desperate, and I hoped to throw him off-balance and risk all on a last gamble while we were all present in the house. I invited Tolliver to the party because I knew it was an excellent chance to clear him of suspicion, and so it proved.

"Bradshaw had a foot in both camps. He was the only person who could move easily about both The Briars and Tolliver's home, and he would be the last person suspected. When he badly miscalculated with the mamba, due to Miss Mortimer changing rooms with the Colonel, I felt sure he would try again. He knew the house intimately and would have had plenty of time to secrete his loathsome charges."

"And the Ipi Idol, Pons?"

"So much rubbish, Parker. Bradshaw had another office in Colchester. It is not worth the proving now, but he undoubtedly posted the package containing his badly sculptured creation from there."

"This is quite astonishing, Mr. Pons," said Miss Mortimer.

Is it not, dear lady?" said Pons, rubbing his hands together. "I have seldom met a more cunning adversary. Of course, in the normal run of events he visited both the Colonel here and Tolliver. In the one case he had ample opportunity of abstracting specimens—the police have found padded baskets, thick gloves, and drugs to put the specimens in a comatose state, at his house—and in the other equal opportunity to bait his horrific traps.

"He saw his last chance in the long weekend you arranged to celebrate your engagement. And when I invited Tolliver—deliberately, of course, in order to get everyone under the same roof—he thought he had his golden chance. I blame myself that it almost ended in tragedy; I did not, for example, realise that the mamba had already been secreted in your bedroom, far less that your fiancé had exchanged rooms with you."

"No one could have foreseen that, Pons," I said.

Solar Pons shook his head.

"Nevertheless, Parker, it was a close thing. When that attempt failed, I realised that Bradshaw would almost inevitably try again that same night. It takes a great deal of nerve to stage these things, and Vickers' activities in snooping about must have worried him. When I learned that Bradshaw's room was next to yours, Colonel, it became a hundred percent certainty in my mind."

"Some more brandy, Mr. Pons. It has been an experience to watch you at work."

Solar Pons smiled. He looked at the crudely carved statuette on the table, which our client had given him as a souvenir.

"Do not forget my good friend Parker here. He showed quite exceptional courage in facing that tarantula. And his cool head in blowing the mamba to pieces prevented tragedy."

"Pray forgive me, Dr. Parker."

I flushed, for in truth Pons' warm words had touched me deeply.

"You forget your own part, Pons," I said. "When I saw you drive that brute back with the cane..."

203

"With unexpected results for Bradshaw," said Solar Pons slowly.

"A highly appropriate conclusion from our point of view. And as my great predecessor said in the matter of the Speckled Band, I am not likely to let this man's death weigh very heavily on my conscience."

The Adventure of
Buffington Old Grange

🙟 1

IT WAS IN the spring of 1923 that one of the most extraordinary cases my old friend Solar Pons ever handled came about. Pons had been extremely busy the previous winter and had been absent in Bavaria for some time, engaged in the affair of the Archbishop of Metz's candlesticks. Other important cases which claimed his time had been that of the Giant Anaconda, in which the notorious Dashwood, the private zoo keeper, had gone down for fifteen years; the Great Copper Alloy Scandal; and the murder of the Honourable Roger Fosdyke on the towpath of the Grand Union Canal, which had aroused such dismay and horror in high places.

Yet of all the notes I kept on Solar Pons' brilliant handling of these affairs, one matter stands out in particular, that of Buffington Grange. There had been showers overnight, and the early view from our windows at 7B Praed Street had presented a chill and damp aspect. But the sun shone as I came down to breakfast, and our good-natured landlady, Mrs. Johnson, was beaming with pleasure as she put the covered dishes on our table.

"A fine morning, doctor, after last night."

"A fine morning indeed, Mrs. Johnson," I said, keenly appreciative of the crisp and pleasant aroma of fried bacon and eggs. Mrs. Johnson's smile broadened even further as I rubbed my hands and seated myself at the table.

"Mr. Pons not down yet?" I asked.

Our landlady's eyes widened in surprise.

"Bless you, sir, Mr. Pons has been up for hours. He was out at dawn as I was black-leading the stove, but said he would join you for breakfast."

I raised my eyebrows, but since Mrs. Johnson did not volunteer any further information I decided to dismiss the matter. No doubt Pons would relieve my curiosity in due course. Indeed, I had no sooner started breakfast and was reaching for my second piece of toast when I heard his light and athletic footstep on the stair.

The door flew open and a dishevelled and ruffianly figure erupted into the room. Though I knew it was Pons, I should have been hard put to it to recognise him in the street. He wore a striped jersey and a coarse pair of velveteen trousers such as porters wear. His hair was matted and tangled; dirt streaked his face and a black eye patch over one eye gave him a villainous aspect. He laughed at my expression, revealing a gap-toothed mouth, where he had evidently blacked out several teeth.

"Don't look so dismayed, Parker. I shall wash and change before breakfast."

"I should hope so, Pons," I said with some asperity. "Except that it is the wrong time of year, I could be charitable and suggest that you had been up all night at the Chelsea Arts Ball."

Pons smiled and threw down the canvas holdall he had been carrying.

"Just a small matter of rounding off a few details in a case which had been nagging me of late," he said carelessly. "I have been down to Smithfield Market. It is true that the carcasses came from Surrey. I think that we have our man."

"What on earth are you talking about, Pons?" I said, making decisive inroads into the toast.

"Pray do not bother your head in the matter, Parker."

He rubbed his thin hands briskly together.

"That bacon smells good. Give me five minutes and I will be with you."

I was pouring my second cup of coffee, and only four and a half minutes had passed, before a surprisingly transformed Pons sat down opposite me and proceeded to devour the contents of the second heated dish. His face shone with health, his strong teeth were normal, and all the raffish detail had been erased. Even his frock coat looked as though it had just come from St. James'.

"Well, Parker," he said, reaching for the coffeepot. "I do declare that the English breakfast is one of the major contributions to civilisation in the Western world."

"You may well be right, Pons," I conceded, refilling my own cup.

"Even though there are minor irritations in life," he continued, "such as the failure of the light bulb near the shaving mirror in the bathroom. And your forgetting your new supply of razor blades again."

I put down my fork.

"How did you know that, Pons?"

"I noticed yesterday that the light was fluctuating due to a faulty filament. I have not yet shaved this morning due to my little disguise. But when I see that the left-hand side of your face is all stubbled, I conclude that the lamp has finally failed, for it certainly favours the left-hand side. When I further observe that you have cut the right side of your face not once but three times, then it is obvious that you have not yet replenished your supply of blades."

"You are correct on both counts, Pons," I said crossly, running my hand across my face. "I am taking a day off from my practice today and will run down to Braithwaite's the chemists, directly after breakfast, to stock up."

"And I will ask Mrs. Johnson about the bulb," said Pons. "I understand she keeps a supply in her kitchen cupboard somewhere."

He put down his coffee cup and immersed himself in *The Times* for the next few minutes. I looked up at his muffled exclamation.

"Have you seen the racing news, Parker?"

"I was never a great one for the turf," I said. "And I did not know that you followed it with any real interest."

Pons smiled faintly.

"Ordinarily, no, my dear fellow. But when I note that Mulcallah has again failed in yesterday's Doncaster fixture, I begin to smell a rat."

"I do not quite understand, Pons."

"The favourite has failed three times in a row, Parker. Even the Jockey Club cannot overlook that. Bryant has been doping again, mark my words. I must telephone Jamison."

He threw down the newspaper with a grunt and finished off his coffee. We had just drawn back from the table, me to finish my last cup of coffee, Pons to enjoy an after-breakfast pipe, when there came a ring at the front doorbell. Pons' face assumed the alert expression I had come to know so well.

"A client, Parker? I hardly dare to hope so. It has been far too quiet of late."

"It is more likely to be the carpenter about Mrs. Johnson's kitchen improvements," I said.

Solar Pons held up an admonitory finger.

"Your mundane mind again, Parker. Carpenters do not usually arrive in taxis."

I put down my coffee cup with a small clatter in the silence.

"I did not hear anything."

"That was because you were not listening, my dear fellow. The engine of the London taxi has a distinctive note that is unmistakable. Ah, I thought as much. Mrs. Johnson is coming up."

Even as he spoke there was a deferential tap at the door and our landlady appeared, a serious expression on her face.

"A Mr. Horace Oldfield to see you, Mr. Pons. The poor gentleman seems much agitated."

Pons rubbed his lean hands together briskly.

"Show him up at once, Mrs. Johnson."

He turned to me.

"Pray do not go, Parker. Unless my client desires the utmost secrecy, I would be glad of both your company and your opinion."

I settled myself back in my chair, considerably flattered at Pons' words and awaited the approach of the heavy tread on the stair with ill-concealed impatience.

The man who presented himself at our threshold was indeed a pitiable object. Tall and thin, he was immaculately dressed in a fur-collared overcoat and a smart check suit, but the effect was marred by his wild, staring eyes, dishevelled hair, and generally distraught demeanour. He staggered as he got inside the door and almost fell. I rushed forward to his assistance and helped him to a chair, noting his chalk-white complexion.

209

"Your department, Parker," said Pons, rising from his seat and looking anxiously at our client.

I loosened his collar and turned to Mrs. Johnson.

"If you would be so good as to pour a small glass of brandy . . . You will find the bottle on the sideboard."

I put the glass to Mr. Oldfield's lips and the colour was soon returning to his cheeks. He tried to get up but I pushed him back.

"Just sit and drink that, Mr. Oldfield. Nothing but shock, I think, Pons."

Solar Pons reseated himself at the table while Mrs. Johnson briskly cleared the breakfast things. When she had withdrawn and we were alone with our client, he blinked once or twice and looked from me to my companion.

"Mr. Solar Pons?"

"I am he," said my friend gently. "Just take your time, Mr. Oldfield. It is obvious that you have been the subject of some unnerving experience."

Our visitor nodded. He gulped once or twice and when he had indicated in grateful tones that he had recovered himself, I reseated myself near Pons and examined our visitor carefully.

He was a man of about forty or forty-five years of age; of a studious aspect, with gold-rimmed pince-nez. His features were regular and would have been pleasing had it not been for his agitated expression. He had a thin wisp of fair moustache on his upper lip, and his teeth were regular and even. His sandy-coloured hair was receding a little; his grey eyes wore a sad expression as he gazed at us.

I had unbuttoned his overcoat, and now he took it off and put it down on a chair at his side. He ran his hands over his hair once or twice as though suddenly conscious of his unkempt appearance and flushed as he reseated himself, fingering his collar.

"I don't know what you must think of me, Mr. Pons . . . "

"Nothing detrimental at all, Mr. Oldfield, I can assure you. Apart from the fact that you are an accountant, that you live in Berkshire, and that you have suffered a grievous shock your nervous system, I know little of you personally."

Our client's eyes opened wide in owlish astonishment.

"Mr. Pons, you amaze me. I do not know where you got those facts, but they are true. As to shocks I have had enough to shatter a man with three times my nerve in the past year. Mr. Pons, I am accursed! My home is infested with ghosts!"

✒ 2

There was a long and oppressive silence.

"Indeed," said Solar Pons mildly. "I think you had better tell me a little more, though you might do better consulting an occultist if you believe in such things." Mr. Oldfield held up his hand.

"Forgive me, Mr. Pons, ghosts are outside my purview also. Please hear my story."

Pons nodded and settled himself back in his chair.

"You made some deductions about our visitor, Pons," I said mischievously. "Would you mind elucidating?"

"Elementary, Parker," said Pons airily. "Mr. Oldfield is well and expensively dressed. Therefore I conclude from that that he is a professional man, and not employed by others. He has an impressive array of pens glistening in his breast pocket. This fact, combined with the ink stains on his right-hand fingers, which brisk scrubbing will not always remove, incline me toward accountancy."

"Perfectly correct, Mr. Pons."

Pons smiled maliciously at me.

"But Berkshire, Pons."

"Mr. Oldfield sports a tie belonging to an old and exclusive Berkshire college, Parker. Very often people are educated in the area in which they also live. When I see evidence of wet sand and gravel on the soles of our visitor's golfing shoes—terrain common to Berkshire—I make an inspired guess and venture that he still lives there."

"Again correct, Mr. Pons."

"There is no getting round you," I retorted.

Solar Pons gave a faint smile and turned to our visitor.

"Come, Mr. Oldfield. You obviously have a strange and unusual story. You will feel better for the telling of it."

"You are right, Mr. Pons."

Our client passed a shaking hand across his brow and put down his brandy glass.

"For some years I practised as an accountant in Reading, Mr. Pons. Then, desirous of a change, I removed to Melton, a small town not far from where I was born, and built up another practice. I married late, when I was past forty, but my wife, who is some thirteen years younger, and I have been very happy and now have two small daughters. With the needs of my growing family, and our home being rather on the small side, we decided last year to buy a larger house."

Oldfield paused a moment, lifted his brandy glass, and drained the residue of its contents. His colouring was quite normal now and his breathing low and steady.

"Buffington Grange was on the market and my wife and I

212

went to inspect it. The building had been derelict for years, but for some reason both my wife and I took an enormous fancy to it. It has a wealth of beams, a good deal of space, and large grounds for the children to explore. I bought the place for a song, Mr. Pons, and spent the money I might otherwise have laid out on the house itself, on restoration work."

"You would appear to have acted wisely, Mr. Oldfield," said Pons, who sat motionless, his fingers tented before him, his eyes fixed on our visitor's face.

Oldfield nodded.

"One would have thought so, Mr. Pons," he said soberly. "But events turned out otherwise. It is a melancholy catalogue and may well try your patience before I have finished."

"I think not, Pons," I protested, casting a reassuring look at our visitor.

"Patience is a virtue this agency has a great deal of," said Pons gravely. "Pray continue, Mr. Oldfield."

"Well, Mr. Pons, the Grange had a bad reputation in the village when I bought it and, as I said, it had been derelict for a number of years. But my wife and I are modern, forward-looking people, and we laughed at the village stories. Any house, even a fairly new one, acquires legends when it is empty for any length of time, and Buffington Old Grange was no exception."

"Before you go any further, just what were these stories, Mr. Oldfield?"

"Stories that often grow up around old houses, Mr. Pons. Murder and jealousy in the distant past. Nothing concrete, you understand; though some twenty years ago an old man, a reputed miser, lived there. He was found hanging in one of the upstairs rooms, I understand. There was talk in the village of both murder and suicide."

"That should be easy enough to determine," said Solar Pons crisply.

Our client looked surprised.

"Quite so, Mr. Pons, though it did not occur to me. I had my mind set on a bargain."

"How long had the house been empty, Mr. Oldfield?"

"Oh, about twenty years. Since the time the old man died, I believe."

"Were there other stories?"

Oldfield smiled diffidently.

"Nonsensical ghost tales. That the miser's footsteps were heard from the ceiling as he passed to his bedroom to hang himself. That he manifested himself as a presence on the landing. That the house was cold and there were certain smells."

"Since no one lived there after the old man's death, that would have been rather difficult to determine," said Pons drily, catching my eye.

"Precisely, Mr. Pons. But my wife and I were anxious to move into the house, and we paid no attention to such rumours."

"Did the estate agents themselves say why the house had been empty so long, or why the price was so cheap?"

Oldfield shook his head.

"I questioned them, of course. But the house had apparently passed to the estate of the old man's cousin. She was a single woman who lived to a great age and had done nothing to it in her lifetime."

"I see. Pray continue, Mr. Oldfield."

"We moved in and at first were very happy. We were comfortable. We had a man for the grounds and a housekeeper and a parlourmaid, which was enough, though there is a good deal to do with such a rambling old property. But some months after we moved in, we began to be troubled. There was a scent of lavender on the landing."

"Nothing odd about that surely, Mr. Oldfield?"

"Except that my wife hates the odour of lavender, Mr. Pons. We made a point of that to the servants. Yet every day, at some time or other, there it was, hanging about, just as though someone had sprayed the air with perfume. It does not worry me, of course, but it upsets my wife."

"I quite see that, Mr. Oldfield. Always the same place?"

Our client nodded.

"Just the landing. We questioned the servants, of course, but they denied responsibility. Then, one evening last winter as I was returning to the house and putting my key in the door, I heard a low, horrible laugh in the porch. The place is dark, with heavy trees and shrubbery, so you can imagine it is gloomy enough. It gave me quite a shock, I can tell you. I searched but could not find anyone.

"The next thing that happened was that my little girl came rushing to my wife a few days later. She had been playing in the attic. It was just dusk and something had appeared to her. I do not know what it could have been, but it frightened poor little Dulcie half out of her wits. It was an apparition of a woman with a hideous distorted face, so far as Susan could make out. Susan—that is, my wife, Mr. Pons—is a strong-nerved woman, and she searched the attic immediately but could not find anything."

"This is taking a serious turn, Mr. Oldfield. Did this apparition do anything?"

Oldfield shook his head.

"It just appeared in the doorway, stood there looking at the child, making a disgusting sucking noise, and then glided away.

215

It was a considerable shock to the child and nothing will induce her to go to the upper floors of the house now."

Our client paused with a twitching face. I rose to refill his brandy glass, and he resumed his narrative.

"Not a week after that, I had gone to the cellar to fetch a bottle of wine. I was just passing the pantry door and putting my foot on the steps when there came the same low laugh I had heard on the porch, and something gave me a terrific push in the small of the back. How I managed to avoid pitching headfirst in the semidarkness, Mr. Pons, I shall never know. I might well have killed myself, for the steps are stone and tremendously steep. Fortunately I had a handrail installed and managed to save myself, but at the expense of barked shins."

Solar Pons' eyes were gleaming and his face wore a grim expression.

"You searched, of course?"

Oldfield nodded. "I found nothing."

"What was the voice like? Male or female?"

"It was difficult to tell, Mr. Pons. It was rather muffled and guttural. I fancy it was a man's."

Solar Pons rubbed his left ear in a gesture which had grown familiar to me over the years and sat in silence for some moments.

"I am certain of one thing, Mr. Oldfield. We are not dealing with ghosts. They are far too insubstantial to push people downstairs. This is a very sinister and absorbing business. Please continue with your catalogue, as you call it."

Our client passed a weary hand over his forehead.

"Well, sir, as you can imagine, these incidents formed a profound impression on the minds of my wife and myself. We recalled those old stories and tried to get further information.

The more one discreetly questioned people in Melton, the more disquieting it became. We tried to keep a cheerful face before the children but we remembered the stories; the fact that the house had been empty so long; the tale of the last occupant; and the more we thought about it the more we began to feel the legends were right."

"Why did you not go to the police, Mr. Oldfield? After all, a murderous attack had been made upon you."

Oldfield shook his head.

"We were afraid of being laughed at, Mr. Pons. Rightly or wrongly, we decided to stick things out. We had made a considerable investment in the property and we did not want to leave it. We kept careful watch upon the children and an equally careful watch upon things in the house. Why, we have not even had a holiday since the time we moved in."

I was startled to observe an abrupt change of expression on Pons' face.

"That is interesting, Mr. Oldfield."

"I do not follow, Mr. Pons."

"No matter. Other things happened, evidently."

Our client looked grim.

"You may well say so, Mr. Pons. There was a fire only two months ago, which might well have been calamitous. It apparently began in the kitchen while there was no one in the house. In fact, if it had not been for my housekeeper, the house would undoubtedly have burned down. She was alone and smelled burning. She rushed into the kitchen almost at the same time as I arrived home from business. Together we put it out without the necessity of calling the fire brigade, though Mrs. Salmon's hands were badly burned, poor thing."

"You were all out, then?"

"That is correct, Mr. Pons. My wife and children had gone to see relatives. The gardener was in the grounds, it is true, but he saw no one about. It was the maid's day off and Mrs. Salmon—that is the housekeeper—had gone to Melton shopping. She discovered the fire on her return and I arrived a short while after."

Solar Pons made an odd little clicking noise with his tongue and sat forward in his chair.

"It is a pity you did not call the fire brigade, Mr. Oldfield."

Our client looked bewildered.

"I do not quite follow, Mr. Pons."

"They are highly expert at detecting the causes of fire."

"Oh, there was no doubt about that, Mr. Pons. There was a half-empty gallon can of paraffin in the kitchen, and an opened box of matches on the floor. The arsonist had made his escape by the back door. There is thick shrubbery nearby, and he could have had cover all the way to the edge of the grounds."

"I see."

Solar Pons pulled at the lobe of his ear again and shot me a piercing glance.

"What do you make of it, Parker?"

"Ghosts do not use paraffin and matches, Pons."

"My opinion exactly, Parker. This is part of a campaign against you, Mr. Oldfield, undoubtedly."

"In truth we did not know what to think, Mr. Pons," said our visitor earnestly. "My wife had read of poltergeist activities and was convinced it was all part of the same manifestations."

"She was undoubtedly right. What other events have occurred recently?"

"Voices in the night, Mr. Pons. Whispering and footsteps. But last night something terrible occurred. Something so awful that I decided to come to see you. My wife had been to the cellar for a bottle on this occasion. She had got to the head of the steps when the pantry door silently opened in her face."

Our client's voice had dropped to a whisper and beads of perspiration were starting out on his forehead.

"Imagine her terror, Mr. Pons, when a hideous visage, grey, corpse-like, was thrust into her own. She was so terrified that she screamed and started backward. She fell down the steps, Mr. Pons. By a miracle, only a week before, I had placed some wicker hamper baskets and some straw as packing for the bottles in the well of the staircase. These broke her fall and she was unharmed apart from shock and bruising. But she is so upset by this that she is still in bed under the care of our family doctor."

Pons had risen rapidly to his feet and was knocking out his pipe on the fender.

"This is something which cannot wait, Mr. Oldfield. You have done well to come to me. I will return with you immediately to Buffington Old Grange."

He looked at me, his face alert and alive, his eyes bright and piercing.

"I suggest your razor blades can wait, Parker. Are you free to come? You will need your revolver. Though ghosts are impervious to bullets, I fancy Mr. Oldfield's apparitions may prove to be of rather more solid construction."

I rose from the table.

"Give me three minutes, Pons, and I am your man."

3

Buffington Old Grange proved to be only a few minutes' drive from the village of Melton and since our client had his own car waiting at the station, we arrived at our destination well before lunch. Oldfield had offered to accommodate us at his house, but Pons declined and we first stopped at The Crown Inn, a pleasant hostelry in the village, and secured rooms for the next few days. Our initial view of the Grange was unprepossessing indeed.

Our client's story had prepared us for something sombre but I was startled at the strange house which rose out of the thin mist which blanketed this part of Berkshire. The grounds were considerable and well-kept, but the woodlands and the great banks of rhododendrons gave them a gloomy aspect. The house itself, timbered and with dark stone, had fantastic turrets and curious crenellated towers which had been added to the original ancient Tudor structure in the nineteenth century, said Oldfield.

We got out before a large, oak-timbered porch, which made a sort of gallery and sheltered the massive oak front door from the weather. Pons looked keenly about him.

"This is the place where you had your unpleasant experiences with the voice?"

"Indeed, Mr. Pons."

Pons' manner was transformed now that he was on the scene of our client's bizarre and horrific adventures. He crossed swiftly to the porch and went rapidly up and down it, his keen eyes observing the details closely. Oldfield and I stood near the front door, our client obviously absorbed by my companion's manner. Pons stopped by some lattice windows at the far end of the gallery.

"What apartment is this, Mr. Oldfield?"

"The kitchens, Mr. Pons. It is a curiously constructed house."

"So I see. Well, there is little more to be learned here. We may as well go inside."

We were met in the dark, panelled hall by a striking-looking woman of about fifty, with jet-black hair coiled at the back of her head.

"The doctor has just been again, Mr. Oldfield. Your wife is resting comfortably."

"Thank you, Mrs. Salmon. These are old friends of mine, Mr. Burton and Captain Parker."

These were sobriquets Pons had insisted on in the train coming down, and now I observed the approval in his eyes as our client introduced us in this manner. The housekeeper, who was smartly dressed in a tweed suit, gave us a half-bow.

"Delighted to meet you, gentlemen. Will you be staying?"

Pons shook his head.

"We are in the neighbourhood for a few days only, at a hotel in Melton."

"Very well, Mr. Oldfield. Lunch will be ready in an hour."

Pons held up his hand and drew the housekeeper to one side.

"Mr. Oldfield has been telling us something of the strange goings-on in this house. Tell me, Mrs. Salmon, what do you think about the matter?"

The tall woman had a faint smile on her lips.

"I do not believe in ghosts, Mr. Burton. Old houses make strange noises, and I am sure Mr. Oldfield will forgive me if I say that both he and Mrs. Oldfield are sensitive people."

"And the perfume on the landing."

Mrs. Salmon shrugged.

"I have smelled it, it is true. It is a very pleasant odour. Perhaps there was once a linen closet there and the aroma of the sachets lingers."

Pons gave the housekeeper an approving look from his deep-set eyes.

221

"You are a sensible woman, Mrs. Salmon. But what of the fire in the kitchen quarters?"

A shadow crossed the housekeeper's face.

"Ah, that is a different question, Mr. Burton. It could have been serious had I not been at hand. There has been much vandalism around Melton in the past two or three years."

"Well, well, you may be right," said Pons with a shrug. "Thank you, Mrs. Salmon."

He turned to our host as the housekeeper's footsteps died out across the hall.

"There goes a very practical woman, Mr. Oldfield."

Oldfield laughed.

"I don't know what we would do without her, Mr. Pons. She has been a great help in our present troubles. In fact we have minimised the problems since we did not want her to think us hysterical or over-fanciful. I told her Mrs. Oldfield had tripped on the cellar steps and did not mention the incident concerning myself. Grace, our other servant, is very nervous and easy to upset and there was no point in creating a fuss."

"Very wise, Mr. Oldfield. Grace has seen nothing?"

Oldfield shook his head.

"Nothing, Mr. Pons. I should have heard of it otherwise."

"That is somewhat curious, I would suggest, Parker," added Pons, turning to me. "I commend it to your attention."

We were interrupted by a sudden scurrying of feet in the passage.

Oldfield's face lit up.

"Come and meet the children, gentlemen."

He led the way into a bright and airy morning room whose dark and low oak beams were offset by the white walls and light-coloured furniture. Two little fair-haired girls were standing shyly inside the door, waiting to be greeted by their father.

"Dulcie, Sally," said Oldfield. "This is Mr. Burton and Captain Parker—two old friends of mine who will be about here for a few days."

The two little girls smiled gravely and then ran forward to embrace their father.

"How do you do, gentlemen?" they chorused, and our client so far forgot his current anxieties as to burst into laughter— a laughter in which pride was mingled with parental affection.

"You will forgive me, I'm sure, but I must just run up and look after my wife. The freedom of the house is yours. We lunch in an hour; in the meantime look about as much as you want. If there is anything special you require to know, Mrs. Salmon will be most helpful."

"Thank you, Mr. Oldfield," said Pons. "Come, Parker."

He waited until the children's eager footsteps and the more measured tread of our client had ascended to the first floor and then seized me by the arm.

"Gently, friend Parker. I think we will first try the cellars, though I fear the scent may be cold."

He put his hand to his lips and led the way through the morning room in the direction of the kitchen quarters. This was empty for the moment, though dishes and pans were simmering on the big range. The fire damage had long been repaired, but Pons spent some time examining the room, deep in thought, while I stood by, secretly irritated by the melancholy dripping of a tap in the sink.

When he had finished, Pons unlatched the door and led the

way into the garden where a light mist was still billowing, though the sun was struggling to break through. He found, as Oldfield had indicated, that thick bushes extended up to the window, and the flagged path would normally have borne no indentation of footprints. We followed the path, which zigzagged through the grounds until it joined the main gravelled drive.

"It would have been too easy, Parker," said Pons, creases of concentration appearing on his brow. "Let us see what the cellars have to offer."

The third door in the kitchen proved to be the one we sought, and we descended the large stone steps, which evidently belonged to the foundations of the older house. There was a narrow landing lit by a dusty electric bulb and Pons spent some time there. He was particularly interested in the pantry door. I was astonished to see him produce his magnifying glass and study the hinges.

"Freshly greased, I see," he observed. "That is significant, Parker, as I'm sure you will have noted."

"I do not follow you, Pons."

Solar Pons clicked his teeth in a manner I always found irritating.

"Come, Parker, you are not living up to my training. Surely it is elementary. Someone deliberately greased those hinges so that whoever hid in the pantry with murderous intent could open the door and creep silently up on Mr. and Mrs. Oldfield without being detected."

The image Pons conjured up in that dusty place was so sinister and oppressive that I instinctively started back.

"Heavens, Pons! There is a diseased mind at work here!"

Solar Pons smiled grimly.

"Diseased perhaps, but devilishly cunning, Parker. And I think we have come just in time to avert tragedy."

We next descended to the cellar, and Pons spent some time looking through the wine bins and pacing the musty aisles between the ancient pillared archways. There was electric light here also, and he spent some time examining the flagstones. An area of newer cement also interested him, and his alertness and concentration increased, if anything, during this time.

We were returning up the steps when our host himself came hurrying down.

"Lunch is ready, Mr. Pons," he said in low tones. "Have you discovered anything?"

"All in good time, Mr. Oldfield," said Pons with a thin smile. "I have a number of hypotheses but insufficient data. If you are agreeable, I will tour the remainder of the house after lunch. I should also like a word with your wife, if she is strong enough."

"By all means, Mr. Pons."

"Then," said Solar Pons as Oldfield led the way up from the cellars, "friend Parker and I will take a little trip into Melton. I have a mind to undertake some research at the local library."

"Research, Mr. Pons?"

Our host looked astonished.

"I have often found that old newspaper files are an excellent guide to the locality, and Melton seems a most interesting part of Berkshire," said Solar Pons, his smile broadening at the look of dismay and disappointment on Oldfield's face.

He put his hand on the other's arm.

"I am looking for causes, not effects, Mr. Oldfield. A little patience, and a great many things will be made clear."

4

"Now, Parker, let us just hear your views on the strange events which have befallen Mr. and Mrs. Oldfield."

Pons and I were walking across a narrow stone bridge spanning a stream, which meandered across the approaches to the small town of Melton. The sun was shining now and the mist had quite dispersed, the golden rays sparkling on the moisture on the red-tiled roofs of the neat and prosperous community. We had lunched with Oldfield and his daughters in an ancient panelled dining room and, immediately after, Pons had discreetly toured the building while I had remained chatting with Oldfield and his housekeeper, who seemed a highly intelligent and resourceful woman.

We had not spoken of the strange events at Buffington Old Grange and neither had Pons made any direct reference to it until now. I waited until a single-deck omnibus whose destination was Reading had thundered across the bridge, before I again ventured into the road and continued walking toward Melton High Street.

"Well, Pons, I must confess none of it makes much sense. The whole thing seems pointless."

"Does it not, Parker. But a pattern is beginning to emerge."

"This nonsense about the miser..." I began, but my companion interrupted me.

"There, Parker, is one of your graver defects, if you do not mind me saying so."

"The legends are preposterous, Pons," I went on. "Hanged men and footsteps on the ceiling..."

"Pshaw, Parker," Pons broke in, his brows knotted in concentration. "Look beneath the legends, man. There is a solid basis of fact. That is why we are going to Melton Library. I find that an hour among the files is highly conducive to the ratiocinative process."

And so saying, he clamped his empty pipe between his teeth and led the way down the busy main shopping street of the bustling little town.

The library itself was surprisingly large, and when Pons produced his card and had it sent in to the chief librarian, we were admitted to an inner room, where there were extensive files of the *Melton Chronicle* which went back into the mid-nineteenth century. Pons rubbed his hands with satisfaction, selected one of the dustiest of the files, and laid it down on the table.

He looked at me quizzically.

"This may take some time, Parker. There is really no necessity for you to stay. I am sure you have urgent matters of your own to attend to."

"Well, I would like to look around the town, Pons, now that we are here," I said.

Pons' eyes twinkled.

"I understand from the guidebook that they serve an excellent sherry at The Saracen's Head. Give me an hour or so, there's a good fellow."

I left him chuckling drily to himself and spent an agreeable interval wandering around that pleasant Berkshire town. I took Pons' advice; both The Saracen's Head and the sherry were extremely good, and I returned to the library a little before three o'clock considerably refreshed both in mind and body. Pons had an expression on his face that I knew well.

"What do you make of this, Parker?"

He indicated a page of the local journal, yellowed with time and blotched with the imperfections that cheap paper reveals as the years go by. I noted the date: it was 1902. The long-winded, single-column headings in the style of those times said:

RECLUSE FOUND HANGED...
SUICIDE VERDICT ON JABEZ KEMP,
THE SQUIRE OF BUFFINGTON GRANGE

Encouraged by the expression in Pons' dancing eyes, I read on.

"The Berkshire coroner, Dr. Hugo Moules yesterday returned a verdict of suicide on Mr. Jabez Kemp of Buffington Old Grange, near Melton, who was found hanging in the attic at his home on March 4th last.

"Sitting with a jury at the Temperance Rooms, Melton, Dr. Moules, said that Mr. Kemp, who was known locally as 'The Squire of Buffington', had been of a reclusive nature and had shunned intercourse with his fellow townspeople."

"Seems quite straightforward, Pons."

"Does it not, Parker. Do read on."

I turned again to the yellowing page.

"The seventy-three-year-old retired tea merchant had for some years shunned his neighbours and, attended by only one servant, had retreated into the upper storey of his home, where his meals were left on a tray outside his door.

"Because of the illness of the housekeeper, Mrs. Theodisia Goodman, no one had been in to look after Mr. Kemp. He had not been seen for some weeks when the housekeeper returned to her duties. As a result of what she suspected, she called in the police. The attic door was broken down, and Mr. Kemp's body was discovered, suspended from a hook by a length of rope taken from a toolshed in the grounds. Medical evidence was to the effect that Mr. Kemp had been dead at least a fortnight.

"Death was due to asphyxia, caused by the noose constricting the neck, and the coroner, expressing sympathy with the surviving relatives, concurred with the jury's verdict that the deceased took his own life while the balance of his mind was disturbed."

There was a good deal more, including evidence from the doctor, a local policeman, and the housekeeper, but I skimmed through the rest with increasing bewilderment. At length I turned from the file with a grunt. Solar Pons sat rubbing his hands with satisfaction.

"So much for the legends, Parker."

"It all seems quite straightforward, Pons."

"Naturally, my dear fellow. Apart from motive, Jabez Kemp's suicide had nothing extraordinary about it at all. Always return to the original sources, whenever possible, Parker. It saves a deal of time."

"But how does this help?"

"By eliminating the encrustation of tomfoolery that has gathered around our client's home. I have been through these files for the past twenty years in the last hour and a half."

"That seems a remarkable feat, Pons."

My companion smiled.

"I knew what I was looking for. Only the extraordinary interested me. And even such a publication as the *Melton Chronicle* does not stint the size of its headlines when it comes to that."

"You are on to something?"

Solar Pons nodded.

"I think I have both the motive and explanation for the sinister web in which our client finds himself entangled."

"You cannot mean it, Pons?"

"Just glance through these later files, Parker. I am saving my trump card for our return to the hotel this evening."

But Pons' researches in these later issues seemed to me to be trite and disappointing indeed. There were elaborate advertisements prominently displayed in estate agents' announcements of the desirable estate known as Buffington Old Grange; apparently there were no takers, for the announcements, becoming progressively smaller, were repeated with increasing monotony until they petered out in about 1904.

"It is disappointing, Pons."

"On the contrary, it is fascinating, Parker. When one knows what to look for."

I tapped with an exasperated forefinger at the group of advertisements he had just pressed upon me.

"All this nonsense about a Grand Circus at Melton, Pons," I cried irritably. "And back in 1912 too. What bearing can this possibly have upon the matter?"

Solar Pons smiled a maddeningly irritating smile and leaned back in his chair.

"Does this not suggest anything to you, Parker?"

I looked in bewilderment at the blurred picture of a handsome woman in tights who faced the camera with a confident smile. Heavy black type proclaimed:

MADAME MANTALINI . . . THE WOMAN
WITH A THOUSAND TALENTS!

I read on with growing bewilderment. Apparently Madame Mantalini was a strong woman, acrobat, clever mime, ventriloquist, and I don't know what else besides.

"She was a lady of many parts, Pons," I said cautiously.

Solar Pons chuckled.

"Was she not, Parker? However, I think we have taxed your brain enough for one day. We will return to our client for tea. I think he and his wife are safe enough for the time being, now that we are on hand. This evening I shall let you see the fruits of my research this afternoon, and we will test how far my methods have impressed themselves upon you. Now, I suggest we will both benefit from a healthful stroll through this agreeable town back to our host's dwelling."

5

"An excellent dinner, Parker."

Solar Pons put down his coffee cup with a satisfied smile and looked carefully around the half-empty dining room of The Crown Inn. It had indeed been a first-rate meal, and for perhaps the first time since we had arrived at Melton, I felt in a mellow, even convivial, mood. We had taken tea with our client and his family as Pons had suggested and afterward had been introduced to Mrs. Oldfield, a pretty, fair-haired woman who was much comforted by our presence. She was still abed and attended by the local doctor, who reassured Oldfield and said she would be up and about within a day or so.

Afterward, Pons had spent some time conversing first with the housekeeper, then the parlourmaid, and finally the gardener, a middle-aged, grizzled man who puffed dourly at his pipe but was evidently captivated by Pons' conversation. The spring dusk had already fallen when we strolled back to the little town and Pons had been unusually preoccupied and silent.

But during dinner he had resumed his gregarious manner and

had run over a few salient points regarding our client's adventures, though without enlightening me much further. I knew he would not fully reveal his thoughts until he had every thread in his hand, and so I had purposefully refrained from questioning him.

Now, as we rose and left the dining room, Pons excused himself.

"I just have to make a telephone call to Brother Bancroft. I desire some information from the Home Office, and I fancy only he can help me there."

I went on into the bar and partook of another glass of sherry, though I found this not as good as that stocked by The Saracen's Head. Pons still had not returned, so I went up to my room and read for a while.

After half an hour there was a light tap at the door and Pons reappeared, rubbing his hands and wearing a satisfied expression.

"Bancroft has his uses," he chuckled, answering my unspoken question. "Now I fancy that the stage is set for the last act of the drama, providing Mrs. Oldfield's health improves by tomorrow and I can persuade the family to leave."

I shot him a puzzled glance.

"What on earth are you talking about, Pons?"

"All in good time, Parker. Just cast your eyes over this. Now, I think we shall need to enlist the help of a local detective officer. It is as well to have the official law on our side when we net our men."

I gave the matter up and glanced at the newspaper Pons had thrust into my hand. My companion sank down at the end of my bed and was soon puffing contentedly at his pipe, emitting long ribbons of blue smoke, which lingered acridly in the corners of the room and gathered in a thick swathe below the ceiling.

I was exasperated to find that my companion had handed me yet another yellowing newspaper from the file of the *Melton Chronicle*. I first noted another circus announcement, again featuring Madame Mantalini.

"Really, Pons," I said. "I cannot see the point in all these old journals. I hope you have not stolen it from the library."

Pons chuckled.

"Put your mind at rest, my dear fellow. I am keeping well within the law. The librarian had a spare copy of this issue in the cellar. I shall return it to him when the case is over. Just cast your eyes over it if you would be so good."

I soon saw what he meant. In fact the headlines of the main item were so large that it would have been difficult to have missed them. They occupied nearly half the top of the front page of the newspaper, which was dated 1912. I shot a sharp glance at Pons, who puffed away unconcernedly, his eyes on the ceiling.

The heading read:

TEN YEARS FOR MELTON ROBBERS...
SECRET OF £100,000 BURGLARIES
GOES TO PRISON WITH THEM

And underneath, in smaller type:

WALTON AND ROBERTS DEFIANT AS JUDGE SENTENCES THEM

Pons remained silent so I read on. The report began: "Mr. Justice Strange sentenced the convicted robbers, John Roberts and Ezekiel Walton, to ten years' imprisonment for burglaries in the Melton area totalling £100,000, at Reading Assizes yesterday.

"The convicted men, who confessed to robbing a large number of country estates in Berkshire of cash and valuables, had steadfastly refused to say what they had done with the stolen property. Ezekiel Walton, the elder of the accused and admitted ringleader, defiantly abused the Judge when sentenced and Mr. Justice Strange referred to him as 'one of the most dangerous rogues in England'. Walton's wife, Elizabeth, is also accused of complicity in the crimes but has fled and her whereabouts are not currently known."

I read on in mounting bewilderment, and at length threw the newspaper down.

"Interesting, is it not, Parker?"

"Well, yes, Pons," I said. "But I don't see how it could help us."

"Do you not, Parker? Surely it would give your mind some interesting facts to work on."

"I fear not, Pons. Old robberies and burglars in prison, to say nothing of hanged misers and ancient auctioneers' advertisements, suggest little to me!"

Solar Pons shook his head with a wry chuckle.

"You may well be right, my dear fellow, but I must just follow this matter through. We shall need that newspaper so take good care of it. I suggest you turn in early tonight because we may have a long day tomorrow. I am just going to stroll down to the local police station and have a chat with one of their detectives. These people usually have long memories."

"Really, Pons," I said. "Your mind works in peculiar ways, sometimes."

"I cannot deny it," he said with an enigmatic smile. "Meanwhile, just think about things. I am sure all will become clear to you."

And with a mischievous wave of his hand he left the room.

We breakfasted early the next morning and were soon back at our client's home. He had put off his business affairs for a few days, partly because of his wife's health and partly to be at Pons' disposal. When we were closeted alone with Oldfield in his study, Pons came quickly to the point. It was a warm, sunny day, and the light spilling in through the mullioned windows gave Pons' lean, feral face an unaccustomed glow.

"I have come to certain conclusions about your case, Mr. Oldfield. So far as I can see there is but one way to resolve it. You and your family must leave the house as soon as possible. Can you be ready to travel by tomorrow?"

My own face must have looked as astonished as our client's.

"You cannot be serious, Mr. Pons! I thought you did not believe in ghosts."

Mr. Horace Oldfield's features were the very picture of dismay and apprehension.

"I have not changed my opinion in that respect, Mr. Oldfield. Pray do not distress yourself. The removal is temporary only and entirely for your own good."

The accountant's attitude changed to one of relief. He leaned forward at his desk.

"Ah, I follow you, Mr. Pons. You are on to something?"

Solar Pons nodded, rubbing his thin hands together with suppressed excitement.

"I have a theory, Mr. Oldfield. How it will work out I cannot be exactly sure. But to put it into operation, Buffington Old Grange must be absolutely deserted to all intents and purposes."

He held up a warning finger to stop the obvious flow of questions that were on the brink of our client's tongue.

"No one must know of this but ourselves. That is imperative. Not even your wife. All I require is a key of the house, preferably to one of the back doors. Leave the rest to Dr. Parker and myself."

"Delighted, Mr. Pons. Anything to clear up this dreadful mystery. But what about the servants?"

"Everyone must be out, Mr. Oldfield. I do not care what excuse you give. That should not present any great problem."

"No, indeed, Mr. Pons. I could say that we are going on holiday and that the entire place is being redecorated."

Solar Pons shook his head.

"That will not do at all, Mr. Oldfield. An empty house is the only bait that will serve. Well, well, I must leave it to you. But the servants must take a holiday too."

"Very well, Mr. Pons. Mrs. Salmon has relatives in London to whom she could go. There is no great difficulty about the maid. Her home is in Melton."

"There is no problem about the gardener, I take it?"

"No, Mr. Pons. He lives out. But I cannot very well exclude him from the grounds. He would think it most odd."

"Of course not, Mr. Oldfield."

Solar Pons was silent for a moment, his hand pulling reflectively at the lobe of his ear. Then he turned to me.

"We shall have to risk it, Parker. He will leave the grounds at dusk, I take it?"

"Certainly, Mr. Pons."

"Very well. There is little more to be said. I think the sooner you are out the better, Mr. Oldfield. Can you be ready by tomorrow afternoon?"

"If you wish it, Mr. Pons."

"That is settled, then. We will leave you to make the necessary arrangements. But I cannot emphasise strongly enough that your entire family must be seen in Melton publicly on the point of departure, whether you go by train or motor car."

"It shall be done, Mr. Pons," said our obedient client.

Solar Pons rose and Horace Oldfield fervently shook his hand.

"I trust you implicitly, Mr. Pons, and I am hoping that this black cloud which has been hanging over us will soon be lifted."

"Leave it to us, Mr. Oldfield. Come, Parker. We have much to do before tomorrow, and I must just check our arrangements with the local police. Remember, Mr. Oldfield, not a word to anyone about the real purpose of your departure."

And Solar Pons strode out of the room so briskly that I had a great deal of difficulty in keeping up with him.

✍ 6

"Everything is going according to plan, Parker."

Solar Pons handed me the binoculars with an approving smile. We had borrowed them from our client, and they were of powerful magnification. Pons and I were sitting on a fallen log in a clearing on a hilltop about half a mile from Buffington Old Grange. From our commanding position, concealed ourselves, we had an excellent view of the road, the surrounding houses, and the Grange itself. I focused the eyepiece and the image of the drive, bluish and sharp in the clear afternoon light, sprang into clarity.Mrs. Salmon, the housekeeper, accompanied by the maid, was walking down Mr. Oldfield's drive. Both carried suitcases and their steps were evidently bent toward

Melton: the housekeeper for the railway station, the girl to her own home. They paused for a while to chat with the gardener, whose wheelbarrow was stationed near the main gates. I watched them for a while, as they resumed their journey, until a bend in the road cut them off.

Pons sat next to me, the blue smoke of his pipe rising in aromatic spirals in the still, sunny air. He was in a mood I knew well; his tense, set face indicated that his mind was engaged in some problem and I knew better than to interrupt him at these times. So I contented myself with idly scanning the road and the surrounding countryside with the glasses, while my own mind pondered on the strange nature of the mystery surrounding the inhabitants of the Grange—so baffling to me, apparently so clear to my companion.

My musings were presently interrupted by the sound of a car in the driveway, and I saw at once that the master of Buffington Old Grange and his family were themselves on the point of departure. A saloon car, brought round from the stable block, was in front of the main door, and the members of the family were loading suitcases into the interior.

I handed the binoculars to Pons and he watched silently while the preparations went forward. Presently the engine of the car started; the car started and it accelerated down the drive and drove off in the direction of Melton. Silence again descended on the quiet country scene. The gardener, deserted now that everyone had disappeared, stood forlorn for a few moments, poised on his broom, and then wheeled his barrow back down the drive, sulkily it seemed to me, even with the naked eye.

Pons had taken the eyepieces from his face and smiled at my expression.

"Why, yes, Parker, I do expect Smithson is a little put out."

"Whatever do you mean, Pons?"

Solar Pons chuckled.

"The gardener, my dear fellow. He did look desolate, did he not? And no doubt he will miss his meat pies, his cups of tea, and glasses of cider, now that the house is deserted."

I joined in Pons' amusement.

"Well, yes, Pons, I was thinking somewhat on those lines. But how you can read my mind in such a manner..."

"Your mind is quite transparent in these matters, my dear fellow."

Pons rose from the log and I followed him along the path across the field. To my surprise he took the fork which led back toward the town.

"We are not going to the Grange, then, Pons?"

My companion's eyes flashed and an expression of irritation, hastily suppressed, passed across his mobile features.

"Have you learned nothing from my methods, Parker? Secrecy is vital, as I indicated. The Grange is watched, I have no doubt. We cannot go there until after dark. We can safely employ ourselves in Melton for the few hours of daylight remaining. And I have an appointment to meet the local C.I.D. inspector at six o'clock."

"I am sorry, Pons," I said. "My confusion comes from not knowing what is going on."

Pons' expression softened as he pulled steadily at the stem of his pipe.

"All will be made clear in good time, Parker. You must just contain yourself a little longer."

We soon reached the outskirts of Melton and, passing over the bridge, once again plunged into that busy little metropolis. I did not see much of Pons after tea, but dusk had long fallen when he at length appeared before me as I sat reading in front of the fire in the hotel lounge.

"All is ready, Parker. I trust you have your pistol?"

I nodded assent and followed Pons as he strode through the narrow streets. Once across the bridge, a shadowy figure detached itself from the leafy hedge and came forward to join us.

"Dead on time, Mr. Pons."

"Punctuality is the keystone of good detective work. Allow me to present my old friend and colleague, Dr. Lyndon Parker. Inspector George Oldale of Melton C.I.D."

"Delighted to meet you, Dr. Parker."

Inspector Oldale was a tall, vigorous man in his mid-forties with jet-black hair and an alert, terrier-like expression. He evidently knew little more than I about the affairs of Buffington Old Grange, but he fell into stride alongside us and listened carefully as Pons outlined our dispositions for the evening.

"We will circle the grounds, gentlemen, and approach the house from the rear. We must be as silent and circumspect as possible. I have a key to the kitchen door. Once inside the house, we shall secrete ourselves in the cellar and await events."

He tapped his pocket with a thin smile. "I have brought a flask and sandwiches. We may be in for a long wait. Or they may not come at all tonight, though after such a time I would think it highly unlikely that they will delay further."

Oldale's face was set in a frowning mask as he stared at Pons. He did not venture any comment but I could not contain myself.

"Who are 'they'," Pons? And what on earth are we doing in the cellars of Buffington Old Grange?"

Pons only smiled again and laid a finger alongside his nose

to enjoin caution. The wind was rising steadily, and the air was fresh, as though it presaged rain. We were coming to the end of the gas lamps now, and beyond them there were only dancing shadows and the patterns thrown by leaves upon the uneven pavement. There was a small lane on our right and Pons took it unerringly, walking as though he had known this neighbourhood all his life.

Presently we found a gap in the hedge and, squeezing through with some difficulty, found ourselves in the grounds of Buffington Old Grange. Crossing a wide lawn to a gravelled path, which we skirted cautiously, we waited for our eyes to adjust to the darkness before Pons located the flagged walk which led through gloomy banks of rhododendrons and, eventually, to the kitchen door.

The detective officer and I waited uneasily in the rising wind, listening to the creak of branches and strange night sounds, until Pons had placed the key in the lock. Pons' eyes glinted with the excitement of the chase as we found ourselves in the darkened kitchen. He relocked the door and then we followed him through the cellar entrance and down the steps. We had to tread carefully; Pons was now using a pocket torch with great caution.

He kept it low, illuminating only the steps, until we reached the floor. He ran the torch beam across the cellar, selecting a hiding place with care. He stationed Inspector Oldale behind one of the Gothic arches, waiting until he had made himself comfortable on some dry straw. Pons then divided the packet of sandwiches and left the officer several fingers of whisky in the silver cup of his flask. He glanced at his watch.

"We must be prepared for a long wait," he whispered. "No smoking and no talking, Inspector. Parker and I will be among the wine bins yonder."

Oldale nodded and drew his thick overcoat about him, for the air was chill in the cellar. I followed Pons over and we secreted ourselves in one of the aisles between our client's wine racks, so that we could, with a little effort, get a good view of the cellar beyond.

"You have no objection to drinking direct from the flask, Parker?" asked Pons, passing me the packet of sandwiches.

"By no means, Pons," I whispered, biting into a cheese sandwich.

Pons switched off the torch. Munching and sipping agreeably enough, we settled down to wait in the pitch darkness while the creaking noises of the wind, audible here through windows high up at ground level, formed a sombre background to my thoughts.

7

I was jerked awake by the insistent pressure of Pons' fingers on my arm. I must have momentarily dropped off to sleep because I felt chilly and heavy-eyed.

"What is it, Pons?"

"It is one a.m., Parker," my companion whispered back. "And something is happening."

Even as he spoke I could hear a faint crunching in the gravel driveway outside the house, and the dim beam of some light source shone across one of the barred windows of the cellar, high above our heads. A long silence followed and then the heavy, echoing slam of the front door.

We had no time to exchange a word with the police inspector before the sharp, brittle beat of footsteps sounded along the corridors above. The kitchen door opened with a sudden crash

242

that set my nerves fluttering. Mindful of Pons' exhortations, I already had my revolver in hand, the safety catch off. The cellar was flooded with light from the overhead fitting.

I just caught sight of Inspector Oldale pressing farther back into the shadow behind the arch as Pons and I moved cautiously into the darkness of the aisle between the wine bins. We were well concealed here, and I pressed my eye to a space between the bins near ground level, which commanded a good view of the cellar.

Footsteps were descending, and the naked bulb in the vaulted ceiling cast grotesque shadows across the wall.

"It's been a long time."

There was exultation and expectancy in the harsh voice.

"It has that. But worth it."

Silence then, as though the owners of the voices had stopped. Now they came forward again. I shrank back, but the two roughly dressed men who descended the steps so confidently had no eyes for anything but that cleared part of the cellar between two of the high windows. I had noticed before that there was a large patch of lighter cement there, but I now realised its full significance and why Pons had given it particular attention.

His lean, feral features were completely absorbed as he studied the two men who advanced with heavy canvas bags. They carried picks and shovels in their right hands, and there was urgency and purpose in their every movement. I noticed that Pons had his own pistol out and ready for use at his side. The men knelt on the cellar floor and were busy unbuckling the bags they carried. They had their backs to the arch concealing Inspector Oldale, so I knew there was no danger of them seeing him; they were far too absorbed, in any event.

243

The taller of the two men had black hair turning silver and as he turned toward me under the light of the bulb, I could see that he had a dirty white scar running down the side of his face. He wore a heavy knitted jersey such as fishermen wear, dark trousers, and what appeared to be rope-soled sandals.

His companion was slightly smaller but still looked formidable; built like a boxer, he had fair hair and appeared to be a good deal younger than his companion. He had a white, set face in which his eyes burned like tiny sparks of fire. He wore coarse blue overalls and dark trousers similar to those of his companion. Both men were rummaging in the canvas bags now and were consulting a slip of paper, conversing in low whispers all the while.

The bigger man looked anxiously up at the two cellar windows, as though he had just noticed them for the first time. Then there followed another interval while the two men paced out certain measurements between two of the arches and carried on a fierce argument in menacing tones.

When that was over, the big man carried one of the pickaxes over and made a few trial blows at the patch of light cement. Chips rained about the cellar floor. He was then joined by the second man and they worked on steadily for a quarter of an hour, dealing blows that seemed to make the whole cellar shiver. Dust and chippings drifted about, and a gaping crack gradually spread under their expert efforts. Both men were evidently in hard condition because they never paused or hesitated, once they had begun to work.

I glanced at Pons but he was completely absorbed in the scene before him and made no comment, though we could easily have conversed undetected, such was the noise the two men were making. After a while they stopped, and both stooped and tugged at a long slab of cement which was proving difficult to dislodge. It finally gave with a loud cracking noise, disclosing a dark hole some six feet long and about four wide.

This caused some excitement because the pair stopped and held a whispered colloquy; then the bigger of the two fetched a bottle from one of the bags and they drank a silent toast before falling to their work again. They were into earth now and the going had become comparatively easy; they were able to work in relative silence as they shovelled up the layers of black mould and heaped them on the cellar floor of Buffington Old Grange.

The wind was rising heavily and made an uneasy background to the strange scene in front of us. Pons' eyes were shining with excitement and he could not resist a glance of satisfaction at me, as if to reproach me for my scepticism earlier.

I shifted my knee, for I was becoming cramped in one position and was suddenly aware that a relative silence had fallen. I again applied my eyes to the space at the bottom of the bins and saw that some discovery had been made. There had been a metallic clatter a short while before and now it came again as one of the men cautiously tested the pit with his shovel.

Both recommenced digging, this time with their bare hands, scooping up the earth like dogs and throwing it behind them in their abandoned excitement. Then they were bending over the hole in the cellar floor, levering at something; a few seconds later it came in sight—a large, oblong metal chest, with dry earth still clinging to the sides of it.

It made a shrill, grating noise as they dragged it out of the hole they had made and across the rim of the surround. The two men were silent now, crouched and looking down at the metal box, and there was an air of stillness in the cellar as though something tremendous had happened. Then one of the men let drop a ringing oath answered by a laugh from the second. The burlier stepped forward and the pickaxe rang on the padlock as he smashed the chest open.

The man with the scar let out a deep sigh and dipped his hand into the box.

"Ten years, by God!" he said in a shaky voice. "Ten years!"

I had moved my position slightly because of my cramp and had become so absorbed in the scene that all caution was forgotten. A sudden stab of pain shot through my calf as I moved and I was caught off-balance, my pistol barrel falling against a metal upright with a ringing crash. The immobile pair flanking the chest parted with the suddenness of disturbed water.

The tall man with the scar clapped his hand to his pocket as Pons and I started up. The hollow boom of the explosion seemed to rock the cellar and a bullet went ricocheting away among the casks and boxes, sending the splinters flying.

"Your shot, Parker, I think," said Pons calmly.

The second man was already running for the cellar steps as Inspector Oldale's police whistle shrilled. I had my revolver ready as the tall man brought up his pistol again. My shot caught him in the calf of his right leg and brought him painfully to the ground.

The running man was at the cellar door before the athletic figure of Oldale brought him low with a rugby tackle. The two rolled over as Pons ran up the steps to the detective's assistance. The night was full of pounding footsteps and the cellar suddenly seemed full of men in blue uniforms. The smoke of the two shots still hung in the air as Pons joined me, and we hurried to where the tall man lay twisted, cursing and groaning,

246

his pistol fallen far out of reach in the hole the two men had so painstakingly dug.

Pons stood silently looking down at him for a moment as Oldale made his way to our side with the second prisoner, securely handcuffed. My companion's eyes flickered to the bundles of bank notes and the packets of sovereigns within the metal box. The eyes of the man with the white scar met ours unflinchingly.

"Mr. Ezekiel Walton if I am not much mistaken," said Pons grimly.

He turned to Inspector Oldale.

"And there is his fellow conspirator John Roberts. Both men out of prison only a year and certainly two of the most dangerous and enterprising rogues in England, as the judge so aptly described them."

Inspector Oldale's eyes were wide open in astonishment, and there was consternation on the faces of the constables gathered around him.

The man on the ground spat in disgust and struggled up into a sitting position. I already had my pocket handkerchief round the clean wound in his leg, which was pumping blood copiously. I tightened it to staunch the flow and fastened Pons' own handkerchief over the top to secure it.

"That will do until we get him to hospital," I said.

There was mingled rage and admiration in the eyes of the man known as Ezekiel Walton as he stared at Pons.

"All in vain!" he said bitterly. "Ten years and all in vain, mister. Though how you got on to us I don't know . . ."

"A little coincidence and a great deal of common sense," said Pons with a dry chuckle.

He turned to Oldale.

"You had better take charge of this money, Inspector. It represents the proceeds of a number of daring robberies. I have no doubt you will receive an official commendation from a certain quarter, which you will find no hindrance in your career."

"You are most generous, Mr. Pons," said the Berkshire detective.

A startling change had come over the face of the man John Roberts, and he now ceased his struggles with the two burly constables who held him. The man on the ground was being helped up, his wounded leg stiff and helpless. He smiled grimly at Pons.

"Mr. Solar Pons?"

Pons nodded.

"I have that appellation."

"The most brilliant private detective in England," said Inspector Oldale.

Ezekiel Walton gave a second twisted smile.

"I don't feel so badly, then," he said.

Pons had drawn Oldale aside.

"This matter is not yet finished, Inspector. Remain here for a few minutes longer while I seek the lady in the case."

"Lady, Pons?" I asked as we hurried up the cellar steps.

"Certainly, Parker. Madame Mantalini, of course."

I had no opportunity to make sense of this baffling statement before Pons was leading the way at a breathless pace through the darkened rooms of Buffington Old Grange. The police had come in through the kitchen door to gain the cellar and the rooms were silent and deserted. But as we mounted the staircase to the upper floors hurried footsteps were heard.

"You have been long enough. What was that disturbance?" a woman's voice hissed.

A heavy door faced with baize opened on the landing before us and the owner of the voice peered anxiously through. Pons bowed politely.

"It means that the game is up, Madame Mantalini," he said mockingly. "The police are in possession and your husband and his companion in custody."

For a moment the woman's face stared at us in the half-light of the staircase like a white, waxen mask. The lips moved with trembling motions but no words came. Then the door was slammed savagely in our faces, and the bolt thrust home. The retreating footsteps died out on the staircase to the attic floor as Pons and I flung ourselves at the panels.

"A resourceful woman, Parker," said Pons breathlessly, at the fourth shoulder-bruising charge. Then he had his pistol out and deftly shot the lock away with two well-placed bullets. I stumbled through on to the landing and found the brass light switch. Radiance blinked ahead of us as Pons crossed to the door of a room almost opposite. I stood in the opening and watched as he moved to a chest of drawers at the far wall. It was a woman's room, with chintz hangings and pink-shaded lamps, and I looked on in bewilderment as Pons started turning out drawers and cupboards.

"Ought we not to follow her, Pons?" I asked, eyeing the narrow stair behind me.

"I think not for the moment, Parker," said my companion evenly.

"If my reasoning is correct she cannot escape that way and a few minutes more will not matter. I have a notion to satisfy my curiosity. Ah, here we have something."

He picked up a glittering object from the back of a drawer and held the crystal container up to the light.

"It is nothing but a scent spray, Pons."

"Is it not, Parker?" Solar Pons chuckled.

He operated the rubber bulb and sniffed critically with flaring nostrils.

"Lavender, if I am not in error. There is your ghost on the landing."

He handed me the spray and was rummaging in the back of a cupboard as he spoke. He straightened up with a grunt. He held a battered book with a leather cover in his hands. He turned over the leaves hurriedly. I caught a glimpse of yellowed newspaper extracts pasted into the pages. Pons lifted his eyebrows.

"Listen to this, Parker. 'Madame Mantalini's Second Successful Visit. Brilliant Ventriloquist Appears Locally'."

"I am still at sea, Pons," I said helplessly.

Solar Pons made an impatient clicking noise with his tongue.

"Tut, Parker. The matter is clear as daylight. I need only one thing more now and we have these rascals in the net."

He thrust the book into my hands and pounced into the darkness at the back of the cupboard. He turned back to me and I could not repress a shudder. I recoiled as a dead grey face, contorted in a hideous leer, stared soullessly into mine.

"A carnival mask, Parker. A simple but effective device to frighten the wits out of Mr. and Mrs. Oldfield, let alone that poor child."

He ripped the papier-mâché creation from his face, his features stern and set, his eyes blazing.

"You cannot mean, Pons..." I began when we were interrupted by an echoing clatter from the rooms beyond the narrow staircase. Pons hurried up, with me following close behind. He ascended the last flight two steps at a time, so that

I had a job to keep up with him. He found another switch and the landing ahead of us sprang into light. We were evidently in the old servants' quarters. There was no sound from our quarry now. Unless there were a back stairs, the woman Pons had called Madame Mantalini could not escape us.

Nor had she, for as I stepped through into the last of the dusty boxrooms a few minutes later, a pale moon shining through the skylight outlined a dark shadow swaying in the gloom. The overturned cane-bottom chair told us the meaning of the clatter we had heard.

Pons supported her weight as I struggled to get her down. She had hanged herself, with the belt from her dress, on a rusty hook protruding from an oak beam in the ceiling. Pons' face was white and he was visibly shaken as I loosened the ligature from around the neck of the woman he called Madame Mantalini and whom we had known as our client's housekeeper, Mrs. Salmon.

"Poetic justice, perhaps, Parker," he said, as I shook my head slowly. "If that woman is not a murderess, it is only by the grace of God."

He rose to his feet, dusting the knees of his trousers. He glanced around the attic room, his face once more alert and clear-minted.

"Though I would not have wished things to end like this. Ironic that it is probably the same beam from which the old recluse, Jabez Kemp, hanged himself."

He smiled thinly at my expression.

"We had better get some of Oldale's constables up to get Mrs. Walton to the ambulance. Then I think that a few explanations are in order."

8

"It has been an incredible experience, Mr. Pons. I do not know how to thank you." Horace Oldale looked beaming around the table, while his wife's smiling face echoed his own satisfaction. Solar Pons toyed with the stem of his wineglass and glanced approvingly at me.

"It has been a case not without some extraordinary points of interest," he admitted. "And one that I would not have missed for a good deal. Eh, Parker?"

"Certainly not, Pons."

We were seated in the dining room at Buffington Old Grange, the debris of an excellent dinner on the table before us, while the firelight flickered redly on the faces of our host and hostess and their children. Inspector Oldale sat alert and diffident at one side, thoughtfully piercing a cigar with a small instrument on his pocket-knife.

"The two men have talked right enough this past week, Mr. Pons," he observed. "But I would like to hear the whole thing from your own lips."

"And so you shall," observed Solar Pons coolly, taking a sip from his glass of port.

"You may recall, Mr. Oldfield, when first you sought my advice, that I then told you I did not hold with ghosts in any shape or form. It was obvious to me from the beginning and before ever I came to Buffington Old Grange, that a human agency was behind the diabolical happenings within these walls. What interested me even more was the reason for these manifestations."

Solar Pons shot me a penetrating glance from his deep-set eyes.

"You may remember, Parker, that when we examined the cellar I was particularly interested in the patch of light-coloured cement. That had special interest for me."

"I must confess its significance had escaped me, Pons," I said. "Though with hindsight I realise its importance."

Pons smiled thinly.

"It was already clear to me, even in Praed Street, that someone wanted possession of Buffington Old Grange. For what purpose was not at that time evident. But the house had been empty for a long period before Mr. and Mrs. Oldfield purchased it, and it seemed logical to assume that something in the house had great interest for a person or persons unknown. Hence the campaign of terror to which the occupants were subjected. And on my arrival it did not take me long to realise that the housekeeper, Mrs. Salmon, was admirably suited to this role.

"She had *entrée* to every part of the house; the whole strings of the *ménage* were in her hands; and she further impressed me as a woman of very great daring and steady nerve."

"Oh come, Pons," I protested. "I saw only a very competent woman devoted to the interests of her employers. Why, she even risked her own life to put out the fire in this very house."

Mr. and Mrs. Oldfield stared at me and even the inspector looked discomposed.

Pons slowly shook his head, a strange smile hovering about his lips.

"That she had first started, Parker. Remember that."

Before I could interject any further remark he went on rapidly.

"My conversations with the maid and the gardener, the only other two members of the domestic staff, quickly convinced me that they could not possibly be responsible. I concentrated therefore on Mrs. Salmon. It was further obvious that some event in the remote past held the key to the bizarre occurrences within this house. It had been empty a long while, so there had been ample opportunity for anyone to explore it in the past. But it became clear as the case progressed that Mr. and Mrs. Oldfield had purchased the property at a time when some exterior event had occurred. To make sense of this I had first to find out what happening in the remote past might be responsible. I therefore consulted the newspaper files at your excellent library, Inspector."

"I begin to see your drift, Pons," I said.

Solar Pons leaned back at the table and tented his fingers, his eyes twinkling as he looked at me.

"Do you not, Parker? Let us just recapitulate. Mrs. Salmon was intent on driving her employers from the house. To do that she deliberately indulged in a campaign of terror which did not shrink from frightening a child half out of her wits and even went on to attempted murder. She capitalised on these old stories of the miser, Jabez Kemp, and his hanging himself in one of the upper rooms of the property. I'm sure you'll forgive me for mentioning this in front of these children of tender years, Mrs. Oldfield?"

Mrs. Oldfield, a handsome woman now quite recovered from the strain of the past months, smiled indulgently.

"Children are more resilient than you might think, Mr. Pons. They are quite absorbed in your narrative, now that they know there is nothing supernatural within these walls."

"There was nothing supernatural, Mrs. Oldfield. Mrs. Salmon was the all-too-human agent. It was she who sprayed the lavender perfume on the landing; she who supplied the whispering and footsteps; she who donned that hideous mask to frighten your children. That was why you heard a guttural voice, Mr. Oldfield. And when that failed to drive you out, she hid in the pantry and tried to push you down the stairs, in turn. Whether either or both of her employers were crippled or killed was a matter of complete indifference to her. She had to drive you out in order to get at that money."

"I quite see that, Pons," I said. "But I don't understand about the fire."

"Elementary, my dear Parker. Mrs. Salmon set it herself. She was the only person who could have done so. The gardener, who was working in front of the house, told me he had seen no one. Mrs. Salmon therefore came back to the house by the kitchen entrance, unseen. She had just lit the paraffin when Mr. Oldfield unexpectedly returned home. She had no option but heroically to attempt to save the property by putting out the blaze herself. In so doing she undoubtedly genuinely burned herself, which added to the verisimilitude of the story she told Mr. Oldfield, of an intruder."

"But what was the point, Pons?"

Solar Pons clicked his tongue again.

"If the house were destroyed, Parker, Mr. and Mrs. Oldfield and their family would have to leave. Whether permanently or for a few months made no difference. The fire would not affect the cellars. If Buffington Old Grange had been gutted, all the gang had to do when the fuss had died down would be to move in one dark night and remove the stolen money."

"And the voices, Mr. Pons?" said Oldfield. "We heard strange voices. They were not hallucination."

"Mrs. Salmon was a woman of many parts," said Pons drily. "She had been an acrobat, a ventriloquist, and a circus performer among other things. I found that out from a perusal of the newspaper files, and an old photograph of her as Madame Mantalini clinched the matter. To a trained ventriloquist the thing would be child's play. As soon as I arrived at the house, I saw that the voice you heard on the porch that dark night, Mr. Oldfield, could easily have emanated from the open kitchen window farther along. All Mrs. Salmon—or rather, Mrs. Elizabeth Walton—had to do was to wait in the darkened kitchen until you returned and put your key in the door."

"You keep saying Mrs. Walton, Pons."

"That was self-evident from the newspaper files, Parker. A series of daring robberies in the Melton area ten or eleven years ago was the most startling and outstanding event which had happened in this quiet place this century. Apart from the death of the recluse in this house. I soon saw from the newspaper account that there was nothing unusual in the old man's suicide. Instead, I concentrated on the robberies. John Roberts and Ezekiel Walton, two of the most desperate rascals who ever embarked on housebreaking exploits were the culprits. Walton was married to Madame Mantalini—or Mrs. Salmon as you knew her, Mr. Oldfield. The trio travelled the country with fairs and circuses, Madame Mantalini providing the façade of circus performer, while the other two worked as stevedores. We have that from their own lips. I soon saw from the advertisements in the local newspaper that the fair or circus had played in the vicinity of Melton when country houses were robbed. The trio would first familiarise themselves with the new district, mark down a particular house, and commit the burglary on the last night they were in the neighbourhood. By the time the crime was discovered, the circus would be miles away."

"I see, Pons!" I said. "I should have paid more attention to those advertisements."

Solar Pons exchanged a slow smile with Inspector Oldale.

"Do not blame yourself, Parker. I already knew what I was looking for before I ever went to the library. The gang had their biggest haul at Melton when the fair played here again. They had marked out the empty house as an ideal cache. They spent the night concealing their booty and cementing it into its cellar hiding place, while the country was turned upside down for them. But later they were caught and sent to prison for ten years, though Mrs. Walton disappeared."

He stopped to take another sip of the port before resuming.

"The people hereabouts had only seen her in make-up as a fair or circus performer. It was a simple matter for her to change her name, personality, and identity and find work in the area as a housekeeper."

"She was watching the Grange to see that no one disturbed the money, Pons!"

"Exactly, Parker. Which she did admirably. She was an extremely patient woman. Imagine her dismay when Mr. and Mrs. Oldfield bought the house and commenced to renovate it. But being a woman of great resources and nerve, she did not despair. She knew the new owners would need someone to run the place and with her excellent local references she was first on the scene to offer her services as housekeeper and to prepare the tragi-comedy."

"But why did she wait so long, Pons?" I said.

Solar Pons shook his head.

The men were still in prison, Parker. She could do nothing until they were released. I called on Bancroft who obtained some Home Office information for me. Walton and Roberts were released a year ago."

"Exactly the time the ghostly manifestations began?" I said.

Solar Pons nodded.

"Mr. and Mrs. Oldfield did not take a holiday the first year they were at the Grange. There was too much to do. That gave me a vital clue. The check with Bancroft revealed the men's release date. They waited a while until the occupants should go away on holiday. The Oldfields, however, showed no inclination to do so and hence the conspirators had no alternative but to then begin the campaign to drive them out."

"Which led me to seek your advice, Mr. Pons," said Horace Oldfield fervently. "It was the most sensible thing I have done in my life."

"Well, well, Mr. Oldfield," said Pons soberly. "It has been a terrifying experience but all has come right in the end. Justice has been done and more than done in the case of Mrs. Walton, who would undoubtedly have killed one of you if it had not been for a merciful providence. I hope that it has not put you off living at Buffington Old Grange?"

Oldfield exchanged a long look with his wife.

"It has certainly not done that, Mr. Pons. I am sure we shall be very happy here now."

"There, Parker," said Solar Pons. "We have achieved something at least. I for one will remain extremely content with that."

He leaned forward and raised his glass in a silent toast to our host and hostess.

"And it will be good to get Dr. Parker spruce and tidy again."

I stared at him in bewilderment.

"I am not sure I know what you mean, Pons."

Solar Pons chuckled. He held out his hand to me and placed something in my palm. It was a packet of new razor blades.

The Adventure of
the Hammer of Hate

1

"A FINE DAY, Parker."

My old friend, Solar Pons, rubbed his thin hands briskly as he sat down to breakfast in our comfortable bachelor quarters at 7B Praed Street.

"Exceedingly, for the time of year, Pons," I agreed.

Though it was January, the weather had been extremely mild and a strong sun shone redly on the hatless and somewhat bewildered throngs of pedestrians in the street below, who were obviously unaccustomed to such benevolence on the part of London weather.

"Croci already out at Kew."

I looked at Pons suspiciously, conscious of the faint smile lurking about his lips.

"You seem to have a remarkable interest in horticultural matters, Pons, if you don't mind me saying so."

Solar Pons cracked an egg with delicate precision and put his spoon fastidiously into the white.

"Ah, Parker, if you had been communing with nature as I have been recently, you would not think it quite so remarkable.

259

My vigil in the Paxton glass-houses and my subsequent apprehension of Mullett have made me more appreciative of the extraordinary flora of this planet."

Light broke in.

"You mean this business of the Kew murder and the arrest of the Head Keeper, Pons. I thought the deductive reasoning behind it too brilliant for Jamison. I did not know you had been retained."

"I had to work in the utmost secrecy, Parker. And my innate modesty prevented me from taking any credit in the public press. I was content to leave the official limelight to our old friend, Inspector Jamison."

"You are too generous sometimes, Pons," I said.

Solar Pons smiled diffidently, leaning forward to pour himself coffee from the silver-plated pot.

"Perhaps, Parker. It is kind of you to say so. But what have we here?"

He sat forward in a familiar attitude, and a moment later I caught what his keen senses had already discerned, the beat of running footsteps in the street below. Then there came a crash as the front door slammed and the scrambling rush of someone in a tremendous hurry on the staircase.

The door suddenly burst open without so much as a knock and a dishevelled figure almost fell forward onto the breakfast table. I sat with my coffee cup poised halfway to my lips, staring in astonishment at a young man, hatless and coatless, who glared at us with wild eyes.

"Mr. Solar Pons? You must help me, Mr. Pons. I am the unhappy Eustace Fernchurch. I tell you, sir, that I did not commit the murder!"

Solar Pons had risen from his seat, a half-smile on his face, and now went forward to proffer a chair to our agitated visitor.

"Pray compose yourself, Mr. Fernchurch. You have the advantage of me. No, it is all right, Mrs. Johnson."

The alarmed figure of our landlady had appeared in the doorway, but on being reassured by Pons, withdrew with a worried look at the young man slumped in the chair. He looked grey and exhausted, and I rose to offer him a cup of coffee, which he accepted with an expression of mute thanks in his hunted eyes.

"Now, Mr. Fernchurch," said Pons, reseating himself and gazing intently at the pitiful figure before us. "You seem to think that we should know you."

"I should have thought the whole world would have known me by this morning," said Fernchurch bitterly. "It was in all the newspapers."

"Ah," said Pons. "We have not yet perused them. It is only a quarter past eight. You took an early morning train, then?"

Our visitor looked startled. He put down his coffee cup and struggled up in his chair with a somewhat more animated air.

"You know me, Mr. Pons?"

My companion shook his head.

"But you still have a return ticket clutched in your right hand. If I am not mistaken, it is one issued by the London and North Eastern Railway. If you have come from the north, it naturally follows that you took a train at an early hour to arrive in London at this time."

Fernchurch appeared to recollect himself, shook his head painfully once or twice, and put the ticket slowly in his pocket.

"You are perfectly correct, Mr. Pons. I caught the express as soon as I knew the police were closing the net around me."

Solar Pons made a little clicking noise with his tongue. He

tented his long, sensitive fingers before him and looked at our visitor expectantly.

"That was extremely unwise, Mr. Fernchurch, if you will allow me to say so. The British police, though they may sometimes be slow and occasionally obtuse, are seldom corrupt in their larger workings. If you are innocent, as you say you are, you will have little to fear."

Our visitor shook his head again.

"You do not know the circumstances, Mr. Pons. Everything is against me. The whole town thinks I killed Bulstrode. I had to flee."

"And by so doing, proved your guilt in the eyes of the world," said Pons crisply. "Indiscreet, Mr. Fernchurch. However, it is past mending now. You must just tell me your story, and we will see what we can do to right things as we go along."

"You will take my case then, Mr. Pons?"

"I did not say so, Mr. Fernchurch. But you have the look of a young man more distressed than guilty. If, as you say, you are innocent, and it appears so from your discourse, then I will certainly take your case."

Eustace Fernchurch sprang up impulsively and pumped Solar Pons' hand fervently.

"You will have my undying thanks, Mr. Pons. That is all I ask."

He glanced at me inquiringly and Pons suddenly seemed to become aware of my presence.

"I beg your pardon, Parker. Pray continue with your breakfast. This is my old friend and colleague, Dr. Lyndon Parker, Mr. Fernchurch. I take it you have no objection to us continuing our meal while you talk?"

"By no means, Mr. Pons."

Pons again drew up his chair to the table, and between sips at his coffee our visitor commenced his story.

"I come from the small town of Maldon in Yorkshire, Mr. Pons. It is some miles from York and a pretty, historic place, with a stream running through the centre. I started work as a mason, but as I have a bent for design, I have been fortunate enough to be taken on as an architectural apprentice with Truscott and Sons of that town. Part of my work is concerned with overseeing the activities of builders.

"One of them, the biggest builder in Maldon, was Sebastian Bulstrode. Cursed be the day that I ever set eyes upon him, Mr. Pons."

"Pray compose yourself, Mr. Fernchurch."

"It does no good I know, Mr. Pons, but I cannot help thinking what this man has reduced me to. I had become engaged to a charming young lady, Mr. Pons. A girl called Evelyn Smithers. She is the daughter of the curator of the Castle Museum and a fine young woman in every way, even if a little flighty."

Our visitor broke off and sat staring gloomily into the dregs of his coffee cup. Then he blinked and roused himself with some difficulty.

"I was at my office one day when my fiancée came in. We had arranged to meet at the Market Cross, but I was delayed a little and she had grown tired of waiting. I happened to be discussing some work with Bulstrode and I could not very well avoid introducing him to her. I noticed he seemed very taken with her, but I did not attach much significance to it. She is a striking girl, tall, with long golden hair and an open, good-hearted nature. Everyone who knows her in the town loves her."

Here our visitor broke off again with an audible groan. I coughed to cover the awkward pause and shifted my eyes onto Pons, whose intent gaze had never left Fernchurch's face.

"Nothing has happened to your fiancée, I trust?"

The young man looked startled.

"Good heavens, no, Mr. Pons. God forbid. But I cannot help thinking that her nature has helped to bring me to the present pass."

I got up to pour our visitor more coffee and, having finished my breakfast by this time, pulled my chair back from the table and gave all my attention to Fernchurch's story.

"I noticed a change in Evelyn's attitude after that, Mr. Pons. It was subtle, it is true, and manifested itself in small criticisms of myself; then she was late once or twice for appointments. She pleaded illness on several occasions. I thought little of it at the time.

"Then, one evening, at a time she was supposed to be visiting a sister in York, I was crossing a side street on my way for a drink at a nearby hotel when a dogcart passed me. There was a street lamp opposite which threw its light across the road, though I was in shadow. Laughter attracted my attention; the light shone across the cart, which was driven by Sebastian Bulstrode. Laughing at some remark he had made, my fiancée was sitting beside him."

"I am indeed sorry to hear it," said Solar Pons soberly. His intent eyes looked sympathetically at Fernchurch, who again paused as though in the grip of strong emotion.

"I cannot really blame Evelyn, Mr. Pons. I am a dull fellow who works late and sticks to his last. Bulstrode was a man of great energy and vitality; short-tempered but not bad-looking, about forty-five years of age, and certainly rich. He had been married once before, but the couple had separated and a divorce had been granted some three years ago."

"Nevertheless, Mr. Fernchurch, the circumstances would seem to cast some doubt on the suitability of this young lady as the choice of your heart," said Solar Pons evenly. "To put it no higher."

Fernchurch was silent for a moment, his eyes downcast; he was calmer now, his ruffled hair smoothed by his hands, though his expression was hard to make out as he sat with his back to the flood of golden light which came in through the window.

"There is justice in what you say, Mr. Pons. Evelyn is flighty, as I said, though I do not really blame the girl at this distance in time. Bulstrode had set his cap for her and she is easily impressed."

"You remonstrated with her?"

Fernchurch nodded.

"We had a dreadful row. In short, the engagement was broken off. Some weeks later I heard she had become engaged to Bulstrode. There was some delicacy in the situation, Mr. Pons. My feelings can be imagined; I could see my former fiancée and Bulstrode together as I went about my daily business—Maldon is a small town—and in addition to this my work threw me in constant contact with the man."

"You have my sympathy, Mr. Fernchurch. Pray go on. You did not come into open conflict with him?"

Fernchurch shook his head.

"I am no coward, Mr. Pons, but Bulstrode is an absolute bull of a man; fearless and short-tempered, as I have said. I would have been no match for him physically and I did not go out of my way to provoke him. But we had words about his conduct, and our business affairs thereafter were conducted with icy indifference on either side. That was the situation which obtained until some six weeks ago when my former fiancée sought me out in great distress. I am going into this matter at some length, Mr. Pons, because I am anxious that you should get the true background of this affair. I trust I am not boring you."

"I am not bored, Mr. Fernchurch," said Pons crisply, looking across at me with a smile. "And I am sure I can speak for Dr. Parker also. Eh, Parker?"

"Certainly, Pons," I said. "It is absorbing."

"You may well say so, gentlemen," said our visitor wearily. "But the whole thing is too close to me to be anything but a nightmare. Evelyn was in some distress, as I said. She sought my help and forgiveness. She had seen Bulstrode's true nature within a short space of time and had tried to break off her engagement. She encountered difficulties she had never found with me. Bulstrode was a headstrong man, with a filthy temper. Reading between the lines, I should have said he had something sadistic in his nature also."

"He used physical violence against the girl?"

"Absolutely, Mr. Pons. He went berserk, quite beside himself with rage. Evelyn ran from his house and went home to her father. When she had recovered a little, she sought me out. It was a difficult situation, Mr. Pons; but the rupture was healed within a few days. Last month we again became engaged."

Solar Pons leaned forward in his chair, his fingers pressed together in front of him, engrossed in our visitor's face.

"And Bulstrode's attitude?"

"That was the strange part, Mr. Pons. I heard about the town that he had beenin black rages over me. Stealing his fiancée, he called it. He had been in some hotels declaiming to the company what he intended to do to me. I must confess I was in some trepidation when business again threw me in his way. But to my surprise, apart from a certain stiffness and reserve in his manner, Bulstrode said nothing. We were back on the familiar footing that had obtained for some years. It was a strange position, Mr. Pons; to hear that a man had been blackening and vilifying one in public places about the town in the evenings—even to the point that I had been threatening him—and to work with him in the day in quite a normal manner."

"Most trying," said Solar Pons soothingly.

"Indeed, Mr. Pons. So you can imagine my feelings a week ago to be suspected of Bulstrode's murder in a most shocking manner!"

2

There was a brief silence in the room. Solar Pons leaned forward.

"Before you go on, Mr. Fernchurch, I think I will just see what the public prints have to say on the subject."

"Certainly, Mr. Pons. There is a long piece in the *Telegraph*."

"Just so."

Solar Pons turned to me.

"The newspaper is at your elbow, Parker. If you will be so good as to favour us with a reading. The salient details only."

"The bottom of the front page, Dr. Parker," said Fernchurch.

I turned to the section of the newspaper indicated. There was indeed, as Pons' client had indicated, a good deal about the affair. The article was headed: MALDON CASTLE MURDER...SEARCH FOR MAN IN BUILDER'S DEATH. I looked at Pons, who replied somewhat snappishly, "Yes, yes, Parker, spare us the journalistic clichés of the headings. Pray read us the account shorn of all the colourful detail so beloved of the general public."

"It is most soberly written, Pons," I protested.

Pons gave a faint smile and sat back in his chair, his hands cradled beneath his chin, as I commenced to read the article.

It ran:

> Yorkshire Police, assisted by Scotland Yard, are searching for a man believed to be able to help them in their inquiries into the murder of Mr. Sebastian Bulstrode, aged forty-six, a builder, of Maltby Road, Maldon, Yorks.
>
> The body of Mr. Bulstrode was found in broad daylight beneath the West Tower of Maldon Castle on January 3rd, the skull crushed and extensively damaged. The murder weapon was a large mason's hammer, belonging to Mr. Bulstrode's own firm, which lay beside the body.
>
> A man was seen on top of the tower a few minutes before, and a Maldon Police spokesman said last week that the inquiry was being treated as murder, the inference being that the hammer was flung or dropped onto Mr. Bulstrode's head as he inspected work in progress.
>
> Mr. Bulstrode's firm was engaged in carrying out renovation of the ancient Castle tower at the time, and the death weapon was believed by members of his staff

to have been in use on the battlements, where scaffolding and building materials had been erected.

Helping the police with their inquiries recently has been Mr. Eustace Fernchurch, a local architect's assistant, who was on the tower at the time of Mr. Bulstrode's death. Mr. Fernchurch said he had an appointment with his fiancée, Miss Evelyn Smithers, daughter of the Curator of Maldon Castle, to meet her on the tower, a regular place of assignation for the couple.

Miss Smithers, aged twenty-five, confirmed this, but said she was late for her appointment since she was having a talk with her father over her becoming re-engaged to Mr. Fernchurch. The couple had been engaged before, but the association was broken off when Miss Smithers became briefly engaged to the murdered man, Mr. Bulstrode.

"Concise and to the point, Parker," said Pons, his eyes still closed. "An admirable summary of what Mr. Fernchurch has just told us with the even more succinctly described circumstances of the actual death."

I read on.

The inquiry has been hampered by a lack of clues and a large number of possible motives for the crime. Police favour revenge, and it is understood that the late Mr. Bulstrode had many enemies, both business and personal, in the town.

"He was a man of most violent temper and an inflammable personality," said a local shopkeeper, who asked not to be identified. Bulstrode had quarrelled with a number of people in past months, including Mr. Fernchurch, the subject of the latter arguments being Miss Smithers.

Inspector Robert Fitzjohn of York C.I.D., who is heading up the Maldon investigation, told our Yorkshire correspondent yesterday, "We are further hampered by there being no fingerprints on the handle of the hammer used in the crime. It is made entirely of metal, the sharpened end of the metal handle being capable of use as a crowbar. The handle was covered with plaster dust, which would normally retain fingerprints. But the shock of the impact with the ground, and the hammer ricocheting from the Castle wall, shook all the dust off it, so that the remnants of the prints were quite useless for our purposes."

I read on for another two paragraphs but Pons opened his eyes, lazily stretched himself, and commented, "You need not go any further, Parker. I have heard enough."

His face wore the alert and animated expression I had grown to know of old.

"The fingerprint details are distinctly ingenious. Either we have someone extremely clever here—or careless. I cannot decide which at the moment."

"There is something in the Stop Press, Dr. Parker, if you will be so good," interjected Pons' client nervously.

I turned to the right-hand bottom of the page and read aloud: "Maldon Murder. Police currently looking for Mr. Eustace Fernchurch in connection with murder of Sebastian Bulstrode. Disappeared from home yesterday. Story Page 1."

Solar Pons made a little deprecatory noise with his tongue.

"Tell us about that, Mr. Fernchurch. You obviously did not abscond today, or the newspaper could not possibly have this Stop Press. The page would have gone away at about three o'clock this morning."

Fernchurch flushed slightly and shifted in his chair.

"I had a talk with my fiancée yesterday, Mr. Pons," he said. "We agreed it would be best if I sought your advice. I could feel the net closing in about me."

"She knows you are here, then?" said Pons.

Fernchurch nodded.

"In that case the police will not be long in tracing you," Pons murmured.

He smiled as Fernchurch held up a protesting hand.

"It is no criticism of Miss Smithers, Mr. Fernchurch. But I have never yet met the woman who was able to keep the truth from a patient and persistent police officer of the right sort. The police would have gone to Miss Smithers straight away. And I know Fitzjohn. He was a very efficient C.I.D. man at the Yard for some years."

"You are right, Mr. Pons," said Fernchurch in a subdued voice. "I knew I was under observation. I managed to elude surveillance after dark last night. I drove to York and stayed in lodgings where I was not known. I got the first available train from York this morning."

Pons pondered in silence for a moment or two longer.

"You are positive that you have told me everything, Mr. Fernchurch?"

Pons' client nodded.

"Everything relevant, Mr. Pons. If anything has been missed it will be through sheer inadvertence."

"That is a fair answer, Mr. Fernchurch. I will take your case

271

and I think the sooner we return to Maldon together the better. How are you placed, Parker?"

I was on my feet.

"I can telephone my locum, Pons. I would not miss this for the world!"

Solar Pons chuckled.

"Just give us a quarter of an hour or so and we will be at your service, Mr. Fernchurch. We will talk further in the train."

The relief on our visitor's face was evident. His eyes were shining and some of his haggardness had lifted.

"There is an express from King's Cross for York within the hour, gentlemen."

Before our arrangements were completed, however, there was a dramatic interruption. The bell rang and we could hear Mrs. Johnson in muffled colloquy with someone on the stairs. There was the tread of heavy boots ascending. I had finished my call and had returned to the sitting room to find Pons standing near the door with an irritated expression on his face.

"That sounds like Inspector Jamison, Parker."

He turned to our startled visitor, who looked as though he actually might attempt to climb through the window.

"It is too late, Mr. Fernchurch. Pray do not be afraid. We must just face it out."

He had no sooner spoken than there was a curt rap at the door, and it was flung open to admit the acid figure of Inspector Jamison.

⁊ 3

"You are quick off the mark, Inspector," said Solar Pons pleasantly. "Won't you come in? I would like to introduce you to a friend of mine."

Jamison smiled sourly, a satisfied expression on his sallow face.

"That won't be necessary, Mr. Pons. I already know the gentleman."

His manner changed to its most curt and official.

"You are Eustace Hornbeam Fernchurch?"

Our client looked appealingly at both of us in turn, swallowed heavily, and nodded mutely. Jamison gave us a fleeting look of smug satisfaction.

"Eustace Hornbeam Fernchurch, I have here a warrant for your arrest on the capital charge of murder. I have to warn you that you are not obliged to say anything, but if you do it may be taken down in writing and used in evidence."

Fernchurch gave a strangled cry and looked appealingly at Pons again.

"Not so fast, Inspector," said Pons curtly. "I do not think this will be necessary. My client and I, together with Dr. Parker here, are just about to return to York to face this charge. My client maintains his innocence, and I hope to prove it once I see Inspector Fitzjohn."

Jamison gave an ingratiating smile.

"That may well be, Mr. Pons, but I have my duty to do. This warrant..."

"It will wait," said Solar Pons coolly. "Mr. Fernchurch will give you his parole and I will undertake to see him safely delivered. If this is not sufficient, you have only to telephone Fitzjohn and tell him I am delivering his prisoner, and I am sure he will be satisfied with the arrangement."

Inspector Jamison hesitated.

"That is all very well, Mr. Pons. But how do I know Mr. Fernchurch will be on the train?"

Solar Pons took the Scotland Yard man by the arm and propelled him toward the door.

"Because you are coming to King's Cross to see us safely off, my dear fellow. You may leave the warrant with me if you wish, and I will see that Fitzjohn gets it."

Jamison hesitated fractionally again. Solar Pons smiled faintly.

"I know what you are thinking, Inspector. The train stops at Doncaster and other places, I believe. No doubt you could have your local men on the platform in each case, and I will identify the prisoner."

"Very well, Mr. Pons."

Inspector Jamison inclined his head stiffly and handed my companion the warrant. He looked over Pons' shoulder to Fernchurch.

"Think yourself lucky, young man. If we had taken you before you arrived here, you would have been in custody by now."

"How did you get on his track so quickly?" asked Pons as we all descended the stairs. There was an unctuousness in Jamison's voice, as he replied, which I must confess grated on my susceptibilities.

"We had a call from York, of course, as soon as Fernchurch disappeared. One of our bright-eyed lads at King's Cross spotted him this morning. It wasn't difficult, since he was dishevelled and obviously upset. His colleague followed while he telephoned me. I told them to see where the quarry went, and he led me to you."

"Admirable, Jamison," said Pons affably. "You have the makings of a detective yet."

Little spots of red burned on the Inspector's cheeks as Pons went imperturbably on.

"Oh, Mrs. Johnson, we are planning a little expedition into Yorkshire. We expect to be away only three days or so at the most."

"Very good, Mr. Pons."

We were in the sunshine of the street now, and Jamison led the way to the police car which stood at the kerb, keeping a tight hold on the unfortunate Fernchurch's elbow. Pons slipped the warrant into his pocket, we put our valises on the luggage rack, and were off to King's Cross.

The journey north passed in moody silence for the most part. We had a compartment to ourselves and Pons' probing questions and Fernchurch's artless answers apparently satisfied my companion, for he soon immersed himself in the pages of a magazine, the reek of his pipe sending blue clouds of smoke about the carriage, where it lay shimmering in the shifting bands of sunlight.

Jamison was true to his word, for there were police officers evident on the platforms of each of the major stations at which we briefly stopped. Pons got out on each occasion and held short conversations before bringing the senior detective to the window so that Fernchurch could show himself. Fernchurch bore the inquisitions with great patience, and now that I knew him a little better the possibility of his innocence was growing with every mile that brought us closer to York.

When that great terminus was reached and we had passed over the bridge under the vast glass roof that spanned the platforms, Inspector Fitzjohn, a tall dark man impeccably dressed in a tweed suit and raglan overcoat, was waiting beyond the barrier and came slowly forward as we descended the steps. Though the sun was still shining, the sky was a little overcast here and once again I caught the raw, bracing air of the north.

After a cordial exchange of pleasantries between Pons and the inspector, which included my introduction, Fitzjohn gave a slight bow to Fernchurch, glanced carelessly at the warrant Pons handed him, and thrust it into his pocket.

"Let this unpleasantness rest for a moment," he said. "A few informal words over a drink would not be out of place."

It was astonishing what a change had come over Fernchurch at the Inspector's words and now he cast a grateful glance at Pons. Inspector Fitzjohn chuckled drily.

"Come, Mr. Fernchurch, you surely did not think I was going to clap you into the Black Maria?"

"I did not know what I expected," stammered Pons' client as the inspector led the way through the long glass corridor which connected the terminus with the Edwardian opulence of the Station Hotel.

Once across the broad foyer with the vast staircase sweeping its elegant balustraded ironwork up to the first floor, the inspector led us into a luxuriously fitted bar where a cheerful buzz of conversation rose from the well-dressed clientele gathered for lunchtime drinks. We sat down at a corner table while Fitzjohn ordered our choices; beyond the glass doors an orchestra had struck up a Strauss waltz.

"A little different from your last case, Pons," I observed as my companion's lean form relaxed on to a banquette opposite. Fernchurch sat huddled in a corner, up by a partition, but the hunted look had gone from his face. He flushed as Inspector Fitzjohn raised his glass and included him in the toast.

"To a successful conclusion."

"I am innocent, Inspector."

Fitzjohn seated himself next to Fernchurch and opposite Pons and myself. His clipped black moustache twitched sympathetically as he muttered deprecatingly, "That may well be, Mr. Fernchurch. You have been indiscreet, nothing more. And the press have perhaps made too much of it. But you are in a serious position, you understand that."

"He does understand it, Inspector," said Solar Pons soothingly. "Which was why he consulted me. You have no objection to my surveying the field of operation, I take it?"

Inspector Fitzjohn's smile was frank and open.

"By no means, Mr. Pons. I should be honoured and delighted. Though I fear you will not make much more of it than we have been able."

Solar Pons rubbed his thin fingers together briskly.

"We shall see, Inspector, we shall see," he murmured.

Fitzjohn smiled faintly as though he doubted that even Solar Pons could do better and observed, "I have taken the liberty of reserving rooms for you and Dr. Parker at The Saddler's Arms. It is one of the best establishments in the town and highly recommended."

"Excellent," said Pons. "I was particularly interested in the matter of the hammer which felled Mr. Bulstrode."

The Inspector's grey eyes looked at Pons ingenuously.

"I thought that aspect would not escape you, Mr. Pons. That was extremely unfortunate as we would otherwise have been able to establish conclusively whether Mr. Fernchurch had handled it."

"You have not ruled out the possibility that the dead man might have been attacked on the ground?"

Fitzjohn raised his eyebrows.

"It had occurred to us," he said easily. "But our medical people said it was quite impossible. The hammer hit him almost squarely on the crown of the head with such force as to completely disintegrate the skull. Bulstrode was a tall man and unless his attacker had been a man about nine feet tall it would have been impossible for him to have struck Bulstrode on top of the head. The forehead or the base of the skull would have been the obvious place."

"I see."

Pons remained silent for a moment, looking absently at the crowded life of the bar about us. Fernchurch sat breathlessly, first looking at Pons' face and then at the Inspector's, as though he expected to read his innocence in the expression of their eyes.

"What was the weight of the hammer?"

"About three pounds, Mr. Pons. A formidable weapon but it would have had to come from a height to inflict that damage. I have the medical report here, if you wish to see it."

Pons waved away the document the Inspector had produced.

I am quite content to accept your word for it, Inspector. From your earlier remarks, I take it you do not intend to incarcerate Mr. Fernchurch?"

"Certainly not, Mr. Pons. Though things do look black against him. I shall have to insist that he does not leave Maldon under any circumstances, of course. And I shall make you responsible for seeing that he keeps his promise. Our local magistrates will have my scalp if he gives us the slip again."

Fitzjohn accompanied his last sentence with a dry chuckle and Pons looked at him approvingly.

"I am happy to give that assurance, Inspector. And now, I think that a speedy journey to the scene of the crime would not be amiss. Parker does not like to be late for lunch and it would never do to upset so valued a colleague."

4

A drive of about twenty minutes in the car the Inspector had parked in the grounds of the hotel brought us to our destination; a small, charming town, with the Castle set on a hill and a broad, sluggish river meandering through undulating countryside below. Fitzjohn drove skilfully through cobbled streets, where timbered houses alternated with more recent ones of the mellow Yorkshire stone, and deposited us at The Saddler's Arms.

Waiting only to register and leave our luggage, we returned to the car and Fitzjohn drove the four of us up a winding road that led to the precincts of the Castle itself. Pons insisted on descending from the vehicle several hundred yards away and prowled about, seemingly casually, his sharp eyes missing nothing. Due to the mild winter, no doubt, there were many tourists about, and cameras on shoulder straps and anxiously flourished guides were much in evidence.

"Interesting, Parker, is it not?" said Pons as we came to a halt in the shadow of the West Tower, whose frowning pile was surmounted by scaffolding and surrounded by tubular girders. "Mainly Norman, I should say, with some particularly hideous late Victorian additions."

Inspector Fitzjohn, who had parked his car against the base of the tower and had now rejoined us, smiled wryly.

"Correct, Mr. Pons. The Town Council used to meet in the annexe, but that part is now being demolished and completely restored under the energetic supervision of the Curator, Professor Smithers."

"Ah, yes, Inspector. The young lady's father. I should like a word with him in due course."

"That can be easily arranged, Mr. Pons."

We had now walked toward the tower and Pons was busy darting about, first glancing upward at the battlements, partly obscured by scaffolding, then down to the ground at the base, where a grassy bank swelled out for a few feet. We had come to the foot of the tower beneath an arch, and a buttress of the wall immediately in front blocked off the adjoining street. Pons paid particular attention to this and to the opposite building, which was nothing but a blank stone façade, broken here and there by very small windows.

Fitzjohn answered the query in his eyes.

"The Guildhall, Mr. Pons. It faces the square on the other side. Most of these small windows give on to store-rooms."

"A pity," observed Pons drily. "Had there been spectators at these casements, they might have had a story to tell."

"Indeed, Mr. Pons. We have been all through that, I can assure you."

Solar Pons stood with his feet planted astride, the pipe which he had just placed in his mouth well alight, a thin plume of blue smoke ascending in the sunlight which penetrated this quiet precinct.

"What do you make of it, Parker?"

"An ideal spot for a murder in broad daylight, Pons," I said, craning my neck upward to the tower from which the fatal hammer had been flung.

"Is it not, Parker? This was one aspect which puzzled me and on which mere armchair theorists would come to grief, I fear. Thus it is so often impossible to form a valid theory without visiting the location. Relate me the course of events as you see them, Parker."

"Well, Pons," I said, aware of Fernchurch's imploring look in my direction. "Supposing someone—not Mr. Fernchurch—had wished Bulstrode harm he could hardly have chosen a more perfect setting. Mr. Bulstrode is making an inspection at the base of the tower to see how the men are progressing. Anyone on the tower would, I imagine, have a complete view of the surroundings. He had only to wait until the precinct was deserted. He could see over the buttress in case anyone was coming along the street; he knew that the Guildhall was opposite and it was unlikely anyone would be in the storerooms. He had only to wait until Bulstrode stopped directly below and then loose the hammer."

Solar Pons put his hand up and stroked the side of his nose while he took the pipe out of his mouth with his disengaged hand.

"Excellent, Parker! It is perfect so far as it goes. Too perfect, perhaps. It first assumes that the aim is dead true. Second, it does not take into account any spectators who might be beneath the archway or standing on the open ground beyond the arch. Third, we know that Mr. Fernchurch was on top of the tower at the time in question and that he saw no one."

I looked round in the direction of the arch, conscious of the Inspector's humorous eyes, and saw that Pons was correct.

"You are perfectly right, Pons. But it does not invalidate my theory."

"I quite agree, Parker," said Pons slowly. "But I think, nevertheless, there is a serious objection. The man on the tower, who must have had an expert knowledge of Maldon, would know there might be people underneath the arch."

"I don't quite follow you, Pons."

Pons made an impatient clicking noise with his tongue.

"You have made a careful study of my methods, Parker. It is

commonsense, surely. Whoever committed this crime afterward had to make his escape from this tower. In order to do so he had to get to ground level. He could not really hope to escape if there had been eyewitnesses to Bulstrode's murder already on the ground."

"That would be an insurmountable obstacle, Mr. Pons," said Fitzjohn, who was watching my companion carefully. There was something reassuring about the vigorous, athletic figure of this obviously very shrewd C.I.D. man which set him apart from the common stamp of police officers—particularly men like Jamison, who was able enough in his own way but frequently wrongheaded.

"Unless the murderer himself lived within the Castle," said Solar Pons mysteriously.

He turned on his heel, suddenly brisk and purposeful.

"Come, Mr. Fernchurch. I should like to see the view from the top, and no doubt you can show me exactly where you stood while you were waiting for Miss Smithers."

Fitzjohn led the way up a series of winding stone staircases in the base of the tower; through broad arrow slits I could see a magnificent view of Maldon unfolding, ever more spectacular the higher we rose. There was a sort of stone landing half-way up, with a series of oak doors leading off it. A uniformed constable was on guard there and saluted the Inspector smartly before opening another door for us.

A brisk walk of two more flights brought us out into the gusty heights of the battlemented tower itself. Pons wasted no time on the magnificent view but went round quickly, casting sharp glances about him. I saw that the top of the tower was littered with builder's material—scaffolding poles and other equipment. I went over to the far side of the tower and looked through the stone embrasure. It was a dizzy height and sombre thought that this was the exact spot from which the death missile had been despatched.

"Where were you, Mr. Fernchurch?" said Pons.

"Just here, Mr. Pons."

Our client went to sit on a large baulk of timber directly in the centre of the tower.

"Were you facing the direction of the Guildhall, or had you your back to it?"

"I had my back toward it, Mr. Pons. I was facing the door through which Miss Smithers would come."

"I see."

Pons stroked his chin and looked thoughtfully at the military figure of Inspector Fitzjohn who stood with one meaty hand resting on the parapet. The golden winter sunshine made a rosy halo round his head.

"You did not move from this position?"

Fernchurch shook his head.

"No, Mr. Pons. The view had no attraction for me. I had seen it many times before."

"You heard no commotion in the street?"

Fernchurch shook his head.

"I was completely absorbed in the thoughts of regaining my fiancée, Mr. Pons. I may have been vaguely aware of some disturbance, but it is always busy and there was a good deal of traffic noise."

Indeed, as he spoke there came the drumming vibration of a heavy goods vehicle through the narrow streets that threaded past the base of the Castle tower.

"Very well, Mr. Fernchurch. So you came up here to meet Miss Smithers. You remained here how long?"

"About half an hour, Mr. Pons. In fact until a number of people crowded up the staircase, including one of the local constables, who began to question me. It was the first I had heard of the death of Bulstrode. I cannot say I blame the police. It must have looked highly suspicious."

Pons nodded approvingly.

"Well said, Mr. Fernchurch. Well, we must just see how events shape and whether or not I can discover something to overturn this distressing theory."

"I shall be greatly interested to see you do that, Mr. Pons," said Inspector Fitzjohn politely, a faint smile hovering round his lips.

There was an answering glint of humour in Pons' eyes. He went quickly over to the other side of the tower, first looking at the street, then carefully examining the stonework with a lens he produced from his pocket. Then he came back and ran his eyes over the jumble of tools which lay about the top of the tower.

"What exactly was going on here, Inspector?"

"General restoration of the Castle, Mr. Pons. Bulstrodes were cleaning and repointing the stonework—generally making good."

Pons nodded, deep in thought. He kicked idly at a mason's hammer which was lying among some coils of rope at his feet.

There was no question the murder weapon belonged to Mr. Bulstrode's firm?"

"No doubt at all, Mr. Pons. It was readily identified. One of the men working on the tower had seen it in use only the day before."

Inspector Fitzjohn stared for a long moment at Pons' probing eyes.

"I have not overlooked that, Mr. Pons. We have been pretty thoroughly into the men's backgrounds. No one had a real grudge against him though I take it he could be a hard master."

"I must congratulate you, Inspector," said Solar Pons mockingly. "You have not missed a trick."

"Thank you, Mr. Pons. That is high praise from you."

Pons was back over to the far side of the tower now. He looked downward casually.

"What have we here, Parker?"

I gave a cry of horror as he put one hand on the coping and launched himself effortlessly into space. His low chuckle came up to us before I could get to the parapet. To my immense relief I saw that he had landed safely on a broad platform of heavy planking about four feet below the battlements.

"That was an incredibly foolish thing to do, Pons," I said testily.

Pons' smile changed from mockery and his expression to concern.

"I am sorry, my dear fellow. It was not my intention to alarm you. Just look at this."

I clambered down to him in less spectacular fashion. I then saw that a ladder led downward from the platform, securely lashed with rope and with wooden handrails. I followed Pons gingerly to an embrasure at a lower level. We stepped through and found ourselves in a dusty corridor. An oak door was ahead of us. Pons opened it to disclose the constable lounging on the stone landing, his back to us. Directly opposite was another heavy door; it bore on it the legend in gold paint: CURATOR'S OFFICE. Pons quietly closed the door and waited for our two companions to rejoin us from above.

"Why, Pons..." I began.

Solar Pons laid his fingers alongside his nose to enjoin caution.

"It gives one food for thought, does it not, Parker? No doubt Fitzjohn has taken it into account."

He became his usual brisk self as Fernchurch and Fitzjohn appeared in the opening behind us.

"I think I have seen enough for the moment, Inspector. A little lunch is indicated. Parker here looks quite famished."

And he led the way down the stairs at a dangerous pace.

5

"Let us just have your views on the matter, Parker."

We had enjoyed an excellent lunch at the hotel and afterward Fitzjohn and Fernchurch had excused themselves—the latter to seek out his fiancée and explain the outcome of his London visit; Fitzjohn to hurry back to the police station, with a final admonition to the suspected man to behave himself.

Afterward we had strolled back toward the Castle as if impelled to the scene of the tragedy by some volition outside ourselves. We had halted at the base of the West Tower and instinctively I glanced up to where windows pierced its frowning mass, finally coming to rest on the battlements where Pons' client had been discovered.

"The hammer is a major impediment to the investigation, Pons," I began cautiously.

"Capital!" said he.

Pons' eyes were twinkling and he strolled about, puffing furiously at his after-lunch pipe, first watching the scudding clouds which were beginning to obscure the sun, then observing keenly the casual passersby and obvious tourists who strolled about the ancient walls of Maldon.

"Everything depends upon the hammer," he continued. "I am glad that point has not escaped you, for it is of paramount importance." He stopped his pacing and halted, looking at me shrewdly through plumes of blue smoke.

We now have two possibilities, Pons," I continued. "It would seem that anyone could have gained the battlements from the tower staircase without being seen, by using the ladder and scaffolding left in situ."

"Excellent, Parker. My training has not been wasted."

"Including the Curator," I added.

Pons looked at me for a long moment.

"What makes you suppose that?"

"It is just a feeling, Pons. Supposing Mr. Smithers did not wish his daughter to marry either Bulstrode or Fernchurch. It would have been an excellent way of disposing of both of them."

Pons puffed steadily at his pipe before replying.

"It is a little farfetched, Parker. Bulstrode had already been removed from the arena and I am sure that a fond parent with his daughter's welfare at heart could well have dissuaded her from marrying Fernchurch if he had been so minded. The engagement had already been broken off once, remember. However, it is a possibility which we should not exclude..."

He broke off as Fernchurch himself appeared beneath the archway. He hurried toward us immediately.

"I have just been talking to my fiancée, Mr. Pons. She is deeply grateful for what you have done. She is eager to meet you and answer any questions you may put. I must get home, now but you have only to step up."

"And where might the young lady live, Mr. Fernchurch?"

Our client looked embarrassed.

"I am sorry, Mr. Pons. I took it for granted you knew. Miss Smithers and her father live in quarters in the tower, just next to Professor Smithers' office. That is Evelyn's window there, just above us."

"Indeed."

Solar Pons drew back and I followed his glance upward to a large open window about fifty feet from the ground. There was scaffolding above it and below it, and I could see that Pons was inordinately interested for some reason.

"We shall be up in a few minutes, Mr. Fernchurch," he said by way of parting. "I have just one or two more inquiries to make, if you will excuse me."

He watched our client hurry away down the street, his bearing much more erect and confident than it had been when he staggered into our rooms in Praed Street. Pons smiled thinly. "It seems to me that that young man seems more pleased at regaining his fiancée than in the prospect of having a charge of murder removed from over his head."

"He is young, Pons," I said. "And when one is in love..."

"Tut, Parker. Pray do not cloud the issue with such romantic irrelevancies. Now, just one thing more to do on the ground."

His next procedure puzzled me exceedingly, but I said nothing, watching in silence as he went over to the builders' materials stacked along the base of the wall. He selected a piece of sacking and carried it out from the wall, first craning his neck up to look at the battlements far above, then adjusting the sacking on the ground. When he had folded it to his liking, he secured it firmly with several heavy stones.

His next action seemed more curious than ever, for he

proceeded to fill his pockets with small pebbles from a pile in a corner. He chuckled as he caught sight of my expression.

"Come along, Parker. All will be made clear in due course."

We ascended the staircase once again but instead of repairing at once to Professor Smithers' quarters, he led me past the stolid form of the constable and up onto the heights of the tower.

"I shall be a few minutes, Parker. If you have better things to do, pray do them."

I looked at Pons sharply but there was nothing on his face to explain the irony in his voice.

"I will just sit here in the sun and smoke, Pons," I said.

Pons nodded affably.

"No doubt you will find it a three-pipe problem," he said.

And with that he stepped round the tangled mass of builders' material and disappeared from view. I sat down on the large baulk of timber once occupied by the unfortunate Fernchurch and set my thoughts roaming in the tangled web in which he found himself. I had been ruminating for some minutes and had been vaguely aware of odd noises from the far side of the tower when a sudden gust of wind drew my attention to the fact that I was becoming chilled. I rose abruptly and moved over to the edge of the battlements. I could not see Pons at first but then made him out, crouched in an embrasure, an intent look on his face.

I quietly crossed to his side, and as I did so the reason for his strange actions on the ground became apparent. The court below was silent and deserted for the moment and as I watched, Pons released a small pebble. It flew true to the dull-coloured patch of sacking below, hitting it with a thump before bouncing against the wall.

289

"Excellent, Pons," I said. "This was evidently the spot from which the hammer was dropped."

"Was it not, Parker," said Pons carelessly, turning away and brushing his hands. He pulled out the remaining pebbles from his pockets.

"Seven direct hits out of thirty is a fair score under the circumstances, though I commend the size of the sacking to your attention."

He said nothing more, and a few moments later we descended to the landing, where the constable pointed out the door to Professor Smithers' private quarters.

Pons' rap brought a tall, fair-haired girl to the entrance. Her eyes widened when she saw us and her smile was just a little forced.

"Mr. Pons? Mr. Solar Pons? Eustace has been talking to me about you. And this would be Dr. Parker? It really is most good of you to help us in this way."

She held out a slim hand for me to take and ushered us into an oak-panelled hall with a flagstone floor which had evidently once formed part of the ancient castle keep. There were several doors opening off the hall and one of them was ajar. Before Pons could reply, a cadaverous, sour-faced individual in a rusty black frock coat darted from the sitting room beyond, with an irritated expression on his face.

"Not 'us', Evelyn. How many times must I tell you. Young Fernchurch is on his own."

Professor Smithers, for it was evidently the Castle Curator, came toward us blinking short-sightedly. He shook hands with Pons and myself in a distinctly chilly manner.

"You must forgive my apparent bad manners, Mr. Pons, but we have been greatly plagued of late. Not only Inspector

Fitzjohn but police officers of every type and description, some of them hardly civil."

He sniffed.

"The press have made so much of this that it has seriously interfered with my work. I hope you are not going to add to my difficulties."

Pons smiled thinly, his sharp eyes taking in every detail of the ill-assorted couple before us.

"I do not think you need worry, Professor Smithers. Publicity is not my forté, as my friend Dr. Parker here will tell you. And I have been retained privately by Mr. Fernchurch. I fancy the official police would hardly care to acknowledge my presence here."

Professor Smithers slightly unbent and relaxed his glacial manner.

"In that case, Mr. Pons, we are at your disposal. Though I fear I shall be able to help you very little. My daughter knows a good deal more about it."

"Indeed."

Pons looked politely at the girl, and there was an awkward pause until our host became aware that we were still standing in the hall.

"We will be more comfortable in the sitting room, gentlemen. Please forgive me."

The girl preceded us into a magnificent apartment, which was lined from floor to ceiling on the far wall with leather-bound books. At the left a stone fireplace contained a massive log fire. Elsewhere the stone walls had been plastered, and in place of the bleak flags of the hall outside, waxed floorboards reflected the flames of the fire. On the far right the wall was curved, evidently forming part of the tower we had observed from outside, and a large curved window was obviously the same one we had seen from below. A quick glimpse at the scaffolding outside confirmed that this was so.

Professor Smithers went to stand impatiently by the fireplace while we seated ourselves on a low divan facing him. After a brief hesitation the girl sat in a high, straightback chair, placed so that she could observe both us and her father. To my eyes she seemed nervous and ill at ease.

I will not keep you long," said Solar Pons, "and my questions are mainly directed to Miss Smithers. Your fiancé, Mr. Fernchurch..."

"You will excuse my bluntness, Mr. Pons," Professor Smithers interrupted harshly. "Evelyn is not Fernchurch's fiancée. She is not anyone's fiancée."

Pons raised his eyebrows while the girl bit her lip.

"I was given to understand differently, Professor. Perhaps Miss Smithers could explain."

"Father was bitterly opposed to our marriage," put in the girl, with a sudden show of spirit.

She tossed her head defiantly, so that the golden curls streamed back over her shoulders. I could then see why Fernchurch was so captivated.

"I have said a thousand times, Evelyn," Professor Smithers went on evenly, "that he is not the man for you. As for that fellow Bulstrode..."

"There I am inclined to agree with you, Professor," Pons put in smoothly, with a brief smile at the girl. "I take it the latter's demise has caused you no sleepless nights."

Professor Smithers' lean form bristled visibly.

"Not to put too fine a point on it, Mr. Pons, Bulstrode's passing is a relief to Maldon."

He hesitated and dropped his eyes before Pons' glance.

"Please do not think me uncharitable, Mr. Pons. Ordinarily I would not wish harm to anyone, but he was a dreadful man. Frankly, if Fernchurch did kill him as they say, then he has done the neighbourhood a favour."

The girl rose to her feet, shock on her face.

"Father!"

She stamped her foot with the vehemence of her emotion. Solar Pons tented his fingers together in front of him and half-closed his eyes as though the professor had uttered a pleasantry.

"So that you would not be bothered if Mr. Fernchurch were convicted of the crime, Professor Smithers? It would, in a way, if I dare venture so crude a suggestion, kill two birds with one stone."

"Or hammer, Mr. Pons?"

Smithers' smile contained icy venom. Then he recollected himself and went to lean against the massive oak mantel.

"I would not go so far as to say that, Mr. Pons. But blind chance has forged a weapon. One might call it the Hammer of Hate for want of a better term. It has removed from my girl's orbit all those undesirable influences I sought to shield her from."

Pons made a mild clicking noise with his tongue.

"Poetically put, Professor Smithers. The Hammer of Hate? You seem to know a good deal about the motives involved here. For all we know the thing might have been a mere accident, instead of premeditated murder."

"Eh?"

Professor Smithers coughed awkwardly and looked discomfited.

"I am only repeating what has been public gossip in Maldon

for some time, Mr. Pons. My views on Evelyn's unfortunate choices are well known in the locality. In fact it may well have saved her from a nasty scandal."

"How so?"

"We were having words about Fernchurch in this very room at almost the instant Bulstrode was killed. I did not know she had an appointment with young Fernchurch on the tower. Our argument delayed her, as you know. If you ask my opinion, she is well out of it."

Pons sat with his chin on his hand, his sleepy eyes apparently fixed aimlessly on a corner of the mantel.

"You may well be right, Professor Smithers. I should like a word in private with your daughter now, if you would be so good. Thank you for your assistance. You have been most helpful."

Professor Smithers drew himself up, glared at Pons for a moment at thus being so peremptorily dismissed, inclined his head stiffly and strode out of the room. The crash of the door seemed to shake the tower. The girl looked at us calmly from clear blue eyes and went to sit down again.

"Don't take any notice of Daddy," she said. "He lives much out of the world."

"Does he not?" agreed Pons, getting up and gliding about the bookcases, scanning the volumes in the swift but thorough way that characterised all his movements.

Nevertheless, your father was correct in some respects. Bulstrode was a highly unsuitable suitor, if you will forgive me for saying so. And the delay at your rendezvous with Mr. Fernchurch did relieve you of an awkward implication."

"Even though it could have cleared Eustace of all suspicion?" asked the girl artlessly.

Solar Pons paused by the far window and frowned.

"I take it your father's account of your argument on the afternoon of the murder was correct?"

"Perfectly, Mr. Pons."

"Your presence on the tower with Fernchurch might have presented the police with a joint case of murder, Miss Smithers. Had you thought of that? It might well have been argued that you both plotted Bulstrode's death."

The girl rose from her seat again and came down the room toward Pons.

"For what possible reason, Mr. Pons?"

"That he was an insanely jealous man, violent when roused. That he was becoming a nuisance and a threat to your resumed relationship with your fiancé."

"Nonsense, Mr. Pons!"

Solar Pons chuckled.

"I quite agree, Miss Smithers. I just wanted to see your reaction. What a charming view you have from your window here. Do you not agree, Parker?"

I got up and joined the two in front of the large window, which was open to catch the sun. It was indeed a fine view, and I saw immediately that it overlooked the spot where Bulstrode had met his death.

"You did not happen to see him that afternoon, Miss Smithers?"

His voice was so quiet, and the question was shot at the girl so quickly that I was almost as startled as she. Evelyn Smithers shifted her weight from one foot to the other and went pink. She stammered slightly as she replied.

"I did see him, as a matter of fact. I was looking out of the window before my interview with Father. Bulstrode carried a hammer and he was tapping about the base of the tower. It was that which first attracted my attention. I presumed he was checking on the workmen."

Pons was very still, one hand on the window frame behind him, as he stared at the girl.

"Go on, Miss Smithers. You did not tell this to the police?"

The girl shook her head.

"I thought it of no importance. They asked me about the actual crime and the time it was committed."

"I see. We will just keep this between ourselves for the moment. Is that all you have to tell me?"

The girl hesitated again, and once more there was the faint flush on her cheeks.

"He looked up at that instant, Mr. Pons. He may have seen me. I do not really know. There was some shouting in the street just then, and I turned away because at that moment Father came in, in one of his tempers, and slammed the door."

"I see."

Solar Pons stood stock-still, pulling at the lobe of his ear.

"You have been most helpful, Miss Smithers. Come, Parker, I have a few more inquiries to make about the town."

6

"Well, Parker, you have seen most of the protagonists in this drama. I should be glad of your thoughts on the matter."

"You flatter me, Pons."

We were sitting in a small rear lounge of The Saddler's Arms, the buzz of cheerful conversation about us. It was early evening and Pons had been unusually preoccupied since our interview with Evelyn Smithers and her father. He had had another talk with Fernchurch before dinner in the smoking room of the hotel, from which he had emerged in a taciturn mood. All through dinner he had remained silent and reserved, and I knew better than to interrupt him on these occasions.

Now, however, when he was sitting back in a comfortable leather chair, a pipe clamped between his teeth, he seemed in a more expansive frame of mind and so I welcomed his remark.

"Come, Parker," he continued, regarding me with narrowed eyes. "You know my methods."

"I know your methods, Pons, but as you are so often reminding me, I do not often know in which direction to apply them."

He chuckled.

"Well said, my dear fellow. How did Miss Smithers strike you, for example?"

"A very beautiful young lady, Pons," I replied cautiously.

"Is she not? I fancy young Fernchurch is not out of the wood there yet, unless I am very much mistaken."

"What on earth do you mean, Pons?"

"Nothing," said my companion carelessly, drawing on his pipe. "But she does not seem unduly concerned at her fiancé's plight."

I sat back in my chair and scratched my head.

"Your line of investigation has succeeded only in confusing me, Pons. Instead of one suspect we now appear to have several. Young Fernchurch had ample opportunity and motive to drop that hammer on his rival's head. Yet you seem convinced that he did not do it."

Solar Pons nodded, his head wreathed in blue smoke.

"Correct, Parker."

"Then you have opened my eyes to other possibilities," I went on. "For example, it seems obvious that Professor Smithers himself could have crossed the landing and have gained the tower by way of the scaffolding without being seen."

Solar Pons chuckled, looking at me approvingly.

"Splendid, Parker. Do continue. You must not leave Miss Smithers out. Her window directly overlooks the scene of the crime."

I stared at my companion in silence for a moment.

"Good heavens, Pons! You surely cannot mean . . . "

Pons wrinkled his brows and his eyes were serious.

"The female mind is complex and convoluted, Parker. I do not exclude anything for the moment. I am about to investigate yet a fourth possibility. And if I am not mistaken, here is my man now."

As he spoke, the door of the lounge was cautiously opened and a small, rather roughly dressed man came blinking in. He stopped before us, looking from one to the other.

"Mr. Solar Pons? Jethro Dobbs at your service, gentlemen. The hotel porter brought me a message that you wished to see me."

"Indeed, Mr. Dobbs. Won't you take a seat? Let me order you a drink. This is my friend, Dr. Lyndon Parker."

That's very kind of you, sir. A pint of bitter if you please."

The little man sank into a chair opposite me and sat looking at me silently until Pons had brought the drink over to him.

He drank greedily, as though he had not tasted liquid for a month. He put the tankard down on the oak table in front of him with a grunt of satisfaction.

"That's better, gentlemen. How can I help you, sir?"

"There is a good deal of gossip in the town, Mr. Dobbs, over the death of the late Mr. Bulstrode. I understand you were in his employ and that you had a tremendous row some weeks before his death."

The little man's eyes were bright and he paused in drawing his sleeve across his mouth.

"That's right," he said evenly. "Only I don't see as how you could know about it."

"It is common gossip, Mr. Dobbs," said Pons easily. "Would you care to tell us about it?"

"It's no great secrecy," said Dobbs bitterly. "I'm one of the best masons in the business and I should think I know my work."

"Indeed," said Pons soothingly. "You are well spoken of in the town as a craftsman. I trust you found a new position easily enough."

The little man brightened.

"Oh, I'm all right now, Mr. Pons. But it rankled, sir, it rankled. Fired me offhand. Never known a man with such a foul temper."

He looked cautiously round the bar.

"I'm not one to speak ill of the dead, but I'm glad Sebastian Bulstrode has gone. Do you know what happened, sir?"

Pons shook his head.

"I'd just finished a section of wall at the base of the tower. Beautiful job. As fine as you could see within a hundred miles. Then Bulstrode came around. He was in a towering rage. He found fault with everything I'd done. The cement was still wet. He got his hammer, the special one with the crowbar handle, and pulled the whole thing to pieces. Made me mad, I can tell you."

Pons' whole expression was one of alertness and engrossed attention now.

299

"Did he indeed! Do go on, Mr. Dobbs."

He tugged at the lobe of his ear and fixed our visitor with piercing eyes.

"Nothing much else to tell, Mr. Pons. We had words. High words, I might say. At the end of it he told me to go to the office and get my money. It was a relief, really. Nasty man to work for. Constant tension and upsets. Is that what you wanted to know, sir?"

Pons smiled.

"Exactly, Mr. Dobbs. I have learned more than I could possibly have hoped for. Eh, Parker?"

"Certainly, Pons," I said, trying to keep the bewilderment from my voice.

"You have been most helpful, Mr. Dobbs. Here is a pound for your trouble."

"Many thanks, Mr. Pons."

Our visitor eagerly grasped the note my companion handed him, drained the last of his beer and hurried out with a friendly smile.

Pons chuckled and sat back on his seat.

"What do you make of that, Parker?"

I shook my head.

"I must confess that I am more confused than ever, Pons. This man had as big a motive for killing Bulstrode as anyone else."

"Did he not? This affair becomes more interesting by the minute. But let us just step up to the bar here. We may learn something further to our advantage. There is nothing like small-town gossip for getting at the heart of the matter."

And with that he led the way up to the crowded bar at the far end of the room. We refilled our glasses, and I glanced round the lounge while Pons exchanged pleasantries with the hotel manager, who had just come in to confer with one of the barmen.

"Oh, it is six of one and half a dozen of the other," said a loud voice behind me. "There was no love lost between the two men. I hear Fernchurch came near to knocking Bulstrode down on one occasion."

The man addressed, a red-faced character with a thick moustache, gave a broad wink.

"Chancing his arm against a man of Bulstrode's size, wasn't he?"

The first man sniggered.

"He thought better of it. Backed away, I hear. But a hammer dropped from the Castle walls would do just as well, I reckon."

There was another snigger and the two men moved away. The manager's face was grave.

"I must apologise for that, gentlemen. People will talk, unfortunately."

He shook his head.

"Murder in Maldon! Who would have thought it. Such a thing is very bad for the tourist trade, gentlemen."

"I can well believe it," said Pons, gently commiserating. His left eyelid twitched momentarily at me as he took a pull at his glass.

I must confess I was more confused than ever when I went to bed that evening.

7

I was up early in the morning but Pons was earlier still. It was a fine, bright morning, the sun shining and still surprisingly mild for January, especially in the north. He came into the breakfast room just as I was sitting down at our table, his face fresh and alert, as though he had taken a long walk. He rubbed his lean hands together briskly.

"Exercise clears the brain wonderfully, Parker. I have just been for a short promenade around the Castle. There is one piece which will not quite fit into place."

"You surprise me, Pons," I murmured, pouring the coffee. "I have a thousand pieces and nowhere to put any of them."

Solar Pons smiled thinly.

"The ratiocinative art continues to elude you, Parker. Ah, well, we are all built differently. But you are a wonderfully stimulating companion."

"Kind of you to say so, Pons," I muttered.

"I have asked Fitzjohn and Fernchurch to join us after breakfast. Light begins to break through. They will meet us at the tower at half-past nine."

And he said no more but attacked his breakfast with gusto.

As we walked up to the Castle afterwards, I could not resist saying to my companion, "I have another theory, Pons. One that should not be discounted."

Pons stopped momentarily, shielding his pipe from a light wind which had suddenly sprung up.

"Pray what might that be, Parker?"

"I have only just thought of it. Could it not be that you were correct about Miss Smithers? That she committed the fatal deed on impulse and that young Fernchurch is shielding her?"

Pons flicked his spent match behind him and looked at me sharply.

"Well said, Parker. That is distinctly ingenious. Your grey cells are working at last. You may have hit close to the truth without knowing it. Ah, here is the Inspector and our client himself."

The two familiar figures had appeared underneath the archway where we shortly joined them, before Pons led the way out to the tower on the other side.

"Well, Mr. Pons, I trust you have come to some conclusions. We cannot keep Mr. Fernchurch here hovering under a cloud."

"Quite right, Inspector," said Pons briskly. "I have followed some lines of inquiry, it is true. But there is some connecting link which eludes me for the moment. I need just that one touch to prove my theory. Until then I prefer not to commit myself."

"Why, Pons," said I. "It should be easy enough. You need only carry out your pebble experiment from the young lady's window, yonder. The shorter distance would not matter so much with such a heavy hammer but would be more accurate, surely."

Solar Pons stared at me as though I had said something of momentous importance. His dancing eyes shot upward to where I had indicated the open window of the Smithers' sitting room.

"My dear Parker, you are, as I said earlier, a veritable transmitter of light! Here the matter has been staring me in the face, and I need only have taken two physical steps to corroborate my theory. If ever I have been obtuse, it is on this occasion. Come, Parker!"

My companions stared at him as though he had gone mad, but Pons had already turned on his heel and was running through the arch. He ascended the tower steps two at a time so that he swiftly outdistanced me. By the time I had puffed my way to the top landing he was already being admitted to their private quarters by Professor Smithers and his daughter.

The Curator had an abashed look on his face as he caught sight of us, but he controlled himself and in quite a gracious manner invited us all in.

"This will not take a moment," said Pons, once we were inside the sitting room. "It is just a small point of corroborative evidence, but which is nevertheless vital. My client's innocence depends upon it."

"Certainly, Mr. Pons. Whatever you wish."

The Professor's amazement was written large upon his features, and he was even more astonished when Pons went across to the open window. A few seconds later there were gasps as he vaulted through, to land safely on the planked scaffolding that was placed just below and to the right of the window.

"Do be careful, Mr. Pons," said Miss Smithers in worried tones.

"Do not fear, young lady," said Pons, kneeling now and intent on the windowsill of the sitting room. He had his lens out and leaned over dangerously, working his way back and forth along the sill before turning his attention to the stones beneath. There was a muffled exclamation and I saw that his face was completely transformed.

"Ah, just as I thought. Allow me to congratulate you, Mr. Fernchurch."

"On what, Mr. Pons?"

"On your innocence and on the clearing of the capital charge against you."

"Oh, come, Mr. Pons," said Inspector Fitzjohn in a sceptical voice. "That is rather a sweeping statement."

"Just fetch me a large mirror, Miss Smithers," said Pons calmly. He sat on the planked scaffolding, dangling his legs in space and looking perfectly at home until the girl returned with the article he had requested. He took the mirror from her and held it so that we could see a portion of the stonework beneath the windowsill.

"There, Inspector. Do you not see?"

"I see a large gash in the stonework, Mr. Pons," said Fitzjohn cautiously.

"Exactly! And the mark is new. It indicates considerable force, for these centuries-old stones are hard as iron. But there is one conclusive point, which you cannot very well see from here. It indicates that the blow was in an upward direction!"

"What on earth are you talking about, Mr. Pons?"

Professor Smithers could not keep the irritation from his voice; so cryptic had Pons been that I almost sympathised with him. Pons handed the mirror back in through the window to the girl with a flourish, and then followed himself, dusting the knees of his trousers.

"But what does it all mean, Mr. Pons?" asked Fernchurch, his puzzled eyes seeking the girl's.

"It means, Mr. Fernchurch, that Sebastian Bulstrode killed himself!"

Pons chuckled at the gasped incredulity from the circle of people around him.

"You cannot mean it, Mr. Pons," stammered Professor Smithers. "Suicide?"

Pons shook his head.

"But you aptly named the weapon, Professor. The Hammer of Hate you called it, did you not? We had better just sit down while I explain."

When we were seated comfortably near the fireplace, Pons went to stand by the mantel, his eyes conveying a far away look.

305

"When Mr. Fernchurch came to me at Praed Street with his distressing story, I rapidly came to the conclusion, from his manner and general demeanour, that he was speaking the truth. He had been caught, as it were, by a large number of people at the top of the tower a few minutes after Bulstrode had been struck down and killed by this heavy iron hammer we have heard so much about. The major difficulties lay in motive and method. First, Mr. Fernchurch had some motive. Rivalry over Miss Smithers, quarrels and—according to some local people— an actual incident when the two men almost came to blows."

"Quite untrue, Mr. Pons," said Fernchurch hotly. "It was mere gossip."

Solar Pons inclined his head.

"I quite agree, Mr. Fernchurch. I have heard a great deal of you about the bars and streets of Maldon. I have long ago learned to ignore gossip, but it can be revealing on occasion. Very rarely it can also help to clear one of suspicion. It has done so in your case. One of the palpable absurdities in the matter—and one which you would have done well to have grasped, Parker—was the obvious difficulty, not to say almost impossibility, of the method used. I made my own experiments by dropping pebbles from the tower top onto a large piece of sacking. Now, although the sacking was a great deal larger than a man's head, I succeeded in hitting it only seven times out of thirty."

Pons paused and relit his pipe, puffing out blue clouds of aromatic smoke.

"So that at an early stage I had discounted premeditated murder in Mr. Fernchurch's case, or indeed his implication in the matter in any way. He was merely unfortunate in that he was at the wrong place at the wrong time. What compounded the difficulties was that Miss Smithers had been delayed in meeting him by some discussion between her and her father on her choice of fiancé. Had both been on the tower top, Miss Smithers could have provided powerful corroborative evidence of his innocence and avoided a great deal of unfortunate publicity."

"I take back nothing I have said," snapped Professor Smithers. Pons gave him a disapproving look.

I did not ask you to," he said gently. "The second difficulty I mentioned was the hammer. It was made of iron, covered with stone dust, and the shock of it first striking Mr. Bulstrode's skull and then rebounding to the ground shook the dust from it, so that no usable fingerprints were found. That could not possibly have been foreseen by any potential murderer."

"You are forgetting the Professor and the other possible suspects, Pons," I could not help putting in.

Solar Pons took the pipe out of his mouth and shook his head.

"I am forgetting nothing, Parker. It is true that there were complications. Professor Smithers could, no doubt, have gained access to the tower from this room and by means of the scaffolding have dropped the hammer onto Bulstrode. But I think it hardly likely, particularly as he could have obtained more accurate results from the window of this room."

Professor Smithers made an angry explosive noise, and I saw Inspector Fitzjohn hastily repress a smile.

"Consider, Parker," Pons went on, as though there had been no interruption. "Motive, my dear fellow. Always consider motive. There were no strong ones in this case. Bulstrode had already been eliminated as a prospective son-in-law. Why risk getting oneself hanged by dropping a hammer on him? The revenge element in Miss Smithers' case would have been ridiculous. She had achieved her object and had become re-engaged to my client. These young people had everything to live for."

"But the mason you interviewed, Pons," I said irritatedly. "He had a grudge, surely."

"Certainly, Parker, but the whole thing was too farfetched. And he made one point of great significance in his talk with us. Two, if one takes into account that Bulstrode was a man who could go absolutely berserk on occasion and do ridiculous things on impulse. You have already heard how he tore down a perfectly good wall in an argument with Dobbs. I made it my business to check that story thoroughly this morning. It was perfectly true and it was corroborated by at least half a dozen of his co-workers."

"What are we left with, then, Mr. Pons?" said Inspector Fitzjohn, somewhat desperately.

"A hammer, Inspector," said Pons, a mischievous twinkle in his eye.

"A Hammer of Hate, as picturesquely described by Professor Smithers. A particularly apt description, though not in the way he intended. The general mistake everyone made, myself included, was that the hammer used in the murder was flung or dropped from the top of the tower. Apart from the impossibility of ensuring accuracy from a hundred feet up and the incredible coincidence of Bulstrode stopping at the exact spot and standing there until Fernchurch had taken perfect aim, the hammer was never on top of the tower."

Fitzjohn's jaw visibly quivered.

"Never there, Mr. Pons? How can you possibly know that?"

"Common sense, Inspector," said Pons calmly. "It was merely assumed, because there were a good many tools on the tower top, that the hammer was among them. But it was a special hammer. Bulstrode's own, in fact, which he habitually carried and with which he tested his men's work. The clue lay in the statement made by Dobbs to myself and Dr. Parker last night, Inspector, and which your own men must have overlooked. Dobbs told us that Bulstrode 'got his hammer, the special one with the crowbar handle'. That made the whole thing perfectly plain in my mind but I could not quite fit the pieces together. The incident of Dobbs and the wall took place weeks ago, but I confirmed from Bulstrode's staff this morning that he always carried the hammer; it was as indispensable to him as a pencil and drawing paper to an architect. When I combined this fact with Miss Smithers' statement, the sequence became more clear. It was not until you directed my attention to the elementary matter of Miss Smithers' windowsill this morning, Parker, that the whole thing came into focus."

"I confess it is not at all clear, Pons."

"My dear fellow, Bulstrode was a vindictive, vengeful man. He considered he had been wronged by Fernchurch and Miss Smithers. It rankled and he was not a man to let such things go lightly. He avoided an open confrontation with my client. But on the morning of his death he was inspecting the work at the base of this tower. You may be sure he had an ulterior motive. That was, I have no doubt, to see Miss Smithers and plead his case again. He had no idea that Fernchurch was on the battlements; he had no reason to know and Mr. Fernchurch himself has told us that at no time did he go near the edge of the tower. I absolutely believe him."

"Thank you, Mr. Pons."

"All very well, Mr. Pons," said Inspector Fitzjohn warily. "But what exactly are you trying to tell us?"

Solar Pons stepped away from the fireplace and his eyes were very bright.

"Just this, Inspector. The whole matter hinges on Miss Smithers here. Bulstrode was anxious to see her. He hung about beneath her window until there was no one in the little square below. Miss Smithers was waiting to talk to her father in this very room about the delicate matter of her engagement to Mr. Fernchurch. She looked out of the window and saw Bulstrode. He was tapping about the base of the tower with a hammer, as she puts it. That is conclusive."

"How do you know this, Mr. Pons?" put in Professor Smithers.

"Because she told me so herself yesterday," said Pons evenly. "The sound had attracted her attention. She said that he looked up and may have seen her. She turned away, quite properly, as she did not wish to be involved with him again."

"It is a pity you did not tell the police this, Miss Smithers," said the inspector quietly.

The girl flushed and lowered her eyes.

"I was afraid of what Father might say," she said. "And it did not seem really important."

"But it was important, Miss Smithers," Pons went on. "You heard some shouting in the street, I think you said; and then your father came in, in a temper, and slammed the door."

"That is so, Mr. Pons."

"Exactly."

Solar Pons looked round the sitting room in the deep silence which had fallen.

"It cannot be conclusively proved beyond a shadow of doubt but it is crystal-clear to my mind that what happened was this. Bulstrode, a vengeful giant with an ungovernable temper, wished to see his former fiancée, with a view to getting her back. He attracted her attention by the tapping of his hammer, and she came to the window. When he shouted to her, she turned away. Blind rage overcame him and he lost control. He hurled the heavy iron hammer at the girl, whether with the intention of killing her or maiming her, we shall never know. But impartial fate works in strange ways. By a weird series of coincidences Miss Smithers providently had gone from the window; his aim was bad, and the hammer struck the wall below the windowsill with tremendous force—the notch just there is more than an inch deep—and literally rebounded onto the head of the evildoer. The weight of the hammer alone, plus the height of the window from the ground and the tremendous velocity with which it was flung, was sufficient to shatter his skull and stretch him lifeless upon the ground."

There was a long silence, broken by Fernchurch, whose face bore a strange mixture of expressions. He went up to my friend and wrung him by the hand.

"Mr. Pons, you have saved my life."

Solar Pons chuckled, evidently satisfied with the effect he had created.

"How say you, Inspector?"

Inspector Fitzjohn came forward slowly, first looking toward the window and then at Fernchurch.

"Brilliant, Mr. Pons. I would be the first to admit it when we are wrong. We must needs have corroboration from our own people on that chip in the stonework beneath the window, of course, but I am convinced that what you have described is substantially correct. There are no other facts that fit. Mr. Fernchurch, you are an extremely fortunate young man."

311

"Well, Parker," said Solar Pons drily. "Have you nothing to say?"

"I will reserve it for Praed Street, Pons," I said. "It will need more than a moment or two to do justice to your reasoning."

Solar Pons smiled as Miss Smithers and then her father came over and shook him by the hand.

"Perhaps we shall be left in peace now," said Smithers sourly as we took our leave.

"Well, Parker, I think our work here is concluded," said Solar Pons. "A decent lunch and then an afternoon train back to town. No doubt the Inspector, Miss Smithers, and Mr. Fernchurch will join us at the inn. Would you have the goodness to book a table?"

✍ 8

"A n interesting little exercise, Parker," said Solar Pons as Inspector Fitzjohn pulled the police car up in front of the imposing bulk of York Station in good time to catch the five o'-clock train to London.

"As you say, Pons," I agreed. "No doubt you will go over the major points with me again on the way back to Praed Street. I am not quite sure I have quite grasped every step of your reasoning."

"Certainly, Parker," said Pons affably as we walked across the concourse to where the hiss of steam made a deafening noise beneath the great canopy.

"Goodbye, Inspector. A pleasure to work with you."

Inspector Fitzjohn's face flushed with pleasure.

"An education, Mr. Pons. We have, of course, already formally dropped the charge against Mr. Fernchurch and he will get an official apology. A statement is appearing in the main Yorkshire evening papers and in the London newspapers in the morning."

"British justice is ever quick to make reparation, Inspector," said Pons. "And we have certainly avoided a dreadful miscarriage of justice on this occasion."

He turned to watch Inspector Fitzjohn as he hurried out of the main entrance.

"Though whether our friend Fernchurch is really so fortunate as Fitzjohn makes out is something only time will tell."

I followed Pons through the barrier and produced my ticket to be clipped. I rejoined him outside the buffet.

"I am not quite sure I follow you, Pons."

My companion seemed abstracted in manner.

"It was just a thought which occurred to me, Parker. Ah, I felt I was not mistaken."

He had caught sight of the willowy figure of Miss Smithers threading her way through the crowd toward us. She seemed embarrassed as she caught sight of us and stopped momentarily. A tall, military figure with her took her by the arm. Her smile was forced and artificial as she came up. Pons raised his hat and I followed suit.

"Quite a surprise, Miss Smithers," he said drily. "To see you so far afield quite so soon."

"A little outing, Mr. Pons."

The tall man with angry eyes and a clipped moustache, dressed in a captain's uniform, looked at us with well-bred indifference.

"Allow me to introduce Captain Gore-Willoughby, Mr. Pons. Mr. Pons, Dr. Lyndon Parker."

"Delighted, gentlemen."

313

The captain's hand was cold and fishlike. He yawned and consulted his wristwatch.

"Ten minutes before our train leaves, Evelyn."

"Very well, Nigel."

The girl turned to Pons again.

"We are going to stay with Captain Gore-Willoughby's relatives at Harrogate for the weekend. I felt I needed to get away."

"A delightful watering place," said Pons ironically. "Pray do not let me detain you further."

And he raised his hat politely as the oddly assorted couple hurried across the bridge.

"Well, Pons!" I said explosively.

Solar Pons took my arm and steered me down the platform as the thunder of the London-bound train sounded in the distance.

"You must learn to take a more equable and considered view of life, my dear fellow. Young Fernchurch has escaped one great peril, and he might well have fallen into another."

"You cannot mean it, Pons!"

"Ah, Parker, you find yourself seduced once again by a pair of winning eyes, a hank of hair, and a passable figure."

"Really, Pons!"

We pressed forward as the London train drew in.

"My dear Parker," Pons went on. "I have hinted it before and I will repeat it now. If that engagement between Miss Smithers and Fernchurch comes to anything I shall be extremely surprised. And if I am any judge of the human condition, that young man will be a great deal better off."

And so it proved.

SOLAR PONS

7B, PRAED STREET
PADDINGTON, LONDON, W. 2   AMBASSADOR 10000